P9-DFP-093

Praise for Keri Arthur

Nominated for the *Romantic Times* 2007 Reviewers' Choice Award for Career Achievement in Urban Fantasy

"Keri Arthur's imagination and energy infuse everything she writes with zest." —Charlaine Harris

Praise for Full Moon Rising

"Keri Arthur skillfully mixes her suspenseful plot with heady romance in her thoroughly enjoyable alternate-reality Melbourne. Sexy vampires, randy werewolves, and unabashed, unapologetic, joyful sex—you've gotta love it. Smart, sexy, and well-conceived."
—Kim Harrison

"A deliciously sexy adventure through a supernatural underworld that pulls you in and won't let go. Keri Arthur knows how to thrill! Buckle up and get ready for a wild, cool ride!" —Shana Abé

"Arthur never fails to deliver, keeping the fires stoked, the cliffs high, and the emotions dancing on a razor's edge in this edgy, hormone-filled mystery...*Full Moon Rising* is a shocking and sensual read, so keep the ice handy."
—TheCelebrityCafé.com

"Keri Arthur is one of the best supernatural romance writers in the world." —Harriet Klausner

"Strong, smart and capable, Riley will remind many of Anita Blake, Laurell K. Hamilton's kick-ass vampire hunter....Fans of Anita Blake and Charlaine Harris' Sookie Stackhouse vampire series will be rewarded."
—*Publishers Weekly*

"Fun and feisty...[An] effective crossbreeding of romance and urban fantasy that should please fans of either genre." —*Kirkus Reviews*

"Vampires and werewolves and hybrids...oh my! With a butt-kicking heroine and some oh-so-yummy men, Keri Arthur...has put her own unique spin on things, and the results are a sensual and energized fantasy brimming with plenty of romance."
—RomanceReviewsToday.com

"Sexy and exhilarating with characters that revel in their sexuality...Provocative and edgy with enough heat to scorch the paper it's written on. It's a pleasure to see that within a genre that is getting crowded with uninspired and repetitive stories it is still possible for this author to create a unique and very strong heroine."
—*A Romance Review*

"Unbridled lust and kick-ass action are the hallmarks of this first novel in a brand-new paranormal series.... 'Sizzling' is the only word to describe this heated, action-filled, suspenseful romantic drama....*Full Moon Rising* sets a high bar for what is now a much-anticipated new series." —CurledUp.com

"Keri Arthur has done a wonderful job with *Full Moon Rising*. It's a great story that's suspenseful, has hot were-wolves, sexy vampires, a huge amount of butt-kickin', and no-holds-barred sex. If you like a twist to your paranormal romance, you'll love this book."

—FreshFiction.com

"Grade A, desert island keeper... I wanted to read this book in one sitting, and was terribly offended that the real world intruded on my reading time!... Inevitable comparisons can be made to the Anita Blake, Kim Harrison, and Kelley Armstrong books, but I think Ms. Arthur has a clear voice of her own and her characters speak for themselves.... I am hooked!" —AllAboutRomance.com

"*Full Moon Rising* is a sinfully erotic tale filled with heart-pounding suspense.... Move over, Anne Rice, Keri Arthur is here to stay!" —RavenEntertainmentPromotions.com

Praise for *Kissing Sin*

Finalist for the 2008 Fantasm Award for Best Werewolf Romance

"Strong world-building, vivid personalities and the distinctive cultures of each of the various paranormal strains combine for a rich narrative, and Arthur's descriptive prose adds texture and menace."

—*Publishers Weekly*

"The second book in this paranormal guardian series is just as phenomenal as the first.... I am addicted!!"

—FreshFiction.com

"Riley Jenson returns with a vengeance in Keri Arthur's *Kissing Sin.* . . . The sex is hot and intense, but it doesn't detract at all from this fast-paced story."

—*Romance Reviews Today*

"Arthur is a marvelously creative author, and has built a solid world for her characters to reside in. Fast-paced and filled with deliciously sexy characters, readers will find *Kissing Sin* a fantastic urban fantasy with a hot serving of romance that continues to sizzle long after the last page is read." —*DarqueReviews.com*

"*Kissing Sin* will captivate readers from page one with its kick-ass heroine's struggle to do what's right without losing herself. Riley's sensuous nature and her lack of inhibitions will tantalize readers and make them sympathize with her. . . . Keri Arthur's unique characters and the imaginative world she's created will make this series one that readers won't want to miss."

—*A Romance Review*

Praise for *Tempting Evil*

"Riley Jenson is kick-ass . . . genuinely tough and strong, but still vulnerable enough to make her interesting. . . . The secondary characters and creatures are rich and diverse. The plots are involved, the action dramatic. Arthur is not derivative of early [Laurell K.] Hamilton— far from it—but the intensity of her writing and the complexity of her heroine and her stories is reminiscent."

—*AllAboutRomance.com*

"This paranormal romance series gets better and better with each new book . . . an exciting adventure that delivers all you need for a fabulous read—sexy shape-shifters, hot vampires, wild uncontrollable sex and the slightest hint of a love that's meant to be forever." —FreshFiction.com

"*Tempting Evil* is an amazingly awesome book that completely blew me away. Ms. Arthur's world-building skills are absolutely second to none. Her take on the legends of vampires and werewolves is utterly unique and mind bending. Riley and the men who inhabit her world fascinate me totally. I did not want this stupendously superb story to end and I cannot wait to see what happens to Riley Jenson next. I simply must have more, please, as soon as humanly possible. Five cups."

—CoffeeTimeRomance.com

"If you like your erotic scenes hot, fast, and frequent, your heroine sassy, sexy, and tough, and your stories packed with hard-hitting action in a vividly realized fantasy world, then *Tempting Evil* and its companion novels could be just what you're looking for." —SFRevu.com

Praise for *Dangerous Games*

Finalist for the 2008 Fantasm Award for Best Urban Fantasy Romance

"*Dangerous Games* is by far one of the best books I have ever read. . . . The story line is so exciting I did not realize I was literally sitting on the edge of my chair seat. . . . If you are a lover of all things paranormal, read this extremely magnificent book as soon as you possibly can. Five cups."

—CoffeeTimeRomance.com

"This series is phenomenal! *Dangerous Games* is an incredibly original and devastatingly sexy story. It keeps you spellbound and mesmerized on every page. Absolutely perfect!!" —FreshFiction.com

"Keri Arthur's captivating supernatural world and her wonderful characters always deliver a story that is worth reading. As always I am greatly looking forward to reading the next installment in this great series. Keri Arthur is sure to win a faithful and strong following to her Riley Jenson series." —*A Romance Review*

Praise for *Embraced by Darkness*

"There's never a lull in the action and danger that surrounds Riley's life. . . . Ms. Arthur is positively one of the best urban-fantasy authors in print today. The characters have been well-drawn from the start and the mysteries just keep getting better. A creative, sexy and adventure-filled world that readers will just love escaping to."
—DarqueReviews.com

"Four stars! This may be the fifth book of the series, but new readers will not find themselves totally lost. . . . A compelling story that held my attention well."
—HuntressReviews.com

"Arthur's storytelling is getting better and better with each book. *Embraced by Darkness* has suspense, interesting concepts, terrific main and secondary characters, well-developed story arcs, and the world-building is highly entertaining. . . . I think this series is worth the time and emotional investment to read." —Reuters.com

"Once again, Keri Arthur has created a perfect, exciting and thrilling read with intensity that kept me vigilantly turning each page, hoping it would never end."

—FreshFiction.com

"Arthur's fifth guardian novel is just as fabulous as the first. Her expertise at depicting the interaction between characters like a smart-mouthed clerk and a bossy werewolf insures breathless excitement on every page. Fast-paced and attention-grabbing, *Embraced by Darkness* is a must read and a necessary possession. Five cups."

—CoffeeTimeRomance.com

"Takes on a much more mature tone, at least when it comes to Riley and her men...Add to that plenty of action and intrigue, and readers will definitely want to be *Embraced by Darkness*." —*Romance Reviews Today*

"Reminiscent of Laurell K. Hamilton back when her books had mysteries to solve, Arthur's characters inhabit a dark sexy world of the paranormal."

—*Parkersburg News and Sentinel*

"Packed with fast-paced action, paranormal intrigue and passion at every turn, *Embraced by Darkness* is a steamy addition to this thrilling series." —MediaBoulevard.com

"I love this series." —AllAboutRomance.com

Praise for *The Darkest Kiss*

"The paranormal Australia that Arthur concocts works perfectly, and the plot speeds along at a breakneck pace. Riley fans won't be disappointed." —*Publishers Weekly*

ALSO BY KERI ARTHUR

Destiny Kills
The Darkest Kiss
Embraced by Darkness
Full Moon Rising
Kissing Sin
Tempting Evil
Dangerous Games

Deadly
Desire

KERI ARTHUR

A BANTAM SPECTRA BOOK

DEADLY DESIRE
A Bantam Spectra Book / April 2009

Published by Bantam Dell
A Division of Random House, Inc.
New York, New York

This is a work of fiction. Names, characters, places, and incidents
either are the product of the author's imagination or are
used fictitiously. Any resemblance to actual persons,
living or dead, events, or locales is entirely coincidental.

All rights reserved
Copyright © 2009 by Keri Arthur
Cover art © Juliana Kolesova
Cover design by Elizabeth Shapiro

If you purchased this book without a cover, you should be aware that
this book is stolen property. It was reported as "unsold and destroyed"
to the publisher, and neither the author nor the publisher has received
any payment for this "stripped book."

Bantam Books and the rooster colophon are registered trademarks
and Spectra and the portrayal of a boxed "s" are trademarks of
Random House, Inc.

ISBN 978-0-553-59115-6

Printed in the United States of America
Published simultaneously in Canada

www.bantamdell.com

OPM 10 9 8 7 6 5 4 3 2 1

Acknowledgments

I'd like to thank:

Everyone at Bantam who helped make this book so good—most especially my editor, Anne; her assistant, David; all the line and copy editors who make sense of my Aussie English; cover designer Paolo Pepe; and cover artist Juliana Kolesova.

I'd also like to thank my agent, Miriam. You rock.

And I'd like to send a special thanks to my best mates and crit buddies—Robyn, Mel, Chris, Freya, and Carolyn. Thanks for being there for me when I needed it most.

Chapter 1

The almost ripe moon hung in the midnight sky, and the heat of it sang through my veins. Being a werewolf at this time of the month generally meant fun times, because we celebrated the moon's bloom with a sensual week of intimacy. One that involved much loving and many different partners. Although for me, there was currently only one man, and he was neither an ordinary man nor a werewolf—although as a vampire, he certainly had enough stamina to satisfy the hunger of *any* wolf.

Of course, I wasn't *just* a wolf, but when the moon bloomed toward fullness, it was she who reigned supreme, rather than the vampire half of my soul.

But I was also a guardian, and it was an unfortunate fact that the bad guys of this world had absolutely no respect for the moon or a werewolf's needs.

Which was why I was now stalking through the deserted backstreets of Coolaroo, following a scent that was all death and violence, rather than being curled up beside my vampire, enjoying his caresses.

The night itself was crisp and cold, and I had a killer case of goose bumps. If I'd had the time, I would have gone home to grab a sweater, but Jack—my boss, and the vampire in charge of the whole Guardian division—had insisted it couldn't wait. That lives depended on me catching this idiot before he could kill again.

Of course, I'd felt the need to point out that he had a veritable truckload of leashed killers sitting in the underground floors of the Directorate, every one of them just aching to be set loose on bad guys. After which, he'd kindly pointed out that if I hadn't lost said killer in the first place, he wouldn't be out killing tonight.

A point I could hardly argue with given it was true, so I'd shut up, kissed Quinn good-bye, and driven straight to the crime scene.

Only to discover another dead human. Like the teenager who'd been killed several nights ago, tonight's victim had been drained of blood. But it wasn't a vampire doing this, because their throats had been slashed rather than bitten, and vampires rarely went to that sort of trouble. Not unless they considered mutilating the bodies of their victims part of the fun, anyway.

Besides, vampires were rarely wasteful when it came to blood, and while both these teenagers had been drained, a whole lot of blood had been smeared across their necks, faces, and the ground. It was almost as if someone had slashed, and then tried to gulp down the resulting surge.

I shuddered. Tonight's death was my fault, because I'd let the damned killer escape me days before.

And the fact that he'd seemingly disappeared into thin air wasn't an excuse. I was a trained hunter-killer, and no matter how much I might sometimes rail against it, there was no going back for me now. Therefore, I had to do the best that I could. And letting a killer go free to kill again definitely wasn't my best.

I blew out a breath and studied the night ahead. Evil was out there, just beyond my line of sight. The scent I followed was a foul thing that hung heavily on the cool night air, reminding me oddly of meat left rotting in the sun.

And I had no idea what it was, because he certainly didn't smell like any other nonhuman I'd ever come across.

Although he didn't smell human, either, even if the description we'd gotten off a witness matched that of a man who was listed as human. Only *he* was also very dead.

I'd immediately started imagining scenarios featuring killer zombies out for vengeance, but Jack claimed I'd been watching too many horror movies. According to him, while zombies *could* kill, it wasn't through any basic desire or need of their own. They weren't capable of thought *or* emotion, and were little more than receptacles for the deadly desires of others.

Which was a fancy way of saying someone else was in charge and directing the action. Only there was never any hint of that other person, either at the crime scene or when I'd been tracking the dead man.

If there *was* another nut behind the wheel, though, then he'd found himself the perfect killer. One that did whatever he was raised to do without question or deviation, then fell down dead again afterward.

Except that *this* man, whether he be zombie or something else, didn't seem to be showing any signs of slowing down or dropping dead.

Although surely a dead body could only move around for so long before bits began falling off or rotting started becoming a real problem.

And given the scent I was following, he was *definitely* well on the way to putrefaction. It was surprising he could move so quickly without doing himself serious damage.

I shivered and rubbed my arms, suddenly glad that I made a habit of keeping my laser in the car. Its weight was a comfortable presence in my back pocket.

Once upon a time, a thought like that might have scared me, but I'd been through too much of late. Even a werewolf intent on *not* becoming a mindless killer needed the help of a weapon occasionally.

I walked on. In the distance, a freight train whistled, the lonely sound mingling with the roar of traffic traveling along nearby Pascoe Vale road. Little seemed to be moving through these streets however, although there were lights on in several of the nearby houses.

I sucked in a breath, my nostrils flaring as I sorted through the aromas running through the cold air. My dead-smelling killer had moved into a side street. I followed, my sneaker-clad feet making little noise on the concrete. I'd mostly given up wearing heels for everyday work. The wooden stilettos might come in handy for staking the occasional rogue vampire, but running in the things across some of the terrain we had to traverse had proved too damned dangerous. And heels and ladders definitely *didn't* go together—as I'd discovered a week ago when I was chasing a rogue vamp. I'd earned another scar for that—this one across the top of my left hand. The same hand that was missing its little pinky.

The bad guys seemed to have a vendetta against my left limb.

The dead scent was getting stronger, though there was still no sign of the man. The warehouses that lined either side of this street were dark and silent, and the only life visible was the occasional cat.

The street came to a T-intersection. I paused, looking left then right. Still no sign of him in the darkness. I blinked, flicking to the infrared of my vampire vision, but the night remained devoid of the heat of life.

Which I guess, if he was dead, made total sense.

I followed my nose and headed left. Down at the end of the street was a gate and, beyond that, huge towers of paper and plastic. A recycling plant, obviously.

But why would a dead guy want to go to a recycling plant? It couldn't be an effort to get rid of any sort of evidence, because if he'd been intent on doing that, he wouldn't have left the mutilated bodies of his victims in easy viewing of anyone who happened to pass by.

So was this really some weird form of revenge

killing, as Jack had surmised, or was something stranger going on?

I suspected the latter, but that might be just my pessimistic streak coming out. After all, fate had a way of ensuring shit always got flung my way when I least wanted or needed it.

And in the midst of moon heat, it was most definitely unwanted.

The scent swung right, drawing me onto a smaller street, barely big enough to get a truck through. The wind filled the night with a forlorn moan as it gusted through the many broken windows that seemed to dominate the buildings here, and the shadows became thicker with the absence of street lighting.

Not that I needed light, especially when the moon shone so brightly, but it still felt better to enter a street lit by lights than one without them. Especially when I was alone, and following God-knows-what.

The thought had me touching my ear to turn on the tracker part of the com-link device that had been inserted a while ago. All Directorate personnel involved in field operations, whether guardians or not, now had them. Jack and the other division heads shared a dislike of losing people, and the units gave not only an instant position but allowed communication if things went sour.

Of course, in my line of work, things going sour usually meant death. And, more often than not, the cavalry had been known to arrive far too late. So far, my brother and I had been lucky, but given fate's delight in throwing curveballs our way, I often wondered just how long it would be before she threw us the biggest curveball of all.

Death *wasn't* something I really wanted to dwell on, but I guess when I was dealing it out myself on an almost daily basis, it was hard *not* to think about it hitting closer to home than my twin, Rhoan, and I might like. Especially when his lover, Liander, had barely escaped his end three weeks ago.

I didn't want to die. I didn't want Rhoan to die, either, but the fact was, death would probably come hunting us sooner rather than later. There was no way around it. Not unless I wanted to become a vampire, and really, I enjoyed sunshine too much. I didn't want to wait a thousand years to be able to enjoy it again.

From somewhere up ahead came the slight rattle of metal. I slowed and listened intently. The sound didn't repeat, and the hair rose on the back of my neck. Something was decidedly off—something other than a walking dead man.

I moved into the deeper shadows, hugging the old buildings. The wind continued to moan, and the chill in the air seemed to be increasing. Or maybe that was just an amplifying side effect of the fear sitting like a weight in my stomach.

The street swung around to the left. Factories continued to line either side, but directly ahead was a high chain-link security fence. Beyond it was the recycling plant. I couldn't see my quarry moving through the corridors of paper, but logic—and the slight metallic rattle I'd heard—suggested he'd climbed the fence and was now in there somewhere.

And yet...

I looked at the building to my left. Like the other warehouses in this street, it was run-down and abandoned. Tin rattled on the roof and the wind whistled through the many broken windows. I could smell nothing out of place, and there was no sign of life-heat in the building—which in itself didn't mean anything when I was chasing a dead man.

But he was a dead man with no apparent mind of his own, so he was obviously running into this area for a reason. Given he'd done a quick side step last night to lose me, I was betting he was trying the same thing tonight. And I was *also* betting that he'd probably gone into the warehouse rather than the more obvious recycling plant.

However, if he *was* meeting his maker in that warehouse, why couldn't I see them? Was it because there seemed to be no light source whatsoever in the heart of the building, or was there something blocking it? Even though my infrared vision was far better than the night-vision devices used by the military, no infrared was going to work properly in utter blackness. Both the man-made devices and vampire vision needed some sort of heat or light source available.

If I was the betting type, I'd be putting money on the fact that something was blocking me. After all, a warehouse with *that* many broken windows surely wouldn't have a pit of blackness at its center.

I looked back at the fence. The scent trail and the metallic rattling I'd heard were both indicative of the fact that my quarry had gone that way. But I'd trusted those two things before and had lost him.

Perhaps it was time to trust my other senses, which were pulling me toward the warehouse.

Of course, my clairvoyance was often a nebulous thing that refused to be pinned down to any direct information. Jack and the Directorate magi he'd roped in to train me kept insisting that not only would it become stronger as time went by, but I *would* learn how to fully utilize it. So far, they'd been proved wrong. Although if my ability to see souls was part of my clairvoyance, then maybe they weren't so off the mark. The damn things were now conversing with me as easily as the living, although that was one part of the gift I could have done without.

The ice of the night seemed to intensify as I neared the broken building. I ignored the chills running down my spine, and followed the graffiti-littered wall until I found the main entrance. The door hung off one of its hinges and swayed slightly in the soft breeze. Beyond it was a tumble of glass, smashed boxes, and rubbish. The air drifting out was rank with the smell of urine and unwashed bodies, suggesting this might have been a squat for the homeless, even though I couldn't see any life-heat within. Maybe something had chased them off.

Something that resembled a dead man walking.

I reached back to grab my laser, then turned it on and stepped inside, keeping my back to the wall as I quickly scanned the first room. A half-circular desk dominated the left side of the room, which suggested this had once been the warehouse's main reception area. There were two glass-fronted offices along the wall behind the desk, but there was nothing or no one hiding in either of them. Not that I could see or smell, anyway.

There were several doorways leading off this main room and, after a moment's hesitation, I chose the one directly ahead. That's where the big blackness lay, and that's probably where I'd find my dead man—*if* my psi senses were right and he hadn't actually gone over the fence as my more mundane senses of smell and hearing had suggested.

Glass crunched softly under my feet as I picked my way through the rubbish, my laser held at the ready and every sense I had tuned for the slightest hint of movement or life. But there was nothing. The only sounds were the wind and my own breathing, which wasn't quite as steady as I would have liked.

The doorway led into a short corridor and, at the far end, a set of swinging doors. Two other doors led off the corridor itself, but neither of these were open. I hesitated at the swinging doors, flicking to infrared and searching the room beyond. Once again, there was nothing to suggest there was any sort of life—or unlife—laying in wait, but that strange blackness was filling it.

I went through carefully and quietly, catching the door with my free hand before it could swing back and clip the other door. The less noise I made, the better. I had no idea what lay beyond that blot of darkness, but I wasn't about to announce my presence any more than necessary.

The air in this room was still, untouched by the wind that played about the rest of the building. Despite my earlier confidence that the inner building had to have some light, it didn't. There were absolutely no windows or skylights. It was little more than a big, black metal box. A box that held a heart of deeper darkness.

I scooted to the right, keeping my footsteps light and my back to the wall. Though I still wasn't getting any readings from infrared, I had a sense that something was near. My internal radar for dead things was jumping. Whether it was my zombie or something else, I had no idea. I certainly couldn't smell either the zombie or anyone else up ahead.

I reached the side wall. There were rust stains and small holes on the concrete floor—indications that machinery of some sort had once stood here. The smell of grease was prevalent, and a good inch of it coated the wall. It smelled faintly of age and rot, and made me wonder just what had been manufactured here.

Keeping a few inches between myself and that grimy wall, I padded along, listening intently for any sounds that might indicate I was getting nearer to my quarry. There was nothing. If not for the fact that my "other" senses were insisting that something *was* near, I might have thought I'd lost him yet again. It was almost as if that black blot in the center—whatever it was—was sucking up all sound and motion.

I crept nearer. Power began to slide across my

skin—a tingling, almost burning sensation that some-how felt unclean. I frowned, my steps slowing as the darkness in front of me seemed to grow—deepen—somehow. I reached out with my free hand and felt an odd sort of resistance to my touch before it gave way. My hand moved forward, into that darkness, and became lost. I knew my hand was there, but I could no longer see it.

Great. I was about to walk into a black hole, and who knew just where I was going to come out?

I blew out a breath, then wrapped the shadows of the room around me, using my vampire skill to hide my body from view. I might be walking into a trap, but I had no intention of doing so in plain sight.

I stepped into the blackness. I might as well have walked into a wall of glue. It pulled at me, making every step a battle. I pushed forward, fighting the gluey blackness, until sweat began to trickle down my spine. Just when I was beginning to think the blackness might never end, I was free of it—the suddenness of it leaving me staggering forward for several steps before I caught my balance.

The darkness beyond the black wall wasn't as deep, meaning I could actually see again. Ahead of me was the zombie. By his side were two big, black dogs. Only I didn't think they were ordinary dogs—not if the scent of sulfur was anything to go by. Sulfur was the scent of demons. I'd come across it once before, when I was trying—with Quinn's help—to close down a demon gate. It had been guarded by a hellhound, and the bastard had almost torn me to pieces. I didn't fancy meeting two of them—not without any sort of weapon that would do them damage, like holy water and silver. God, it was tempting—very tempting—just to step back into the gluey darkness and disappear.

Only I had a job to do, and they didn't seem to be noticing me anyway. They were too busy looking upward, just like the zombie. I followed their lead. Above them, a gantry stretched from one side of the room to the other—a rusting metal structure that seemed far older than the building itself. On it sat a crow.

And while it looked like an ordinary everyday bird, I doubted there was anything plain or ordinary about it, if only because whatever it was had the complete and undivided attention of both the hellhounds and the zombie. If it wasn't a shifter, then it was undoubtedly something a whole lot *less* pleasant, and I really *didn't* want to discover what. Especially with the bitter taste of evil that seemed to be rolling off it.

I raised the laser and pressed the trigger. The crow must have sensed the shot at the last moment, because it dived sideways—a very uncrowlike movement if I'd ever seen one—and the bright laser beam shot past its wing.

I fired again. It squawked and avoided the laser a second time, moving faster than I would have thought possible for anything not a vampire.

I swore and shot the zombie instead. The beam hit him neck height, severing left to right. His head rolled slowly off and made a wet splash as it hit the floor. His body crumpled and did the same.

I shuddered. Rotting flesh indeed.

I raised my gaze to the ceiling again. The crow squawked even as I sighted the laser, and the two hellhounds turned as one, their beady yellow eyes gleaming in the darkness and their thick canines bared.

The bird was definitely in control of the beasties.

I pulled the trigger, firing off a final shot at the crow, then turned and ran into the black glue. A howl ripped across the air, but the sound abruptly closed off as the blackness wrapped itself around me.

But I knew they were behind me. I could smell the thick scent of sulfur getting ever closer. It seemed the blackness wasn't quite the hindrance to them that it was to me, and sweat broke out across my brow as I realized that I wasn't going to get out of this before they were on me.

Then a hand came out of nowhere, wrapped itself around my arm, and hauled me none too gently upward.

Chapter 2

As I landed on a metal walkway that groaned under my weight, the hand released me. I spun around, ready to fight, not sure whether I'd been rescued or drawn into deeper danger.

The raw scent of wolf swirled around me, rich with a musk that was all man and totally delicious.

It was also a scent I recognized, even if I'd only smelled it once, and then only briefly.

Kye—the man who'd played bodyguard to Patrin, the son of our pack's alpha, Blake, and one mean bastard.

I couldn't see him in the gluey blackness, but I really didn't need to. Not given how close he was. Not when the heat of his body rolled across mine, sending warm prickles of desire skating across my skin.

Not a good reaction. Not when the moon bloomed

near fullness, and especially not when we were in such a dangerous situation. Danger is an aphrodisiac to a wolf, and my hormones didn't need that sort of prompting right now.

I tried to step back and put some distance between us, but his hand grabbed mine again, pulling me closer, until the heat of him was pressed against me and all I could smell was the tangy aroma of sweat and man and desire.

God, he smelled good.

Don't speak, he said quickly. *The witch can hear through the black shield.*

Shock rolled through me, battering away the desire. How the *fuck* could his thoughts breach my shields so easily?

My shields were vampire tight—I knew, because I'd tested them recently against Quinn and Jack, both of whom were extremely powerful telepaths. If they couldn't breach my shields, then this man certainly shouldn't be able to. Hell, according to his records—which we'd checked after our brief run-in when he'd been Patrin's watchdog—neither he nor any of his pack had ever shown any evidence of psychic skills.

Yet here he was, succeeding in doing the one thing two powerful vampires could not. Come to think of it, he'd been extraordinarily fast that day I'd cornered him and Patrin in my apartment. That might not have been a psychic skill, as such, but it proved there was something going on with this man. Something out of the ordinary for someone who supposedly was just another werewolf.

Your records say you're not telepathic, I said, mind voice tart. *So how the fuck are you conversing with me that way?*

Records often don't contain all the facts. His words ran with warmth, and it spun through my body like a summer storm, heating and electrifying. *And I'm not telepathic.*

So, this conversation we're having is just a figment of my imagination?

His amusement danced through my thoughts, and my hormones tripped along to its tune. My heart was beating so fast I swear it was about to go into a meltdown, and I wasn't entirely sure whether it was desire for the man who was holding me altogether *too* close, or fear of him.

An odd reaction given some of the things I'd faced over the last few years.

Like the zombie, the witch, and those yellow-eyed dogs are figments? he said, mind voice wry. *I think you know better than that.*

Those dogs are hellhounds, and unless you have some holy water on you, we don't stand much of a chance against them.

I have no intention of fighting them. That's why I'm up here and they're down there.

So why else are you up here, exactly? And why the hell did the press of his body against mine have to feel so good?

This closeness had to stop, otherwise I might not be able to.

I stepped back, breaking his grip on my arm and

forcing some distance between us. His scent clung to my skin and clothes, teasing my nostrils and sending my pulse rate into another merry dance. But with the heat of his body no longer pressed so invitingly against me, it felt like I could breathe again. Concentrate again.

I'm tracking a killer, he said. *What are you doing here?*

Same. Only I'm legal.

His smile felt like sunshine through rain. All warm and sparkly as it spun through my thoughts.

Bounty hunters are legal.

Not in this state, buddy boy. I paused. *Why are you hunting the zombie?*

Who said I was hunting the zombie?

The metal platform swayed a little as he moved and I grabbed sideways, wrapping a hand around the railing to steady myself. A stupid reaction really, given I could now achieve seagull form and fly with some semblance of proficiency, but it seemed my stupid fear of heights just wouldn't entirely go away.

The dogs are coming back, he added.

I looked down. There was nothing but an inky blackness to be seen, and the only thing I could feel—and smell—was him.

How the fuck can you see or sense anything in this muck?

I can't see them. I can feel them.

How?

He hesitated. *It's a talent.*

Another talent you supposedly don't have?

Yeah.

The scent of this wolf might be divine, but his

continued avoidance of any real information was getting damned annoying.

Tell me why you're here, before I'm tempted to beat the information out of you.

You wouldn't. You're not the type.

You have no idea what type I am, Kye.

Oh, I think I do. I could feel the weight of his gaze on me, knew without even seeing his face that his expression would be thoughtful. Intent. Like a soldier sighting an opponent and weighing his options. *I saw you in action with Patrin, remember. Given everything he'd done to you and your brother, you would have been well within your rights to kill him. And yet, you let him live. Scared the shit out of him, true, but left him alive. That shows compassion—and perhaps more than a touch of foolishness.*

How do you know of our history with Patrin? How did he know about my brother? It certainly wasn't something I spread around—and Patrin surely wouldn't. Not after we'd so thoroughly busted his ass.

But how else would Kye have found out? He might be able to read my surface thoughts with ease, but he'd gotten no further than that.

I was sure of *that* much.

How else would I know? Patrin boasted to me about it, before you and Rhoan showed him just how foolish such attempts would be now.

Patrin's a bastard. And how *dare* he tell strangers that Rhoan and I were related! In our line of business, that could get dangerous—and giving that sort of information to a man who was little more than a gun for hire was doubly so. *But why would he have told you about us? It had nothing to do with your stint as bodyguard.*

Well, conversations about the weather got boring, he said, mind voice dry. *Your pack mate is not the most intelligent conversationalist around, let me tell you.*

"What the fuck?" The voice rose out of the blackness, thick with anger and very definitely female. "Don't tell me you lost the trail?"

No words answered her, but one of the hellhounds whined.

So, not only could the zombie understand crow, but the witch could understand hellhound. Either that, or they were telepathic—which was entirely possible, given that my knowledge of hellhounds could have filled a teaspoon.

"Well, scents just can't disappear." She paused, as if listening, then added, "No excuses accepted. Finish off the creature. We must get out of here."

I glanced toward Kye. *Who is that?*

My target.

She's the crow?

Yep.

Who put you onto her?

The father of her first victim. He's a friend of mine, and asked me to look into it.

The first victim was only murdered several nights ago. That's not exactly giving us a whole lot of time to solve this case.

If it was your daughter, he said, mind voice patient, like he was talking to a slightly slow child, *wouldn't you take every avenue you could to find her killer?*

He had a point—although it wasn't one I was about to acknowledge. *So technically, you're not hunting a bounty, you're just hunting.*

With intent to kill. Just like me. Except I was supposedly on the side of the angels. Kye was on no one's side but his most recent employer.

Considering hunting is illegal in this state, do you think it wise for me to admit it?

He'd basically done that anyway, which only emphasized the point that this wolf had very little fear of guardians or of the Directorate. Which meant he was either very dangerous or very stupid, and I suspected it wasn't the latter.

This is a guardian case, Kye. Which means I have to warn you to keep your nose out of it.

Warning heard.

And ignored, if his tone was anything to go by.

A soft scraping filled the brief silence. I frowned down at the ground I still couldn't see, wondering what the witch was doing.

Shit, Kye said. *The blackness is fading and lifting.*

He was right, because the ground was suddenly visible—and distant enough that old fears had me stepping back from the edge. The curtain was lifting from the concrete up, and if we didn't do something very quickly, it would leave us altogether exposed.

It wasn't the witch that worried me. It was those hounds.

I stepped forward, wrapped my arms around Kye, and pulled him close. He tensed instantly, and the

warm amusement that had been flowing between us
fled faster than water down a drain.

Now is not a good time for this sort of thing.

Amusement bubbled through me. So, it was okay
for the bounty hunter to pull *me* close, but heaven for-
bid that I do the same. *Don't worry, wolf, I'm not trying
to jump your bones. If I was, you'd know about it.*

So what the hell are you trying to do?

He was still as stiff as a board, and yet despite his obvious displeasure with my sudden action, there were
parts of him that were *totally* enjoying the experience.

Which was a relief, because at least it meant I hadn't
entirely lost my touch in the weeks I'd been with
Quinn.

I'm half vampire, remember? I can cloak us in darkness.

Patrin never mentioned that aspect.

*Patrin knows squat about what Rhoan and I are really
capable of.*

Oh, I think he's got an inkling after what you did to him.

He relaxed a little, his arms going around my waist
and his body pressing harder against mine. As the fading blackness began to expose the walkway we were
standing on, I extended the shadows and wrapped
them around Kye. It took more effort than I thought it
would, and a tiny ache began in the back of my left eye.

But that was nothing against the desire that rushed
through me. Desire that wasn't only fueled by the delicious heat of him or the hardness of his erection pressed
so invitingly against my groin, but by the danger we
were in.

I closed my eyes, trying to ignore the needs of my

body, trying to concentrate on what was going on below us. There was little in the way of sound, even with
the black wall all but gone. Yet the witch was still there.
I could sense her presence.

I shifted a little, and felt the movement ripple across
the shadows that were hiding us. Pain stabbed through
my brain, briefly cutting through the haze of desire
throbbing across my body.

I shuddered, wishing I could rub my temples to ease
the ache behind my eyes, but not daring to move again.
On the concrete below, the two hellhounds were consuming the remains of the zombie. The witch herself
was nowhere in sight, but a pentagram I hadn't noticed
before had been destroyed, its outline smudged and the
candles tipped over.

Then the crow squawked. I looked up and saw it sitting on the gantry again. The hellhounds had all but
consumed the zombie, and all that remained was the
splash of blood where his bits had fallen.

The bird squawked again and launched off the platform, flying so close it was all I could do not to duck.
Then she and the dogs were gone, and silence fell.

I blew out a breath then stepped back, and gratefully
released the shadows. The pressure behind my eyes
eased almost instantly, but the distance I'd put between
Kye and myself didn't do a whole lot to ease the pounding of my heart or the heat of need racing through my
veins.

Even with the black wall gone, it was still darker
than hell in this section of the old factory. But Kye's

amber eyes were very visible, glowing with a heat that was all desire, all need. All power.

And I *wanted* that power. Wanted to feel all that heat and hardness wrapped around me again. Wanted to feel it in me.

But that wasn't an option. I was a guardian, and I had to at least try and act like it—even if it went against my more hedonistic nature.

"What can you tell me about that woman?" I said, perhaps a little more sharply than I should have. I didn't *want* to want this man, but it seemed my wolf soul was having none of that.

"She's a witch and a shifter."

His low, husky tones sent desire skittering down my spine. I loved being a werewolf, but it could sometimes be a real pain in the ass. I mean, I had a good man waiting for me. I didn't need this attraction, and I certainly *didn't* need another man in my life.

Or in my bed, for that matter. Been there, done that, and I'd ended up seriously burned.

"So has she got a name? An address?"

"She has," he said. "But I don't know them yet."

Then he grabbed me, crushing me close, his mouth finding mine almost savagely.

And oh, his lips tasted *so* good. I might not *want* to want him, but I couldn't find the strength to push him away, either. Not when the hunger to taste him was *this* bad.

I wrapped my arms around his neck as the kiss became an urgent, hungry thing, fueled by the need that burned through us both. We were so close I could feel the ripple of muscles across his chest as he breathed and the gun strapped under his arm. So close that every rapid intake of breath filled my lungs with the scent of him and it was all I could do to not tear off his clothes and take him there and then.

I wanted to.

But somewhere deep inside, a sliver of control remained. And no matter how bad the rest of me ached, that sliver would not let go. Not here, not on a walkway barely a foot wide. Not when I still had a killer to catch.

Kye, stop.

The demand sounded weak, even to me. The mind might have good intentions, but the body had other ideas.

His hand slid up my spine, the ring on his finger snagging against my top. There was a brief, sharp pain as something pierced my skin.

Sorry, Riley.

Kye, I mean it. Stop.

But the hunger of his kiss didn't abate and annoyance swirled. I broke away from his lips, but didn't move back, my breathing harsh as I stared into the flame of his eyes. "How did you track the woman here?"

"Followed her scent."

His breath teased my lips as he spoke and sent my hormones on another merry dance. The swirl of anger grew stronger. Not just at him, but at myself. I might be a werewolf and the moon heat might be rising, but damn it, surely I had better control than this!

"She's a bird," I snapped. "Her scent would be dispersed by the air long before it got to a wolf's nose."

"I didn't mean her physical scent. I meant her magical one."

"What?" Maybe my mind was still a little fuzzy from covering us both in shadows, but I had no idea what he meant.

He shrugged. "I haven't the time to explain now."

And no intention of explaining later, either. "Walk away from the case, Kye. This is Directorate business."

He hesitated, but his gaze was calculated, watchful. "And this job is for my friend. Besides, this is my living. This is how I make my money and maintain my reputation. I won't let you take this kill away from me."

"Well, that's just too bad, isn't—"

The words stopped as a cold sensation rolled over me, making my knees want to buckle and my stomach stir. I swallowed against a suddenly dry throat and met his gaze. Remembered the brief flare of pain in my back. I thrust out a hand, twisting my fingers into his shirt and pulling him close.

"What have you done, you bastard?"

"What I had to do." His voice was so annoyingly calm and cool. If not for the heat still burning in his eyes, it would be hard to imagine we'd shared a mind-blowing kiss only moments before. "As I said, I can't let you stop me—and you were certainly planning to."

His arms went around me just as my knees gave way. I wanted to hit him, wanted to break away from his grip, but my muscles refused to obey me and my strength seemed to have slipped away.

"The effects of the drug won't last long," he added. "Maybe an hour or so. You'll be safe up here."

"Unless the witch comes back." The words were indistinct, slurred.

"She has no reason to. Her pentagram and her creature have been destroyed. She'll start up again somewhere else."

"You are in so much trouble, buddy boy," I muttered.

He smiled and, despite the anger, I couldn't help noticing the way little laughter lines teased the corners of his eyes. A full smile would be knee-buckling.

"It won't be the first time," he said, as he lowered me onto the catwalk.

I tried to retain my grip on him, but I might as well have been a baby grabbing at an adult.

"See you later, Riley," he said. His lips brushed my forehead, and then he was gone, his footsteps retreating along the metal walkway.

"Bastard," I said, as the darkness closed in around me.

*R*iley?"

The voice was sharp and concerned. It was also very loud, spearing through the shadows of unconsciousness as fiercely as a foghorn.

I forced my eyes open, but for several seconds, nothing registered beyond the blackness and the cold metal that pressed into my side.

Then memory came back and I sat up abruptly.

Only to have my head just about explode in protest at the sudden movement.

"Ow," I muttered, pressing fingers to my temples and massaging lightly. It didn't do a lot to help the fierce ache behind my eyes.

"Damn it, Riley, answer me!"

Jack's voice reverberated through my head, shooting pain through my brain and making my eyes water.

I flicked my ear, switching the com-link fully on, then said, "I'm here, Jack. No need to shout."

"No need to shout? We've damn well been trying to contact you for the last fifteen minutes."

I rubbed a hand across gritty eyes, then glanced at my watch. It was nearly three. I'd been out for a good half hour. "Why have you been trying to contact me?"

"Because according to the tracker you've been stationary for forty minutes, and given that you're *never* still for that long, Sal figured something was wrong."

"Sal was right." She'd taken over as Jack's chief assistant when I'd reluctantly become a guardian two years ago. She was damn good at her job and had saved the lives of a couple of guardians through her quick response to signs of trouble. It was good to know she had my back as well, despite our somewhat antagonistic relationship.

"What happened?" Jack asked.

"Long story, but I was basically knocked out."

"Who by? And what happened to the zombie?"

I pushed up onto my feet. The warehouse walls seemed to spin around me and I had to grab at the railing to keep upright. The sensation abated quickly enough, but it left a queasy feeling in the pit of my stomach.

"The zombie is defunct. Eaten by hellhounds. There was a witch controlling it, but she took the form of a crow and flew off."

"So that's why there's never any evidence of a second party at the murder scenes. We were looking on the ground rather than up higher."

"Yeah. I didn't get much of a look at her, but I'd recognize her voice if I heard it again."

He grunted. It wasn't a happy sounding grunt, either. "So what happened?"

"Kye Murphy."

"Who's he?"

"A gun for hire. Our paths crossed a year ago, when he was playing bodyguard to the son of our pack's alpha."

"The one you and Rhoan beat up?"

Surprise ran through me, and it took me a moment to reluctantly admit, "Maybe."

He laughed. "Don't sound so shocked. There isn't much that goes on in this place that I don't know about."

Something I'd better remember in the future if I was planning any other little side excursions on Directorate time. I walked left along the railing until I found the tiny excuse for a ladder, then slowly—carefully—began to climb down. When my feet finally hit the concrete, some of the tension that had been riding me eased. I might be able to fly, but my fear of heights had never entirely vanished. I doubted it ever would.

"Look, Cole and his team are just about there—"

"You sent Cole after me?" I couldn't help the surprise in my voice. "Why send a cleanup team rather than a guardian?"

"They were the closest to your position, and Cole and his men can fight, trust me on that." His voice was dry. "He might as well check the zombie remains while he's there. At least we can confirm whether our killer was raised or not."

"There's not much more than blood here, boss. I'm afraid the hellhounds ate nearly everything else."

"What, even the bones and skull?"

"Yep." I walked toward the swing doors. "Was my being stationary the only reason you were trying to contact me?"

Even as I asked the question, I had my fingers crossed for the correct answer. After my near miss with Kye, I really needed to get home to my vampire.

"No. There's a disturbance at a house I want you to investigate, but it can wait until the morning. I'll send you the address."

Relief swam through me. Morning might almost be here, but at least I could catch a few hours alone with Quinn before I had to leave again. That'd be enough to take the edge off the hunger. "What's so special about this disturbance that we're investigating it?"

"He's an old friend of mine."

"How old a friend?"

"We were turned together."

Which made him a very old friend indeed, considering Jack had been turned over 860 years ago. I blew out a breath, then said, "I can drive over there tonight, if you'd prefer."

It was the last thing I actually *wanted* to do, but I owed Jack more than a few favors. Besides, friends *that* old were surely rare, even in the long-lived world of vampires.

Jack hesitated. "No, it should be all right. Armel thinks it may be a ghost of some kind. Things have been moved around or gone missing. Nothing major— just small things. He's just curious as to what is going on."

Hence the reason Jack had called me. He might be good at many things, but the one thing he couldn't do was see ghosts and souls.

Unfortunately, I could.

"Why did he call you rather than a clairvoyant or someone like that?"

"Because we're old friends, and I owe him a few favors."

Calling in the Directorate still seemed like overkill. But maybe that was why he was a long-lived vampire. "No one's broken in, I gather?"

"He believes not. He's got good security and he doesn't sleep all that much. He'd hear anyone entering his house."

Outside, a car pulled up, but the scents of wolf and bird were suddenly strong on the still air. I recognized both.

"Cole and his team have just arrived."

"Good. Once the situation there is sorted, go home and get some rest. I told Armel you'd be there at nine."

"Gee, thanks for letting me sleep in, boss."

"He wanted you there at six," Jack said dryly, "so be thankful for small mercies."

"Why so damn early?"

"He doesn't believe in wasting good daylight."

"He's a vampire. There's no such thing as good daylight, is there?"

"There is when you're old enough to enjoy it."

"Which neither you nor he is, so why the hurry?"

"Just because we can't play in it doesn't mean we can't enjoy it." Jack's voice was amused. "And be careful when you're there. Armel will flirt with anything that breathes, but he's partial to redheads."

"I've already got two old vampires in my life. I don't need another."

He laughed and signed off. I touched my ear to turn off the voice part of the com-unit, then pushed open one of the doors and said, "Cole, I'm down this way."

A second later, he appeared.

"So much for me hoping to save your pretty ass," he said dryly. His gray overalls were still blood-splattered from the previous crime scene and his silvery hair was darkened with sweat. "You just love spoiling my fun, don't you?"

I grinned. "Totally. Especially if it means me not lying somewhere half dead."

I looked beyond him as the similarly garbed Dobbs came into view. Like Cole, he was armed, his laser humming softly in the silence. Unlike Cole, he wasn't relaxing; his gaze constantly moved through the shadows. I was betting Dobbs could fight every bit as well as

Cole. It was evident in the quiet way he moved. He reminded me of a predator about to strike.

I met Cole's gaze, noticing the sweat staining the collar of his overalls and the quick puff of his breath on the night air. "What, did you run here rather than taking the car or something?"

"Basically, yes." He stopped and swiped a hand at the sweat running down his cheek. "Well, I ran and Dobbs flew. Dusty collected the gear and car first."

Jack *must* have been worried to impart that sort of urgency. "Sorry to put you through that hassle for no good reason."

"I think you owe us a beer." He studied me for a minute, nostrils flaring, then said, "I smell another wolf."

He didn't actually say he could smell him on me, but that's what he meant. I smiled. "You know what us werewolves are like—we can find a man in the oddest places."

"Then he's not here now?"

"No." I stepped back, giving him room to enter. "But we have zombie remains—well, zombie blood and little else, really—sitting in a destroyed pentagram."

"The wolf did the pentagram?"

"No, he was hunting the woman who did. She had a couple of hellhound helpers, which proved a bit of a problem for both me and the wolf."

"So you know him?"

"Had a run-in with him last year. I won."

"But not this time." He paused, his gaze amused. "I gather he drugged you."

"Yeah." I stopped as we reached the smudged penta-gram. "Might be worth getting one of the magi out here to look at this. They might be able to tell us what she was using it for."

"Something black would be my guess."

That went without saying. I mean, surely witches on the side of good didn't employ hellhounds or zombies to do their bidding. Our magi didn't—well, not as far as I knew, anyway.

"Our witch took the form of a crow and flew off, but while she was here, she was perched on the gantry above the pentagram." And her human scent still lingered—it was faint, but there, and I'd recognize it if I smelled it again.

Cole nodded. "We'll check it, and see if we can find any droppings or feathers."

"Might be worth doing the same at the crime scene—unless you've already checked the trees?"

"We had no reason to do so." He hesitated again. "Are you feeling all right? Your eyes are very blood-shot."

"Combination of the drug and shadowing, I think."

"I've seen you come out of shadow. It doesn't usually cause this reaction."

"I was shadowing two of us." I shrugged. "Maybe it's just plain tiredness. You'll send me the report ASAP?"

"As usual." He glanced around as Dobbs finished his perimeter check and approached. "You want to get a kit up to that gantry? We probably have shifter traces up there."

Dobbs nodded, gave me a half-smile, then walked away, reholstering his weapon as he went.

"He's a believer in the old adage that it's better to say nothing, isn't he?" I asked, amused.

"Totally," he agreed, a smile crinkling the corners of his blue eyes. "Unlike some guardians who just love to hear the sound of their own voice."

"And this is wrong because . . . ?"

He made what sounded like a disgusted snort and shook his head. "You *can* leave anytime you want."

"You know, the amusement that still lingers on your lips is spoiling the whole stern effect you're trying for there."

"Riley, stop being a pain and go."

I went.

It didn't take all that long to drive back to Quinn's, but finding parking anywhere near the hotel, even at this hour, was a pain. I eventually gave up and just dragged out my Directorate parking tag. They might be for use only in emergencies, but hey, this *was*.

There was no one in the lobby, though I could hear voices in the office near the desk. I took the elevator up to Quinn's suite and walked down the plush, carpeted hallway to his door, dragging my key out of my pocket and swiping it through the reader.

The door clicked open. "You're back early," Quinn said, the rich Irish lilt in his voice sending shivers of delight down my spine.

He came out of the bedroom as I closed the front door, as naked as the day he was born. I couldn't help smiling. I'd once thought of this vampire as staid, but

I'd learned over the past few weeks that staid only ap-plied to new relationships. Once he knew—and, I sus-pected, trusted—his partner, he was as adventurous as any wolf could want.

He was also gorgeous.

It wasn't a term I often used to describe men, but with Quinn, it just fit. With his thick, black hair, sin-fully dark eyes set in a face that would make angels en-vious, and an athlete's body, he was so easy on the eye it was dangerous.

And he was mine to play with. The thought made me want to dance.

"I thought you'd be gone most of the night."

"Thank God I wasn't."

He raised an eyebrow, dark eyes glittering with amusement and awareness. "Oh? Why's that?"

He was an empath, so he knew exactly what I was feeling, even if he was playing dumb. "Because of this."

I pressed a hand against his chest and pushed him back against the wall. Then I claimed his lips, kissing him like my life depended on it. Kissing him hard and urgently, until the taste of Kye was erased and my skin burned with the need for vampire rather than wolf.

"My, my," he murmured, when he could. "Chasing bad guys doesn't usually generate this sort of reaction. Not that I'm complaining, mind you."

"It wasn't chasing the bad guys, it was meeting an-other wolf. Now shut up and get down to business."

He grinned and did as he was bid.

And oh, it was *good*. Not just the way his hands ca-ressed me as he stripped off my clothes, but the smell of him, the feel of him, the press of flesh against flesh. The way his body shuddered as I caressed and nipped him, the taste of his sweat on my tongue.

Then he was in me, filling me, liquefying me. I groaned in sheer pleasure and wrapped my body around his, holding us both still, enjoying the feel of his body pressed against mine and the heat of him deep inside. There was something so very perfect about the way we fit together, something magical. And it went beyond the physical—it was almost as if we were matched body *and* soul.

Almost.

As his lips claimed mine again, he began to move, gently at first but quickly becoming faster, until it was all heat and desperate need. The rich ache blossomed, becoming a kaleidoscope of delicious sensations that washed through every corner of my mind. I gasped, holding on to him tighter, wanting it faster, needing it harder. Needing *him,* and all he could give me. Then everything broke and I was unraveling, and there was no thought, only waves of glorious sensation that went on and on.

He came with me, and as his seed poured into me, his teeth grazed my neck and broke through flesh. A second orgasm hit, the intensity of it stealing my breath and my sanity for too many seconds, the power of it rolling on and on.

I rested my forehead against his and blew out a breath. "That was fantastic."

"That's one way of describing it," he said, voice amused as he lowered me back to the ground. "So, who's the wolf I should thank for this sudden rush of enthusiasm?"

I grinned as I stepped over my clothes and headed toward the coffee machine. Once upon a time, Quinn's voice would have held more than a hint of annoyance while asking such a question, but he seemed to have relaxed a little in recent weeks. Part of this might have been because while I hadn't entirely given up my werewolf ways, I'd willingly restricted them. But I also think the mere fact that we were spending real time together out of the bedroom had helped our understanding of each other.

"The wolf's name is Kye Murphy. He's a bounty hunter, and he's after the witch who's raising the zombies."

"It takes heavy-duty dark magic to reanimate flesh, and that means not only that she's a sorcerer rather than a witch, but that she's extremely powerful. You be careful hunting her."

"That goes without saying." I poured myself a coffee, sucking in the rich hazelnut aroma—a scent almost as tantalizing as the man behind me. "You've met Kye—he was the wolf playing bodyguard to Patrin."

"Ah, yes." He wrapped his arms around my waist and pulled me back against him, then dropped a kiss on the side of my neck, sending little shivers of delight down my spine. "There was something odd about that one. And he could move as fast as a vampire."

He also kissed as good as a vampire...but I shook the thought from my mind and took a sip of coffee before answering. "According to his records, he's all wolf.

But he seems to have a few very different gifts that aren't on file."

"So you're investigating him?"

"We did when he was guarding Patrin. Right now, I've simply warned him away from the case."

"He probably won't listen. Most wolves tend not to."

I grinned and turned around in his arms. "That's a very cutting remark from someone who's planning to have more sex with a werewolf."

"I'm not planning sex. I'm planning a long night of hot and heated lovemaking."

I arched an eyebrow and said in a low voice, "So what the hell are you waiting for?"

Amusement crinkled the corners of his dark eyes. "You're holding coffee, and you tend to get vicious when it's taken away."

I immediately put the cup down. "Only when there's nothing better being offered. You, my darling vampire, are certainly that."

"I'm glad you think so." He swept me up into his arms then walked toward the bedroom. "Because I intend to ravish you senseless for the next four hours."

"Only four? Age must be affecting your stamina."

"There's nothing wrong with my stamina, trust me."

A point he deliciously proved over the next four hours.

*T*raffic was hell the next morning, so I arrived at Armel's ten minutes late. Which I figured was pretty damn good, considering, but Jack hated tardiness and he'd probably chew me out once he found out. Of course, I *could* fly, and therefore could avoid the whole morning traffic situation if I wanted to, but I still preferred to drive. Shifting into my seagull shape had an even worse effect on my clothes than shifting into my wolf, and I wasn't about to face a randy old vampire flashing bits of flesh through torn clothing.

I climbed out of the car and looked up at Armel's house. It didn't exactly follow the expected conventions when it came to the abode of a very old vampire. It was as big as any other house situated in the millionaires-only suburb known as Toorak, but it was also a place of stark white concrete, odd angles, metal monoliths, and huge glass windows. And the garden had the same angular, sparse outlook. There was no grass, just harsh white pebbles, and sharply angled garden beds that were filled with carefully shaped plants.

Not a place I'd want to live, but then, disorder and I were comfortable companions.

I walked through the gates and up the white marble steps, my footsteps echoing harshly in the cavernous entrance. The tall metal doors were stippled, the surface so highly polished that I had to squint against the brightness of the sunshine bouncing off them. I pressed the button to the right of the massive doors, and somewhere deep inside the house a sound rang out, reminding me somewhat of an old church bell.

I waited for several seconds, listening to the silence within the house and wondering if I'd even hear the approach of the old vampire. They could move with ghostly silence when they wanted to, though most vampires never bothered. Stealthy vamps tended to spook most humans, and given that many humans still weren't overly fond of vampires and their current place in society, spooking them often led to violence. That was never a good thing—for both the human and the reputation of vamps in general.

No one seemed to be answering the door, so I rang the doorbell again. Still no answer.

I stepped back and looked up at the massive windows. I wasn't sure what I was looking for, because I certainly wouldn't see a vampire standing there looking down at me. Even one as old as Armel couldn't withstand the sunshine that would currently be streaming in through the glass. Quinn could, but then, he was over four hundred years older than Armel. Which wasn't a whole lot of years in vampire terms, but apparently those extra years made a huge difference when it came to sunshine-immunity.

I looked back at the door, then grabbed my vidphone and rang Jack.

"Don't tell me you're going to be late," he said by way of greeting. "I will not be happy if you are."

"I'm not late—"

"Miracle of miracles."

"I'm at Armel's. He not answering the door."

Jack frowned. "He's expecting you, so he should be there."

"Maybe he is. Maybe he's gone to sleep early." I hesitated, pressing the doorbell for a third time, just in case he *was* sleeping. "What do you want me to do, boss?"

"Try opening the door."

I did so. The knob turned easily in my hand and the huge door pushed open with barely a whisper of sound. "What's his surname?"

"Lambert."

I moved the phone away from my mouth, and said, "Mr. Lambert? Riley Jenson here to see you."

"Any response?" Jack asked, voice terse.

"No." I stepped through the doorway and sucked in the air, letting the various flavors run across my tongue. I quickly discovered one that was all too familiar. "I can smell blood, Jack."

He swore softly. "Investigate. I'll be there in twenty minutes."

"Jack, it's after nine—"

"I'll be fine," he snapped, and hung up.

I blew out a breath and shoved the phone back into my pocket, then stepped farther into the wooden-floored hallway. No one challenged my appearance. The house remained as quiet as a grave.

I hoped that it hadn't become one, too.

Though my footsteps were soft, the rubber heels on my shoes squeaked lightly and the sound echoed across the stark silence. If there *was* someone alive in this place—someone other than me—then I wasn't sensing him. But I couldn't sense anything dead, either. The only reason to suspect something was wrong was the thick scent of blood.

Large rooms led off the hallway—a dining room, living room, and the biggest library I've ever seen. At the far end of the hall stood a staircase, the chrome balustrade curving gently upward to the next floor. Somewhere up there was the source of the blood.

I stopped with one foot on the bottom step. "Mr. Lambert, are you up there?"

I didn't expect an answer and I didn't get one. After a moment's hesitation, I grabbed the handrail and began to climb. There was a runner on the stairs, so the squeak of my shoes was silenced, and a deep sense of gloom seemed to descend. Or maybe that was just my pessimistic nature coming to the fore.

The carpet continued on the next floor. I walked past several doorways, not bothering to look inside, following my nose to the source of the blood.

I found it in the end room, in what looked like a study.

Or rather, I found him.

Chapter 3

I had no doubt it was Jack's friend who lay dead on the floor beneath the open safe. He seemed about the same age, and had a regal sort of look that befitted his name. His face was angular, filled with lines that spoke of a life enjoyed, his skin lightly tanned despite the fact that he wouldn't have been able to take much sun.

In life, he would have been imposing. In death, he looked small and sad.

Especially with his head and legs separated from his body.

The blood I'd smelled had pooled mostly near his legs, but there wasn't a whole lot of it. Not a body's worth, anyway. Someone had cut them off and bled him out before he'd killed him. This in itself wouldn't have completed the job of killing him, simply because a vampire could survive wounds that would kill most nonhumans. Even breaking a vampire's neck wouldn't actually kill him, though it *would* incapacitate him, and this in itself could be deadly. But completely severing the head was a different matter altogether—no vampire could recover from that. Not even one as old as Armel.

I glanced around the room. Beyond the open safe, which only had a few scattered papers in it, the room seemed undisturbed. The windows were locked, and the sunlight streaming in through the glass highlighted the darkening pools of blood and little else. There was hardly anything in the way of mess and yet something felt very wrong here. Not just the death, and not just the fact that there didn't seem to be any reason for it, but something in the air itself. An energy that felt powerful, and yet very wicked.

I shivered and rubbed my arms. Armel might have called Jack about spirits, but I doubted a ghostly apparition had been responsible for this. Besides, how would a ghost cut off someone's legs or head?

This mightn't have started off as a proper Directorate case, but it sure was now.

I stepped around his body and walked over to the safe. Beyond the few scattered papers, there was nothing inside. I doubted Armel would have had a safe installed if he didn't actually put things of value in it, so it was a fair bet that this had probably been a murder-slash-robbery. The safe didn't appear to be tampered with in any way, so either Armel had opened it for the thieves, or he'd caught them in the midst of the job.

But if that was the case, why was there no sign of fighting? No vampire went to his death willingly, and I couldn't imagine Armel simply lying still while someone hacked off his legs and head.

So what the hell had happened?

Frowning slightly, I stepped away from the safe and walked across to one of the large windows. I had to squint against the brightness of the sunlight streaming in through the glass, but it did little to warm the chill from my flesh. Shivering, I dug my phone out of my pocket and called the Directorate.

Sal answered. "What's up, wolf girl?"

"I need a cleanup team sent to my current location."

She didn't say anything for a moment, and when she did, there was a slight catch in her voice. "Armel's dead?"

"Yeah." I hesitated. "You knew him?"

"He was one of my lovers."

That surprised me. Not the fact that she had more than one lover—vampires couldn't survive on each other's blood, so while they often had vampire lovers, they also kept a harem of other races. And while some of them, like Quinn, preferred to keep their harems to a minimum, many did not. What *did* surprise me was the fact that Armel was one of Sal's men. Given that she had the hots for Jack something bad, I would have thought that fucking his best friend was a bad idea. Friends didn't take from friends—and Jack, from what I could gather, was more of a traditionalist like Quinn than the free-for-all man Armel had apparently been.

"I'm sorry to be the bearer of sad news, Sal."

"I figured it was bad when Jack rushed out of here." She hesitated. "Was it at least quick?"

I looked across at the decapitated body, at the blood pooled near the remains of his legs. "I don't think so."

She took a deep breath and blew it out slowly. "Get the bastards for me, wolf girl. Make them pay."

"I think I'll have to beat Jack to that task."

Her laugh had an edge that spoke of barely controlled pain. "Yeah, you probably will. I've reassigned Cole and his team. The boss will want the best on this one."

"Thanks, Sal."

She hung up. I shoved the phone back into my pocket, then grabbed the nearest curtain and pulled it closed. The sunlight retreated from Armel's body, keeping him whole for Cole and his team when they got here.

I walked back out into the hall then stopped. The air out here was no fresher, the scent of blood seeming to drift everywhere, but that wasn't what I was looking for. I sorted through the differing scents, recognizing and discarding a dozen or so before I found the odd one I'd sensed in the study. The scent of wrongness. Of wickedness.

It was strange that such a thing could have an actual scent, but then, fear and anger did, and they were often stronger than life-affirming emotions like lust and happiness.

I followed my nose and ended up in one of the bedrooms. It had to be Armel's—the color scheme and furniture were very masculine, although the four-poster bed and accompanying draperies were not.

The scent stopped midway into the room. The owner of that scent had stood here, possibly staring at the bed but going no further. My gaze shifted to the nightstand. An expensive gold watch sat there, as did a wallet. If robbery was the reason for this murder, why not take those as well?

Frowning, I continued on to the disheveled bed. The dents in the pillows suggested that Armel had not been alone. I couldn't smell the other person's scent, but maybe its sheer evilness was overwhelming everything else. Because I certainly couldn't smell Armel in here, either, and I should have.

I picked up his wallet, blew off some dust—which was also odd—and had a quick look. Beyond the thick wad of cash, there were credit and ATM cards, as well as a collection of cards—both business and personal.

And the thief, who'd come in here and stared at the bed, had left all this sitting here.

This was definitely a weird one.

I turned around and walked back downstairs, checking the other rooms as I went and finding nothing out of place and no indication that someone else had been in the house. Except for that out-of-place scent and the dent in the pillows, Armel seemed to have been alone.

I walked to the front door to wait for Jack. He arrived in a dark van a few minutes later. The driver crashed through the carefully constructed garden beds as he maneuvered the van as close to the front entrance as possible. The van's side door opened, and I had a brief glimpse of Jack before he blurred and raced toward the door.

I stepped back out of his way, then slammed the door closed once he'd entered, stopping the sunshine from streaking into the hallway.

"Where's the body?" he said, face and bald head pink with sunburn despite his efforts.

"Upstairs." I hesitated. "Boss, it's not pretty—"

"I didn't expect it to be." He glanced up the stairs, his expression hard and grim. "Has a cleanup team been called?"

"Cole is on his way."

He grunted. "You need to get back to the Directorate and write up a report for last night. And check break-ins for this area, to see if we've got a pattern occurring."

Normally I would have argued, not only because I hated leaving crime scenes before I got a first impression from the cleanup team, but because I didn't like being stuck in the office doing paperwork. But the pain so obvious in Jack's green eyes suggested he wanted time alone to grieve for his friend.

I turned to leave, then hesitated. "Boss, there's an odd smell in both the bedroom and the study upstairs. You might want to call in the magi to investigate it."

He nodded and I left without another word.

The roads were still clogged with traffic, so it took longer than it should have to get back to the Directorate. I bought four coffees from Beans, the little coffee shop that had opened next to the Directorate building, then headed down to the level that held the guardian division's main office area and the cell we called a squad room. Sal was sitting at her desk in the main room, so I walked in and offered her a coffee. She took it with some trepidation, taking a sniff then saying, "Hazelnut?"

"Cures all hurts, if only temporarily," I said, and headed out.

I'd almost reached the door when she said, "Thanks, Riley."

I gave her a half-wave and continued on to the squad room. Both Kade and Iktar were there, the horse man squinting at the computer and the spirit lizard sitting in the corner, the outline of his body fading into the shadows. It was somewhat disconcerting to see, but given that Iktar preferred to study his case files that way, we'd almost become used to it.

Almost.

I handed them both a coffee, then plonked my butt down on the corner of Kade's desk. Of course, this brought me into close proximity to the heated scent of him. Kade might be out of bounds—thanks to both Jack's rules and my own desire to remain as true as possible to Quinn—but that didn't stop desire from stirring, especially when the moon was heating my blood.

"I think you'd better get your eyes checked. Your squinting is getting worse."

"It's not my eyes, it's lack of sleep," he said, leaning back in his chair and rubbing a hand across eyes that were bloodshot and baggy. "It's the fucking babies. They won't sleep."

I grinned. "Well, you're the one who wouldn't keep his little swimmers to himself. I have no sympathy for you."

He snorted softly. "You're such a bitch."

"And you should be helping your mares out. It takes two to create babies, and two to look after them."

"The whole point of having a large herd," he said, voice holding a hint of irritation, but the gleam in his warm chocolate eyes countering it, "is the fact that there are plenty of mares to share night duty. The breadwinner has no need to get involved."

I snorted derisively. "Sable makes more money in a week than you do in a year."

"That is beside the point." He took a sip of coffee and sighed in pleasure. "Damn, this is good."

"The Directorate's probably saved a fortune since the shop upstairs opened." Certainly we hadn't used the coffee machine much since they had. I took a sip myself, then added, "What's happening?"

"Cole's sent a prelim report in for the zombie killing last night. General impressions and identifications, nothing more."

It was surprising he'd managed to get that far. Between riding to my rescue and then being called over to Armel's, he'd been kept pretty damn busy.

"Any initial similarities to the first murder?"

"Other than the fact they're teenage girls who had their throats slashed and blood drained, no." He reached forward and turned the monitor around enough for me to see. A pretty young blonde dominated the screen. I quickly scanned the report underneath as he added, "Last night's victim was a street kid with convictions for theft and drugs."

The first murder had been Amy Prince, a seventeen-year-old kid who'd recently left high school. There'd been nothing criminal about her. "There's no apparent connection between the two sets of murders?"

"Nothing obvious that we can see. They don't even look alike. The victims appear to be selected randomly."

"But random just doesn't feel right."

Kade raised an eyebrow. "Why?"

"Because these murders are being committed by zombies, and zombies do not rise on their own," Iktar said. "Nor do they practice revenge. Only the living do so."

I looked at him. He was still reading, looking engrossed, but obviously not. "What makes you think these are revenge killings?"

He met my gaze, his all-blue eyes striking against the darkness of his featureless face. "Zombies have no thoughts or feelings of their own. They are mere receptacles for the desires and hatreds of others."

"So?" Kade said.

"So, if mere murder were the motive behind these killings, then why raise the dead? There are a thousand different ways a person with the sort of power needed to raise the dead could cause death, but she chooses decaying flesh to be her instrument. To me, this suggests not only that she *wants* our attention, but that she has a powerful motivation. Revenge is one such emotion."

"So is hatred, or bloodlust," I murmured, and yet I couldn't disagree with him. These killings were linked somehow, I could feel it, and revenge was certainly one possible connection. Revenge for *what* was the question. "Why would anyone actually want to attract our attention? That's just suicidal."

Iktar shrugged. "We won't know that until we find the person controlling the zombies."

I glanced at Kade. "Maybe we're tackling this from the wrong angle. Maybe we need to discover if there's any connection between the zombie and the dead people."

"It's still hard to imagine a connection between a street kid in Fitzroy and a former Broady high school student."

"Street kids weren't born that way. Maybe they all went to the same school or something." And it wouldn't be the first time we'd dealt with the bloody need to avenge injustices done at school. Hell, Liander—the love of my brother's life—still bore the scars after one such episode.

"Has anyone talked to the kids who shared the squat with last night's victim?"

Kade shook his head. "They scattered when I tried earlier this morning. I think I looked too much like a cop for their liking."

He looked about as much like a cop as I did. It was probably more the fact that he was a big, imposing male who looked ready to handle any sort of trouble that had them running.

"Then maybe that's what I need to do next." Jack might have told me to write up a report, but solving this case was infinitely more important. Besides, talking to the street kids got me out of the office and away from Kade's delicious aroma. I might be strong willed, but I wasn't a fool. Even the saintliest werewolf could succumb to temptation during the moon heat, and I certainly had never been a saint. "Could you do me a favor?"

"Look out, Kade. We're about to be asked to do something she was asked to do."

I glanced across to Iktar. "Hey, I brought you coffee. Be nice."

White teeth flashed—an odd sight in his all-black face. "I was. I didn't tell him to say no, although that is what he should do."

"Why don't you just go back to your reading?"

He chortled softly. "If Kade didn't want to get back into your bed, he would say no."

"Kade knows there's no chance of that."

He met my glance with a raised cup. "Doesn't stop me from hoping otherwise, of course. What's the favor?"

"Could you run a check for break-ins in the Toorak area? One of Jack's friends was murdered this morning during a robbery, and he wants to see if there have been any similar occurrences."

"That explains the explosion of anger I felt just before he stormed out of the squad room."

Kade, like Quinn, was an empath, but he was also kinetic, which had definitely come in handy when fighting many a bad guy.

"And it means he'll be in a foul mood for days to come." I hesitated, then grinned. "Another reason for me to be in the office as little as possible. You know how easily I can annoy him."

He snorted softly. "Go. I'm stuck here anyway. The lizard and I have to cross-check the details of everyone in that emo nest you found to make sure there's no illegals or underage turnings."

The emos were a large group of vampires I'd discovered while investigating a previous case. Rather than living on blood, emos fed off emotion. Which, according to Jack, made them even more dangerous than blood suckers, simply because they could amplify emotions like hate and rage, and feed off the resulting chaos.

Not that *this* nest of emos had done anything like that as yet, but it paid to be cautious. Especially when we hadn't even known they existed until I'd stumbled upon them.

"The lizard has a name," Iktar said mildly. "Kindly use it."

Kade grinned. He loved teasing Iktar, and I had a fair idea Iktar enjoyed prodding back—although it was hard to tell because very little expression showed on his face. "I'll stop calling you lizard when you stop calling me horse boy."

"Can it for five minutes, will you?" I shook my head

and took another sip of coffee. "What happens if you find illegals or underage emos?"

"From what Jack said, the vamp responsible will be given a warning and fined, and then the vampire council will get called in to keep an eye on her."

I raised my eyebrows. "I thought the vampire council preferred the Directorate to deal with such matters." Hell, we cleaned up the rogues, and that had once been the council's job.

Although if Quinn was to be believed, the council was still very much involved in such duties, only its cleanups involved vampires far worse than anything we ever saw. Which was a scary thought considering some of the psychos we dealt with on a regular basis.

"We don't police the vamp community, remember," Kade said. "We just hunt the ones who kill humans."

"And nonhumans."

He nodded. "But from what I've seen, it's rare for us to go after vamps who kill vamps."

I frowned. "I'm sure we have." And yet, I couldn't remember a clear example, and wondered if this was because such cases were automatically shunted to the council.

I took another sip of coffee, then added, "Anyway, I'm glad it's you doing the paperwork, and not me." Being stuck in a small room with the luscious smelling Kade during the moon heat was always a test for my resolve, but after my close call with Kye, I just didn't want to push it. Feeding some hungers just made them grow. I slid off the desk. "Let me know when Cole's full report comes in."

"Will do."

I headed out. According to the report, last night's victim had been sharing a squat in an old section of Fitzroy. The building had once been an old machine shop and, like the other factories around it, had been bought out in preparation for a new housing development. But the plans had been caught up in red tape, and the buildings had lain empty for years. Street folk were never shy about claiming such buildings as their own, though, and it wasn't unusual for a whole mini-city to be surviving within the grimy, run-down shells.

I locked the car and studied the building, analyzing the scents that surrounded the place and letting them run across my senses. More than one unwashed body lived in this building, and there was also more than one nonhuman. It was an odd fact that while a lot of humanity still seemed to have problems coping with the vampires living in their midst, streets kids and the homeless all seemed to live side by side with vampires without problems. I guess it helped that most vamps didn't eat at home, and did more than their fair share when it came to protecting the squat and the people who lived with them. The kids and tramps returned the favor, looking after the vamps during their daylight sleeping hours.

I pocketed my keys and headed in. The strongest scent of humanity came from a corner on the upper floor, though there were one or two overly strong aromas coming from different sections of the ground floor. Both suggested wino, and given they weren't my targets, I kept walking.

The metal stairs creaked as I climbed, giving ample warning of my arrival to anyone who was paying enough attention. And they were. Footsteps scattered, boxes scraped across the floor, and doors slammed. I couldn't help smiling. Even regular human cops couldn't have missed those noises, and it suggested the street folk on this level were very young indeed. Those who'd been on the streets for a while tended to meet their fate with a resigned acceptance and smart mouth.

Sunlight streamed in through the grimy windows on the upper floor, highlighting the motes of dust dancing on the air. This section of the building had obviously once been offices, but most of those were little more than broken shells, leaving a wasteland of debris and half-walls. My quarry waited in a far corner, in an office that had two whole walls and two half-walls. With all the smashed windows, it was probably the only part of this floor that provided any real protection from the chill of the wind.

Three boys were waiting for me, though I guess it wasn't fair to call them boys. They might have only looked fifteen or sixteen, but one look into their eyes suggested a life that had been harsher than most.

One boy—a gangly, pockmarked kid with matted brown hair and the most startling blue eyes—took several steps forward and said belligerently, "What do you want? This is our place, and we don't like strangers here."

I stopped and grabbed my ID from my pocket. "Riley Jenson, from the Directorate," I said. "We're investigating the death of Kaz Michaels, and I just need to ask you some questions."

He looked at the ID, then at me. "You're a guardian?"

"Yep."

"But you ain't no vampire."

I raised my eyebrow. "What makes you so sure?"

"You don't smell like no vampire."

I had to grin at that. It was nice to know that I wasn't the only one in the world who thought most vampires stank. "And you don't smell like a regular street kid."

"The water is still connected to this dump, so there's no reason not to use it." He looked me up and down, then said, "What are you, then?"

"Werewolf. You the boss here?"

He shrugged. "Depends on what you want."

"I need to know everything possible about Kaz."

"Why?"

"Because the person who murdered her has murdered someone else, and I need to stop him before he does it again."

"By stop him, you mean kill him." It was a statement, not a question.

I nodded. "That's what we guardians do, I'm afraid."

He cocked his head a little on the side, then said, "You don't look that dangerous."

I grinned again, liking the kid's attitude. "You should see me if I don't get coffee every hour, on the hour."

He snorted softly, and amusement danced in his bright eyes. I had a feeling that despite his young years and somewhat puny looks, he was a force to be reckoned with. At least when it came to protecting "his" kids.

And I was betting now that the ones who were hidden hadn't so much run for protection, but were instead a surprise force ready to attack if and when it was needed.

"Can you help me?"

He shrugged. "I don't know a lot. Kaz kept pretty much to herself. She only came here for protection at night, like."

"So she had no real friends?"

"No." He hesitated. "Joe might know more. He hung around with Kaz a bit."

"Then where can I find Joe?"

"Around. He mostly works the streets during the day. Safer than at night, even if it doesn't pay as well."

I wasn't sure whether he meant working in the prostitution or stealing sense, and wasn't about to ask. "You think you can get him to talk to me?"

"That depends."

I didn't ask on what. We both knew what he wanted out of the deal. "There's two hundred in it," I said. "That's twenty bucks cash for everyone here." And enough money to buy meals for the next couple of days if they were canny.

"Three," he said.

I hesitated. Jack wouldn't approve an expense report, so this money was coming out of my own pocket. In the scheme of things it wasn't much, but I had a brother who liked to overspend and it was often me who picked up the slack to ensure we had food in the cupboard and coffee on the table. "Two-fifty."

"You guardians are well paid. You can afford more than that."

"Did I mention I have a serious coffee habit?"

He grinned. "Two seventy-five."

"You drive a hard bargain."

"Totally." He held out his hand. "We got a deal?"

"Deal." I clasped and shook it. The kid had a good grip for a scrawny human. "If you can you get Joe here this afternoon."

He grinned. "I'll get him here by five."

Meaning Joe probably wasn't working the streets, but hiding out nearby. This kid was a shark. "You got a name?"

He hesitated. "Mike."

I lightly linked to his mind, quickly skimming the surface. I saw no lie in his thoughts, about either his name or anything else he'd said.

"Well, Mike, I'll be back at five, then."

I nodded to the two kids behind him, then walked out. Once in the car, I checked the computer for any messages then leaned back in the seat, wondering what to do. Cole wouldn't have finished his report on Armel's murder yet, and I didn't want to go back to the office. Quinn had business meetings all day, so he was off the list as well. Even my friend Dia wasn't around. She'd gone up to Queensland for a month-long vacation.

I blew out a breath and started up the car. With nowhere else to go, I headed home to grab some lunch.

Liander was sitting in the living room when I arrived, newspaper in hand and his feet crossed on the table. The sun streaming in through the windows made his silver hair gleam like ice, and his normally pale skin took on an almost golden glow.

He finally looked healthy. For a while there, he'd been looking frailer than a ghost, and moving like an old man. Though I guess almost getting gutted would do that to you.

"Some people have a good life," I said, throwing my bag on the table before heading into the kitchen to turn on the kettle and investigate the fridge.

"Some people hate the confinement the doctors are forcing on them," he said dryly. "There's leftover lasagna in the fridge if you want to zap that for lunch."

"Sounds like a plan," I said, pulling out the tray. "How much longer do you have to rest?"

"Until the soreness goes away."

I shoved two slices of lasagna into the microwave, then leaned against the door frame and frowned at him. "I thought it had."

He suddenly looked sheepish and made a show of looking at the paper again. "Well, it did, but then Rhoan and I got a little overadventurous, and I think it strained things."

I snorted softly. "No sympathy from me, then. You want a coffee?"

"As long as you're not going to tell me to get it myself."

"I'm not that mean." I made two coffees and carted them across to the coffee table, then went back to grab the lasagna. I handed Liander his, then plonked down on the other sofa.

"So how's the love life?" he said, after several mouthfuls.

I grinned. "A hell of a lot safer than yours, from the sound of it."

"No problems on the Quinn front?"

"He's being quite the gentleman."

Liander snorted. "That'll change once you start acting like a proper wolf again."

I gave him an exasperated look. "I *am* acting like a proper wolf."

"Have you gone back to the clubs? Taken other partners yet?"

"You know I haven't. I'm happy as I am, Liander, and Quinn and I do share something special."

"He's not a wolf, my girl. And your wolf soul will always hunger for its mate, no matter how happy you might be with Quinn."

"You're not telling me something I don't know. I'm just not ready to venture fully out of the cave yet."

"You know, if I ever meet Kellen again, he's going to get a very large piece of my mind."

"Don't you dare. He was doing what was right for us both."

He snorted softly. I ignored him and continued to eat the lasagna. One of the many good things about Liander coming to live with us was the fact that the quality of the meals we were getting had improved— mainly because he could cook and Rhoan and I couldn't.

I took a sip of coffee to wash it down, then said, "I had something of a close call yesterday, actually."

"Oh?" He raised a gray eyebrow, amusement teasing the corners of his silvery eyes. "Do tell."

"You remember Kye? The bodyguard Patrin employed?"

"The one Rhoan reckons was more than just a wolf?"

"Yeah. Turns out he's a bounty hunter, and he sort of saved my butt."

"Well, it *is* a cute butt."

I grinned. "Maybe so, but I doubt that's the reason he saved it."

"So, you got hot and heavy with him as a thank-you?"

"Not intentionally." Liander's eyebrows rose again, so I added, "I blame the moon heat and the fact that he smelled so good." He kissed damn good, too, but that was beside the point.

"So why didn't it go any further?"

"It's hard to concentrate on loving when there are a couple of hellhounds wanting to tear you to pieces."

"I guess." He took a mouthful of food, then added, "You intending to see him again?"

"No. I don't really like him, and I certainly don't trust him."

"Hey, I didn't like Rhoan when I first met him, either."

"I thought you got hot and heavy on the first date."

"Nope. I thought he had a great body, but a shitty attitude. I still thought that when we had sex a few days later. Of course, attitude or not, he was the one. And he has mellowed, thankfully."

"He's never going to be the perfect man." Even I knew that, and I loved my brother to death.

He waved a hand in agreement. "All I'm saying is you should never write anyone off just because you don't instantly fall in love. Or lust."

I snorted. "Trust me, I don't expect to—although lust is always handy." Especially if you had to spend the rest of your life with him. I took another mouthful, then added, "Besides, if I meet Kye again, I'm going to have to arrest him, because it means he's still investigating a case I've warned him off."

"Well, that probably *would* put a damper on things," he said, his voice wry.

"Totally."

I finished the last of the lasagna and picked up my coffee with a sigh. "I'm so glad you came to live with us."

He grinned. "I think you two are getting the better end of the deal. Do you know how badly you both cook?"

"Absolutely. That's why you and Rhoan are never going to be able to set up house alone. I'd starve on my own." I rose as my cell phone rang, and walked across to grab it out of my purse. "Hello?"

"Riley? Jack," he said, unnecessarily. "We've got another vampire dead. One Garrison Bovel."

I swore softly. "Not someone else you know, I hope?"

"Not personally, no, though I've seen him around

the various bars a few times." He sounded bone-tired. "He was the head of an accounting firm that handled the taxes for many of the dead. It could mean trouble if they got into his records."

"Has his office been raided?"

"Not as far as we know, but we've contacted his partners and told them to check."

"Why would anyone want to rob an accountant?"

"Because he's been a record keeper for three hundred years, and has amassed quite a fortune."

God, he had to have loved his job to have done it for that damn long.

"I'll send you the address," Jack continued. "Mel and her team are already there."

"Has Cole's report for Armel's murder come through yet?"

"He's still working on it, but he believes there were magical influences."

I raised my eyebrows. "In the robbery or the murder?"

"Hard to say. Head over to Bovel's straight away. We need to nip this in the bud quick, before the vamp community gets antsy."

And *that* wouldn't be good for anyone. "Will do."

"Trouble?" Liander asked as I hung up.

"Another dead vamp. Tell Rhoan I probably won't be home for dinner."

"Will do."

I grabbed my bag and headed back out. The address had come through on the car's onboard computer and I drove over to Brighton in record time. The beachside suburb was the local "it" spot for all those who were more than mere millionaires and, because of this, had its fair share of older vamps. After all, any vamp over a certain age had time enough to amass more money than most humans.

Which didn't mean they were good targets. Most vamps protected their fortunes fiercely, and the wise robber went elsewhere. Especially if he didn't love the thought of becoming a vampire's next meal.

I pulled into the victim's driveway. The house was another of those modern ones that always looked like a big white concrete box—and it still surprised me that vampires chose to live in these places. I would have thought something dark and gothic would be more their style. But then, vampires these days were all about breaking expectations.

A dark van with Directorate plates sat in the tree-lined parking lot and the front door was open. A stick-like figure hovered near it, dusting for prints. It had to be Janny. Mel's other team member—Marshall—was a portly soul.

I grabbed my ID as I walked up the grandly arched steps and showed it to the mobile recording unit that had been set up in the doorway to record all movement in and out of the house. There'd be others inside.

"Afternoon, Riley," Janny said without looking up. Her voice was surprisingly mellow and rich, though I don't know why I always expected it to be otherwise. Something to do with her insectlike looks, I think.

I stopped and studied the doorknob she was dusting. No obvious prints. "How bad is it, Janny?"

She shrugged. "I've seen worse."

So had I, but that never made it any easier. "Same method of disposal as the first killing?"

"Seems to be. Mel's inside if you want a fuller report. You'll find her upstairs."

"Thanks." I stepped past her carefully and headed for the stairs. The air inside was alive with the flavors of the house—the delicate aroma of rose mixed with the deeper resonance of vampire. Underneath that, the metallic tang of blood. I couldn't smell the wrongness that had been in Armel's. Not on this floor, anyway. I climbed the stairs.

Mel poked her head out of a doorway, brown hair shining in the sunlight streaming in through the windows at the far end. "You want to check the bedroom on the right for me? There's a scent in there I can't define, and I'm wondering if it's the same as the one you found in Armel's."

I nodded and headed in. The interior of Garrison's matched the exterior, and his bedroom reflected this. The white walls held little in the way of adornment and the bed—with its deep red comforter and matching pillows—was the only splash of color in the room. Even the carpet was white—a bad color for a vampire to have in a place where he fed, I would have thought. Even the smallest of splashes would have been noticeable. The red bed, at least, made sense.

I studied the scents of the room, searching for the one I'd found in Armel's. That powerful sense of wrongness was there, but fading fast. Another hour or two, and there'd be nothing more unusual in this room than the scent of sex and the musty aroma that spoke of vampire. A vampire who washed, I thought, thinking of the kid's comment with amusement.

I walked up into the other room. This was a library rather than a study, as Armel's had been, but it still had a safe. Mel was dusting it for prints.

My gaze fell on a chrome and glass side table and I noticed the dust gathered there. And it wasn't the powder Mel was using—this stuff was coarser, and reminded me of the dust I'd blown off Armel's wallet. I glanced back at Mel. "You taken a sample of this?"

She looked across to see what I was pointing at, then nodded. "Don't know what it is, though I don't think it's regular house dust."

"It looks similar to some dust I saw at Armel's."

"Then we'll add it to the priority list."

"Thanks."

I finally let my gaze move to the body. Garrison, or what remained of him, sat in a plush leather chair next to the side table, a book slumped across his chest and the remains of a glass underneath the fingers of his right hand. Wine stained the carpet, its color almost as rich as the bloody pool that had formed under what remained of his legs.

"Where's his head and the end of his legs?" I asked, suddenly realizing what was missing.

"Your guess is as good as mine at this point," she said, catlike green eyes bright in the semishadows. "But there's a couple of rather large Dobermans in the backyard, and the window behind you is open."

I looked at the window, then back at her. "You

haven't checked whether the missing bits are out there?"

She smiled grimly. "We have two bird shifters and a cat shifter on this team. Sorry, tackling dogs is off all of our to-do lists. But you could always try."

I could, but if those dogs out there were guarding the remains of their master, I wasn't going to interrupt them. The only reason a vamp would have a couple of Dobermans would be for protection, and I rather suspected these two would be trained to tackle most nonhumans. I also doubted that one lone werewolf would faze them, even if that werewolf had alpha tendencies and could back down most canines.

"Have you called in a dogcatcher?"

"Yep. But the vampire's bits would have turned to ash very soon after they hit the sunlight, and they could have been thrown in any direction from that window. It can wait."

I turned away from the window. "Any idea how these people are getting into the house?"

She shook her head. "Marshall can't find any obvious—or nonobvious—methods of entry. But they appear to be walking out the front door with their hauls."

That raised my eyebrows. "They would have to have been covered in blood, wouldn't they?"

"You'd think so. Cutting off someone's head and legs while he's alive would have created spurts of arterial spray, even in a vampire, but other than the pools of blood near the remains of his legs and neck, there's nothing."

"So they used a screen or something?"

She wrinkled her nose. "I doubt it. Arterial spray is something of a misnomer—it comes out with a lot of force when a main artery is cut. Even if they'd used a screen, there would have been residual drips."

"And they couldn't have used any sort of floor cover, because then we'd not have the blood pools."

"Exactly."

My gaze ran around the room, then came to rest again on the pools of blood underneath Garrison's body. They weren't nearly big enough for a body that had been bled out. "Maybe they were collecting the blood."

"Maybe. Hard to imagine anyone sitting still through that sort of thing, though, and they don't appear to have used restraints of any kind."

"Could it have been magic?" I asked, looking at Mel again. "Cole thought there might have been magical influences over at Armel's murder."

She frowned. "If it is, it's not one that I've smelled before. And it would have to be an extremely powerful magic to restrain someone when you're hacking him to pieces."

"Well, there's at least one thing that *is* obvious," I said grimly. "These people have a serious grievance against vampires."

And if they *had,* maybe Armel and Garrison weren't their first kills. Maybe they had a history of it. It was certainly worth checking into.

"You'll get the report to me as soon as possible?"

She nodded. "Won't be tonight, though. The lab is

severely backed up at the moment. Even the priority stuff is going to take longer than usual."

"As soon as you can, then. Thanks, Mel."

She nodded and got back to her fingerprinting. I dug my phone out of my pocket, ringing Jack as I headed back to the car.

"Anything?" he said.

"Just the same odd smell that I noticed at Armel's. Have the magi checked out Armel's yet?"

"They're there now."

"Which means we probably won't have an answer for a while yet." I gnawed at my lip as I opened the car. "Had another thought—"

"That's always dangerous."

Despite his dour tones, he was obviously getting back to some sort of normality if he could throw barbed remarks. Well, as normal as one could get after losing a longtime friend.

"It might be worth checking for similar murders in other states," I continued, "just to see if this is an established pattern. These murders are well practiced, Jack. We're dealing with professionals, not novices."

"Sal's already on that. There's nothing yet, but it's going to take a while. You got anything else?"

I glanced at my watch. It was only four, and it wouldn't take me that long to get back to Fitzroy for my meeting with the street kids. But I was betting Joe would probably already be there, and if not, I'd wait. It was better than going back to the office and doing paperwork.

"I've got a meeting with a kid who knew the latest zombie victim at five."

"What about her parents?"

"She'd been living on the streets for years. I doubt the parents would be able to tell us anything useful about her." And I really didn't want to confront that sort of grief without the hope of getting something useful.

Jack grunted. "Once you finish there, concentrate on your report. I want it on my desk by the morning, Riley."

His tone added the "or else."

"You'll let me know if Cole's report comes in?"

"Yep."

"Thanks, boss."

I hung up and drove to Fitzroy. I got there with tons of time, and walked up to the Macca's on the corner to grab a burger and a shake, downing them both before heading back.

A shiny silver BMW had been parked in front of the building in my absence, and the car looked very conspicuous against the grime and age of the surrounding buildings. Obviously whoever owned the thing had no great love for it, because parking it in an area littered with street kids was nothing short of an invitation for robbery.

I lightly touched the hood as I walked by. Still warm, so it hadn't been parked here long. Inside, there was nothing more than a few folders to be seen. Maybe it belonged to the owner of these old buildings. Maybe the red tape surrounding the building plans had finally been removed, and the street kids were about to find themselves on the street again.

I walked through the old factory doors and drew in a breath as I headed for the stairs. Though I didn't expect it, there was one major difference in the aromas teasing the air.

The kids were no longer alone.

Kye was here.

Chapter 4

I walked up the stairs and through the wasteland of half-walls. The kids were holed up in the far corner again, and Kye was with them. Though his arms were crossed and his stance casual, there was an underlying tension in his shoulders that suggested he was ready to move at the slightest provocation.

"What the hell are you doing here, Kye? You were warned off the case."

"So you know this guy?" Mike asked, his bright blue gaze latching onto mine with some hostility. Like it was my fault Kye was there.

"He's not a guardian, if that's what you're asking."

"Never said I was." Kye's voice was deceptively mild. This man was a fight waiting to happen, and everyone in the room was aware of that fact.

"Then I don't have to talk to him?" Mike continued.

"No, you don't." I glanced at Kye. "Do I have to arrest your ass?"

He gave me a smile. My hormones did a happy little dance, but then they were easily amused.

"You can try."

I met and held his gaze. Something sparked deep in his amber eyes, something beyond the desire raised by the approaching night and the nearness of the full moon. Something that was ancient and basic, and honed deep into our wolf souls.

The need to fight. To prove worth.

I was challenging him, and the alpha within him wasn't liking it.

But I'd done a whole lot more than simply stare when he'd been protecting Patrin, so his reaction here was a little surprising.

Whatever the reason, the fact was that I didn't *want* to fight him. I might be stronger and faster, but I had a feeling Kye had a few nasty surprises of his own.

"Retreat to the stairs, Kye. This is Directorate business, and you shouldn't be here."

He'd hear from the stairs, we both knew that. It was a way for both of us to back down gracefully, avoiding a fight that would do neither of us any good.

He stared at me for a moment longer, then that odd spark was snuffed from his eyes. Desire lingered, however. Maybe he could control that no more than I could.

"This won't end here. You know that."

I didn't answer, simply because I wasn't entirely sure what he was referring to—the challenge, or the attraction. Either possibility was unsettling.

He turned and walked away. I glanced back at the kid. The same two teenagers stood behind him, but the scent of several others hovered in the nearby room, and a few of those were new.

"That was intense," the blue-eyed leader of this motley group said, his gaze flickering between me and Kye. "Felt like you two were about to come to blows."

Given that wasn't actually a question, there was no point in answering. "Where's Joe?"

"Where's the money?"

I smiled and dug the wad of cash out of my pocket. He tried to take it, but I grabbed his hand before it got anywhere near the cash.

His eyes widened slightly. "You're fast."

"Werewolves are. Produce Joe."

"How do I know you'll give me the money afterward?"

"You don't. But I will."

He considered me for a moment, obviously weighing his options. Then he made a motion and a door behind me opened.

"What do you want?" a new voice said.

I turned around. Joe was small and, like most of the kids here, on the thin side. He also had gray eyes that were absolutely startling against the darkness of his skin.

"Mike tells me you were friends with Kaz Michaels."

The kid's gaze slipped past me for a moment, getting, I suspected, the go-ahead from the boss. "Yeah. What of it?"

"Did you see her much the days before she died?"

"Sure. She bunked here, like me."

"Then was there anything different about her behavior in the days leading up to her death? Did anything unusual happen?"

He frowned. "Well, she met a lady about a job, which was odd because Kaz didn't really like to work."

I raised my eyebrows. "Was the woman from employment services?"

The kid behind me snorted. "Yeah, the government's so concerned about us living on the streets that they send employment gurus down here to help us."

"Then who?"

Joe shrugged. "She was just a lady. Well preserved, middle aged, wearing a blonde wig."

"A wig?"

"Yeah. There was a stray lock of brown hair coming out the back of it, like."

The kid was observant, but I guess they had to be. "So you were there as a spotter?"

"Yeah. Kaz never really trusted anybody."

And she was dead—probably because she *did* trust the wrong person. "What was the job?"

"Don't know. I wasn't close enough to hear, but she said later it was worth ten grand."

That raised my eyebrows. What the hell had the kid gotten herself into that she was promised such a large payout? To me, it immediately suggested something illegal—like the rumored underage slash-film ring that had apparently been running in Melbourne for a while now. But Kaz had been killed by a zombie, and I doubted the filmmakers would have the sort of power needed to raise the dead. If they did, they surely wouldn't be making money from sick underground films. They'd have the means to aim a lot higher.

"Wasn't she suspicious of being offered such a large sum of money?"

"All Kaz worried about was *getting* the money. Thought she could do so damn much with it." He shrugged.

"There's nothing else you can tell me about the woman that might help track her down?"

He frowned. "Well, she was posh, like. And she had a very manly voice."

Which could have simply meant she was wearing a voice modulator. "And would you recognize her if you saw her again?"

"Sure." He dug a hand into his pocket and withdrew a grimy piece of paper. "Did this up for you."

I accepted the paper and unfolded it. It was a hand-drawn picture of a woman with a hawkish nose and thin lips. I looked up at Joe, surprised. "This is really good."

He shrugged, like it meant nothing, but a quick flash of pleasure showed in his eyes. "I don't know anything else."

"Then thank you for your help." I turned around and handed the cash to Mike. "And thank you."

He leisurely counted the cash, then pocketed it without commenting on the extra twenty-five I'd given him. "Pleasure doing business with you, Riley."

"If you hear of anyone else being approached by a woman with fake blonde hair, you'll get back to me?" I handed him my card, and he pocketed it as easily as the money.

"If there's cash in it, sure."

"You really do drive a hard bargain."

"Hey, a kid has to live."

I suspected *this* kid would do rather well in whatever profession he set his mind to. Heaven help the police if he decided the criminal life was his thing.

I made my way back to the waiting Kye. He fell in step beside me and we silently made our way out of the building. I stopped at his BMW and turned to look at him. His golden skin was as warm as the sunshine, and the dark red of his hair ran with brighter highlights. He was, in many respects, a golden man with cold, cold eyes—even if those amber depths burned with a desire equal to anything I might be feeling.

The moon might be on the other side of the world at the moment, but she had a hell of a lot to answer for.

"Last warning, Kye. Stay away from this case or I'll report your presence to the Directorate."

His smile was dismissive. He might have heard me, but he wasn't believing me.

"Do you think this wig-wearing woman is the one we're after?"

"What did I just tell you?"

Amusement teased his lips. "Stay away. You didn't say don't discuss."

"It's a very fine point, and not one I'm going to get into. Just get into the car and leave."

His smile grew, even if it never entirely reached his eyes. "Answer me and I will."

I blew out a frustrated breath—although the frustration wasn't due so much to his obstinacy as it was to my own giddy reaction to something as silly as a smile.

"There's nothing to connect the wig-wearing woman with the woman who controlled the hellhounds and the zombie."

"Other than the fact that one woman contacted the kid, and another woman killed her."

"Joe said the woman who contacted the teenager had a deep, almost manly voice. The woman in the warehouse didn't."

"Ever heard of voice modulators?"

"Of course I damn well have." Hell, I'd used the horrible things. "I still don't think they're the same woman."

"Why not? Because you don't want me investigating further?"

Well, yeah. "No. And it's nothing more than a hunch."

He studied me for a moment, and there was something in his look that made me uncomfortable. Like he was trying to get inside my mind and pick it apart. Only he *wasn't* actually doing that. I would have felt the intrusion. Eventually, he said, "Do you often get these hunches?"

"Sometimes."

"And do they often come true?"

"Sometimes."

He smiled again. "You're not very forthcoming with information, are you?"

"You're a bounty-hunting killer who has been

warned off the case. Why is it surprising that I'm not forthcoming with information?"

"I wasn't talking about the case."

"And why would I want to provide personal information?" My voice was dry. "You and I have nothing in common."

"Other than the fact we're both paid to kill, you mean?"

I crossed my arms and resisted the urge to point out that *I* at least was a legal killer. Being on one side or the other wasn't really his point. "Other than that, yes."

"Well, we do seem to have this odd attraction flaring."

"Kye, the full moon is only days away and we're both werewolves. Lust is natural—but I, for one, am not going to act on it."

"I wouldn't bet on that."

Neither would I, actually. "Get in the car and leave, or I'll make you."

There was nothing pleasant or nice about his sudden smile. He considered me for a moment, then raised a hand, lightly brushing his fingertips down my cheek. It felt like I was being branded by fire and, deep inside, my wolf shivered. I wasn't entirely sure whether it was fear or anticipation.

"Don't ever threaten me, Riley," he said quietly, his voice so silky soft, carrying no hint of threat and yet full of it all the same. "Because I *will* kill you if I have to. Nothing personal, of course. I'm just here to do my job."

I stepped away from his touch, but I could still feel

the heat of it on my skin. Part of me wanted to scrub it away, the other half wanted to exult in it.

"You have no idea what I'm capable of, Kye. Don't ever think you'll come out on top in a fight with me."

"Ah, but I have the advantage of knowing what you are. You have no idea what I truly am, and therein lies my advantage."

And with that, he turned and walked around the front of the car and climbed in. The big car roared to life and within seconds he was gone.

Leaving me standing there wondering who was the bigger fool—him or me.

After a second, I grabbed my cell phone and called the Directorate as I walked to the car. Sal answered.

"Of course it would be you," she said tartly. "It's nearly my quitting time."

"I'd hate for you to be bored in your final few minutes, Sal," I said cheerfully. "I need you to start a search for me."

"Of course you do." In the background I heard keys tapping. "Okay, who?"

"Kye Murphy. Werewolf, bodyguard, and gun for hire. Rhoan and I did a basic search on him a while ago, but I need a deep one. I want it all—gossip, secrets, family, the lot."

"And why would you be needing all this?"

"Because he's turned up on a crime scene twice now, and each time he's gotten there before us. I want to know where, or how, he's getting his information."

"You could always arrest his ass."

"I have a bad feeling that would not be easy—and

that's another reason why I need this information fast. He's hiding something, and I want to know what."

"Sounds like you've got a thing for this bad boy," she said dryly.

"All werewolves have a 'thing' for each other during the full moon phase, Sal. It's beside the point."

She sniffed. "I'll initiate it, but it'll take a while to collect the information."

"Let me know when it's there."

"Will do."

I hung up and climbed into my car, then headed home to write up my overdue reports. Neither Rhoan nor Liander were home when I got there, but I found a note on the fridge saying they'd gone out for dinner.

Which made my stomach rumble a reminder that it needed something more substantial than a burger. So once I'd typed up the report and sent it off to Jack, I grabbed my cell and rang Quinn.

"I was wondering when I was going to hear from you," he said.

The sexy lilt in his voice made me want to sigh in pleasure. "I didn't want to disturb any vital business meetings."

"All business meetings are vital, and they all drag on into boredom if there isn't a reason to take a break." His voice was wry. "Am I going to see you tonight?"

"That depends on whether you intend to pay for dinner or not. I gave my last spare cash to a street kid and now I'm broke until payday."

"And I'm sure there's a perfectly good reason for you

doing that. Only it probably won't make sense to the more logical of us."

"That's a rather catty remark from someone who wants sex tonight."

"Not when I'm paying for the dinner you obviously can't afford."

"True. Apology accepted then."

He laughed softly. "Shall I try and book a table at Wren's?"

Wren's was the latest "it" spot for all of Melbourne's high flyers and, as such, had a waiting list months long. Luckily for us, Quinn knew the owner and most times could get us squeezed in. We'd been there five times now, and I adored the food. Mainly because Wren's was rare in the world of fine dining—it actually served enough food to keep even a hungry werewolf happy.

"If you get us a table, I'll love you forever."

"If only you would," he said, with another laugh. The sound washed across my senses as sweetly as a caress and made my body tingle with desire. "What time?"

I glanced at my watch. It was just after six-thirty now, and Wren's was in the heart of Toorak, which was always a hassle to get to.

"I can be there by seven-thirty."

"You really *are* hungry."

"And maybe not just for food," I said cheekily. "I hope you're not wearing an expensive suit, vampire, because I fully intend to rip it off later."

"Be my guest. It'll be worth the loss."

I grinned. "See you in an hour."

I hung up then walked into the bathroom, having a quick shower and drying my hair before heading for my bedroom. Wren's was posh, so I grabbed a form-fitting black skirt that was split up the left side, and a sexy black jacket for warmth. The jacket was short, barely skimming my waist, and the neckline plunged enough to show glimpses of my lacy red bra. I had matching panties, but I didn't put them on. There was something delicious about going without them. To complete the outfit, I chose four-inch red stilettos—the ones with the wood heels, of course. Mainly because Jack had a habit of calling me out to a job at the most awkward times, and the wooden stilettos had come in handy as a weapon more than once.

Quinn was already waiting in front of the glass and chrome building when I arrived. He was dressed semi-formally in black pants and a neat pale-pink shirt that was roughly rolled up to the elbows, and he was holding a black jacket casually over his shoulder. He looked absolutely wonderful.

His gaze met mine for a moment, then swept down my length, and the desire that stirred the air when he looked up again was powerful enough to make my wolf soul want to howl.

"You look fantastic," he said, swinging around and offering me his free arm.

I laughed softly. "I was just thinking the same about you."

"Then we're well matched." The gray-clad door-man opened the door and gave us a nod. Quinn contin-ued, "Frances couldn't give us a table tonight."

Disappointment ran through me, then stalled as I saw the amusement in his bright eyes. "I'm sensing there's a 'but' to that statement."

"But I booked out the starlight function room for us instead."

I stared at him for a moment, then laughed. "That room is *huge*."

"So is, I presume, your appetite, because I have pre-ordered all your favorites. Besides, what is the point of being a billionaire if I cannot splurge occasionally?"

I grinned. "I guess this means we'll have to make sure you get your money's worth."

The look he gave me just about smoked my insides, and it was all I could do to stop myself dancing with excitement.

Frances Wren, owner and chief hostess of the business, approached as we neared the maître d's station. She was a tall, willowy woman with perfect blond hair and sapphire-colored eyes. She was also over five hundred years old, and didn't look a day over twenty. Vampirism did have its benefits.

"Quinn," she said, her Irish accent far more pronounced than his ever had been. "It's lovely to see you again."

He gave her a hug and a kiss on the cheek. "I hope I'm not pushing my luck by booking at such short notice."

"The room wasn't being used, so it's hardly a problem. Besides, I owe you far more than a table a couple of times a week." She turned her attention to me, and

her smile radiated a warmth that had my own lips reacting. "Riley. Lovely to see you again."

"Are you sure opening the starlight room for just the
two of us isn't going to be a problem?"

She gave Quinn an amused look. "Rest assured, it
isn't. And he did tell me it was a matter of life or death.
For his clothes, that is."

"He might have been right."

She laughed softly. "This way, please."

She led us through the packed dining room. The
color scheme was as muted as the light, and the overall
impression the room gave was one of warm welcome.
Wren's decor might be subdued, but the food was spec-
tacular, and that was probably the secret behind its
success.

We climbed the stairs at the back and reached the
barely lit landing. The decor here was richer, all claret
and gold, with plush velvet chairs and tapestries on the
wall. Wren opened the double doors that led off the
wide corridor beyond the stairs and ushered us through.

Like the hallway, the starlight room was plush and
rich. Tapestries and old paintings lined three walls, but
the fourth—the side that looked onto the street—was a
smoky glass through which little could be seen. There
was no ceiling in this room, just more glass. The sky
was clear and bright above us.

The room itself was shadowed, the only light coming from the muted wall lights and the candelabra set
up in the middle of the table. Two wineglasses sat near
the candelabra, and an open bottle of wine waited in a
freestanding chiller.

"Your meal will be up in an hour," Frances said softly, amusement dancing across her lips. "I hope that gives you enough time."

I waited until she'd left, then glanced at Quinn, eyebrow raised. "Time enough for what?"

"To enjoy the wine, of course." He rested his fingers lightly against my spine, guiding me across to the table. The heat of his touch sent little flashes of desire racing across my flesh, until it felt like my whole body was tingling.

"It doesn't take a whole hour to drink one bottle of wine," I said, sitting on the edge of the table rather than on one of the plush chairs.

"It does if you drink it with proper appreciation, rather than merely gulping." He handed me a glass, then picked up the wine and poured it. "Tell me about your day."

He sat down beside me, his long legs stretched out and crossed at his feet, his thighs brushing mine and practically sending my pulse rate into overload. I wanted him so bad the scent of it hung on the air, but the lusty aroma wasn't *just* mine.

He obviously had his seduction all planned, and though my blood practically boiled with the need for him, I wasn't in the mood to hurry tonight. Not when we had this big old room to ourselves, and all night to play.

"Did you know either Garrison Bovel or Armel Lambert?"

"Given your use of the past tense, I take it they've both been killed?"

His gaze moved from my face, drifting downward, until it rested on the swell of my breasts. My nipples hardened under his scrutiny, and it was all I could do not to undo the tiny buttons and allow him full viewing access.

"Yes, they have."

He took a sip of wine, then placed the glass back down on the table and said, "I didn't know Bovel personally, but I did hear he'd been doing well with the importing business he'd set up. Armel was one of the older ones, so yes, I knew him."

His tone had my eyebrows rising. "I take it you didn't like him?"

"He was a player. He took risks. And all too often he included others in those risks—mostly to their detriment." He shrugged eloquently. "On another note, I always thought bright red lingerie wouldn't suit a redhead, but that bra looks lovely against your skin. I don't suppose there's panties to match?"

I took a sip of wine. The rich fruity taste rolled around my tongue and made me want to sigh in pleasure. "That's for me to know and you to find out later. We have wine and food to enjoy first."

His sigh was dramatic, but the effect was spoiled by the twinkle in his bright eyes. "And there's nothing I can do to change your mind?"

He raised a hand as he said it and trailed a finger across the top of my breasts, just above the bra's lace line. Though his touch was light, it seared my system with a heat that was pure and lusty. A tremor ran across my skin and the deep-down ache suddenly leapt into focus.

"Nothing at all," I said, voice husky. "Do you think someone could have held enough of a grudge against Lambert to kill him?"

"Easily," he said, his gaze thoughtful as his fingers slipped underneath the edges of my jacket. "But from what I understand, Bovel had nothing in common with Armel. No similar friends or interests."

His hand slid down lace, until he was cupping my breast. Casually, he brushed his thumb across the nipple, sending a ripple of pleasure across my skin.

I licked my lips, saw the knowing smile play across his mouth. The damn man knew which strings to pull to get me aroused, but I'd be damned if I'd let him win me *this* easily. Besides, drawing it out would only make the result all that more satisfying.

"Well, they do have one thing in common—they died the same way." I took another sip of wine but its taste was suddenly sour compared to the dizzy sweetness of his touch. "Both were drained, decapitated, and had their legs chopped off."

"It would have taken a great force to subdue Armel. He was a powerful vampire." His hand was on the move again, drawing back to the buttons on my jacket. One came undone, then another.

"There was no sign of a fight. It looks for all the world like he caught robbers in the act and they overpowered him."

The front of my jacket fell open. "Lovely," he murmured, then leaned forward and brushed his lips across the red lace. I closed my eyes against the sensation, but couldn't suppress the shudder of delight.

But I wanted to play, to tease, and draw out the time before sex, so I pushed my butt back and put some distance between us again.

He smiled, but there was a determined spark in his eyes that suggested he wasn't about to give up his sensuous assault.

And I certainly didn't want him to.

"Trust me," he said, picking up his wineglass again and taking a sip. It was an action so sensual I practically melted. "Someone like Armel would never be overpowered. Not only was he a vampire, he was an extremely strong telekinetic. He could have blown any attackers into the next suburb had he wished to."

I took a gulp of wine, but it really didn't do a whole lot to quench the fire inside. "We think there might have been magic involved."

"Magic done on the run shouldn't have been strong enough to contain psi elements." He slid forward, so that his legs were pressed hard against mine again.

"Shouldn't being the operative word." I stood up and retreated a few steps.

"True." He smiled lazily and took another drink. "I can hunt around and see if there's any whispers about either of them, if you'd like."

"I think Jack is already doing that."

"Ah, but he is younger than I, and will not be able to push as far."

He rose and stepped toward me. I took several more steps back, flashing a nice bit of leg as I did so. His gaze drifted down and the rich scent of desire increased, until it felt like I was drowning in it. And oh, what a way to go.

"Armel was Jack's friend," I said, amazed my voice was sounding so normal when every inch of me was practically shaking with need. "I think he'll push as far as he damn well needs to."

He continued to walk toward me, and I continued to retreat, all the while sipping my wine and giving him a lazy, come-get-me smile.

"What you forget," he said softly, "is that vampire hierarchy is very feudal in its structure, even in this day and age. He's restricted in what he can say and do to the older ones."

My back hit the glass hard enough to slop wine over my hand. He closed the distance separating us, leaving only a few bare inches between us and overriding my senses with the delicious scent of man and lust.

"Have I told you about these windows?" he said, neatly pinning me in place by placing his hands on either side of my head.

"They're windows," I said, my voice steadier than my pulse, but only just. "Why do you need to tell me about them?"

"Because they're made from a special glass that reacts to heat."

Then they'd be reacting now, because I was burning. And it wasn't just his closeness, but the brush of his breath along my lips and the caress of his desire across my senses. Everything about this man was hot, and everything he did made me want him all the more. And he didn't even have to touch me to achieve this.

"And this is important because?"

"Because when something hot touches them, it becomes visible to the outside world."

My heart began to pound that much harder at the thought. Danger might be an aphrodisiac to a wolf, but so was exhibitionism.

"And will something hot be touching them?" I asked, the words little more than a gasp of air.

He smiled and plucked the wineglass from my hand, putting both of them on the sill. Then he leisurely hooked his thumbs under the bra's underwire, and slowly slid it up and over my breasts, until the lace no longer covered them.

"I think perhaps it will," he said, his voice little more than a low growl as his hands replaced the lace and gently began to press and tease and massage.

God, it felt *good*.

And my resolution to prolong our lovemaking for as long as possible was getting more frayed by the moment. I took a deep breath and tried to remember what we'd been talking about.

"Jack's sister is one of the older ones." She was also the head of the whole Directorate in Australia, and based in Melbourne right alongside her brother. "Surely she'd—" the words came to a sudden halt as he caught both nipples between his thumb and forefinger and lightly began to pinch. A shudder went through me and my knees just about gave way. I licked my lips again, and somehow managed to add, "help him out?"

"Madrilene Hunter will not tie herself to personal vendettas, even for her brother," he murmured, his touch leaving my breasts and moving down my stomach.

I didn't know whether to sigh in relief or whine about the temporary reprieve from the sensual assault.

"Meaning she won't help him, either."

"No."

His hands slid around my hips, until the length of me was pressed against the long, hard length of him. It felt so good I stopped thinking and just started reacting, letting my hands slide down his back to cup his butt and press him even harder against me. Slowly, sensually, I rubbed myself against him, enjoying the heat of him, the hard press of his erection.

He smiled, his dark gaze holding mine, afire with the same need that burned through me. His hands slid up my back and with one clever flick of his fingers, my bra came undone. A second later, he was sliding both my jacket and my bra from my shoulders and dropping them to the floor.

He kissed one puckered nipple, then the other, then murmured, "Turn around."

I did as bid, and found myself pressed against the cool glass, the heat of my body making the surface flare and go clear. Suddenly everything on the street below was visible.

"I want everyone to know that this gorgeous body is mine," he murmured, sweeping my hair to one side and kissing the nape of my neck. "I want everyone to see just how glorious you look when you come."

His words had me shuddering in pleasure, and it was all I could do not to turn around, to take what I so desperately needed.

But this was his game. Mine could wait until later.

His fingertips slid up my bare leg, making my muscles twitch in delight and the deep-seated ache all that much fiercer. When he reached the top of the skirt's split, he hesitated, and my breath hitched in expectation. I wanted, needed his touch to slide underneath the material. To explore where I ached.

Instead, his hand moved down to my thighs and slowly, surely, the skirt slid upward.

For several seconds, he didn't do anything more than simply stand behind me. But I could feel the weight of his gaze on my body, hear the rapid intake of his breath, smell the raging of his desire. And it was as arousing as a touch, making the throb of desire fiercer than I'd ever thought possible.

More minutes ticked by, and sweat began to trickle down the back of my neck. The weight of expectation was not something I'd experienced before, and while it might be sweet, it was also torturous.

Finally, his hands touched my shoulders and moved down, sliding around to my breasts. His body pressed lightly against mine as he caressed and pinched my nipples, and I moaned, thrusting back against him, enjoying the steel of his erection pressed so firmly against my butt.

Then one hand began to move downward, along the flat of my stomach, across to my hip, down the outside of my thigh. My breathing was getting harsher by the moment, and expectation was rising, until it felt like I would surely burst if he didn't damn well touch me *there* soon.

His fingers brushed the inside of my thigh, and my breathing hitched. Slowly, surely, his caress moved upward, and when he finally brushed my clit, I cried out in sheer, aching pleasure. His fingers slid through the wetness, caressing, delving, and all I could do was shudder and writhe and moan. And then he was in me, thrusting hard and deep, and I came, shaking with the sheer force of my climax. And still he thrust, the thick heat of him stabbing deep, the sensation so glorious pleasure rose thick and strong all over again. Then he came, and his teeth were in my neck, and the dual sensations were so glorious I came a second time.

For several minutes we did nothing more than merely stand there, our bodies locked together and the heat of our union clearing the glass. On the street below, several men had gathered, obviously trying to figure out if they had just seen what they thought they'd seen. If I'd had the energy, I would have waved.

"That," I said eventually, "was a brilliant start to the evening."

"It surely was."

He dropped a kiss on my shoulder blade, then stepped back. I turned and followed, letting the glass go smoky again. Quinn placed his hands on each side of my face and gently kissed me. It was a sweet kiss, yet one that spoke of passion not yet sated.

The thought had my hormones coursing in delight.

He leaned down to pick up the drinks, his undone

shirt revealing delicious glimpses of toned stomach muscles as he gave me my glass. I took a sip, enjoying the coolness of the sweet liquid, then said, "So, where was our conversation again?"

"I believe I said something along the lines of Madrilene not going out of her way to help her brother solve these murders."

"Ah yes." I took another sip of wine and idly wondered if it would taste as good if it was licked off his skin. "Why do you call her Madrilene when she's known everywhere else as Alex?"

His smile was sensual and dangerous. A man getting ready to seduce again. "Most older vampires have had several names over the years. I met her when she was Madrilene, so that is what I call her."

"And what does she call you?"

"Ciaran. Quinn is a derivative of my original sur-name, O'Cuinn."

"Ciaran O'Cuinn." The name rolled off the tongue sweetly. "It suits you."

"But it is no longer the name I go by."

"And will your current moniker also hit the dust one day?"

"It's hard to say, because the existence of nonhumans is an accepted fact now. Back when I was young, they were very much a myth, and anyone who lived too long or didn't age was treated with great suspicion—and that often resulted in death." His shrug was an elegant thing. "But enough of me. Continue with your tales of death."

I smiled. Getting Quinn to talk about his past was as

difficult as ever, but at least I was now getting little bits and pieces. Once upon a time, he'd clam up tighter than, well, a clam. "We also happen to have a couple of hellhounds running around. Don't suppose you've some more of that holy water lying about, do you?"

He laughed softly. "It's not something I keep in the cupboard, no. But I can get you some, if you'd like."

"Please." I dipped my fingers into the wine, then lightly sprinkled it across his chest. Stepping away from the window, I pressed myself against him and slowly licked the droplets off. Desire stirred, his and mine, filling the air with its richness. "How much time have we got left before our meal arrives?"

He barely even glanced at his watch, merely wrapped his arms around me and said, his lips so close to mine I could practically taste them, "More than enough time to uncover some more creative uses for the wine."

"Good," I said.

And it damn well was.

Someone was touching my feet. The sensation was feather light, but nevertheless annoying. I twitched my feet away but the annoyance seemed to follow.

"Go away," I muttered, not opening my eyes.

"I will in about five minutes," Quinn said, amusement evident in his rich tones. "You need to wake up."

"Says who?" I grabbed the pillow and hugged it tighter. As if it would chase away the reality of the morning and the fact that I *did* need to get up and go to work.

"I have coffee."

My nostrils flared. "Not in your hand, you haven't."

He chuckled softly and kissed my cheek, leaving it tingling. "I'm not *that* stupid. It's out on the table, along with your bacon, eggs, and toast."

"I don't want to get up." It sounded petulant, but God, I was *tired*. Between the sex at the restaurant and the sex here in his penthouse, sleep hadn't played a major part in our night.

"Trust me, neither did I. Not when you had your warm and luscious body wrapped around me. I have meetings I can't get out of, however."

And I had killers to chase. I blew out a breath and opened my eyes. "Why this sudden rash of meetings? Your airline business isn't in trouble, is it?"

"No, but I am considering shifting the headquarters down to Melbourne so I can see a certain redhead more often."

He was shifting his whole business for me? God, was there ever a greater sign of commitment than that? It made me feel intensely happy, and yet intensely selfish. I couldn't give him the same sort of commitment because there would always be one part of my soul that hungered for—needed—more.

Besides, he wasn't the first man to offer such a gift. Kellen had moved down to Melbourne for me, too, and look how well *that* had turned out. "Really?"

"Really." His dark eyes smiled. "Of course, the move

will be gradual, as said redhead is keeping her options open when it comes to other werewolves."

"It's not like I'm going to the clubs and dancing every night."

"I know, and I appreciate it." He leaned down and kissed me gently. "But we both know there will come a time when I am not enough, and that will be a testing time for us both."

"I won't flaunt any other lovers in your face, Quinn. I promise that much."

He smiled and touched his fingers lightly to my cheek. The caress was tender and yet oddly sad. Just like the brief flare in his eyes. "I know. The problem lies with my instincts, not yours. A vampire doesn't like to share."

"What about an Aedh?"

Quinn had never been entirely human, even before he'd turned vampire. The Aedh weren't flesh and blood, they were beings of energy who sometimes took on winged human form to procreate. His father had been a priest of the Aedh, whose job it was to guard the gates that joined this world to the other.

He smiled. "The Aedh has sympathy for the vampire, but he's certainly the reason for the tolerance currently being displayed."

"Then I need to thank him." I reached up and kissed him again. His lips were warm and delicious, tasting faintly of coffee. "Shame you have business meetings to attend to."

"We have tonight." He pulled away from my grip. "Up woman, or you'll have Jack calling to hound you."

I muttered something unpleasant under my breath, but gave in to the inevitable. By the time I'd showered and dressed, Quinn was gone.

The eggs were cold when I got around to eating them, so I just ate the bacon and toast and then gulped down the coffee. I was almost out the door when my cell phone rang.

"On my way, Jack," I said, answering without bothering to look at the screen.

"Well good," my brother said. "Because it is nearly nine-thirty, and your ass should have been in the Directorate by now."

"So Jack has sent you to track me down?"

"No. Well, sort of. He's sending me undercover later today, so I told him I needed to talk to you first. You feel like breakfast?"

"I've had breakfast."

"What, you've never heard of a second breakfast? We're never going to make a good hobbit out of you, are we?"

I grinned. Rhoan and Liander had been on a Lord of the Rings kick of late, and could practically recite the old movies word for word—although neither of them had gotten around to reading the books. Rhoan wasn't much of a reader, and Liander had never gotten past the first few chapters—although he kept picking the book up, and did get a little bit farther each time.

"I'll be into second, third, and fourth breakfasts, you know that." All this good sex made a gal hungry. Besides, I needed to keep my iron intake up to avoid problems with the amount of blood Quinn was taking.

"Meet you at Beans in ten, then."

"Will do." I hung up and punched the call button. The elevator answered straightaway, zooming me down to the parking levels.

Rhoan was already waiting by the time I got there, and drew me into a bear hug. "Nice to see you again."

"Says the wolf who's always off gallivanting with his mate."

He grinned and took my arm, guiding me to a booth. "The flat does get a little crowded with the three of us there all the time."

I slid into the booth, punched an order of hazelnut coffee and pancakes into the electronic ordering machine, then slid my credit card through the appropriate slot.

"So," I said, as Rhoan repeated the process. "Tell me about the undercover job."

"It's at a gay strip bar." Anticipation glinted brightly in his silver eyes. Like most wolves, Rhoan was an exhibitionist by nature, and he loved flaunting the wares.

But he was also addicted to sex—or rather, the danger of sex with a man who might well be his prey. He might be committed to Liander, but when it came to work, all bets were off. And Liander, knowing of his addiction, had given his blessing.

"Who's the target?"

"No one specific. Apparently the club is one Armel visited quite often. Jack wants me undercover there to see if there's any whispers as to what might have happened."

"Armel was bisexual?"

He nodded. "Apparently many old vampires are. I suppose restricting yourself to one gender does tend to limit your food source."

That was true. But it made we wonder if Jack, or Quinn, ever had male lovers. Neither of them had mentioned it, but I guess it wasn't something you just dropped into casual conversation.

"Why doesn't he just ask the owners himself? Or better yet, go there and do a mind sweep of the patrons?"

A waitress appeared with our coffees. Rhoan gave her a smile of thanks before saying, "Because the club is an underground one, and owned by two powerful vamps who run the business along the same lines as many wolf clubs. He's afraid that if we go in there in an official capacity, everyone will either disappear or clam up."

"So these vampires are older than Jack?"

"Apparently."

Hence Quinn's warning that Jack would be restricted in what he could do and ask. I sipped my coffee then said, "Have you talked to Liander about it?"

He smiled. "He was first cab off the stand. Sorry, sis, I love you and all, but he gives good sex."

I picked up a sugar packet and threw it at him. "Idiot. Of *course* you'd tell him first. He's your mate."

"Yeah." He paused, then said, "It takes a bit of getting used to, doesn't it? Having someone living with us, I mean."

"Yeah. But it's also good, because we have more than just each other now. We have Liander."

"I guess." He paused. "I sometimes miss the peace of you and me, though."

"Because it's only been a few weeks. We've been alone for practically forever." I glanced up as the waitress delivered my pancakes and Rhoan's fried breakfast, thanking her before adding, "You're not getting cold feet again, are you? Because I promise you, I *will* smack you."

He laughed. "No, everything's fine. As you said, it's just taking some adjustment."

"Imagine how Liander feels. He's gone from a supercool, roomy house to a messy two-bedroom apartment. It has to be his version of hell."

"Never really thought of it that way," Rhoan said around a mouthful of food.

I smiled. My brother had always tended to think of his needs and wants first. It was something of a family trait, I guess.

I tackled my own food with gusto, and it was only when I'd finished that I said, "So how long are you actually going to be undercover?"

"Don't know. The full moon is coming up, so I'll be no good to anyone then. Maybe a week, maybe less." He shrugged. "I guess it depends on whether I catch any whispers or not."

"Then Jack hasn't got anything concrete on Armel's murder?"

"Nope. Cole's apparently waiting on the magi to finish up their reports before he submits his complete findings."

I frowned. "They're taking a while, aren't they?"

"Some things do." He shrugged again. "How's the zombie hunting going?"

"About as well as everything else is going," I said, then grimaced as my cell phone rang. "How much do you want to bet that this is Jack?"

Rhoan snorted. "Not biting on that one. The odds are too short."

It *was* Jack, and the news wasn't good. "There's been another zombie murder," he said. "Salliane's sending the details through to your onboard."

"It can't be the same zombie, boss. He was eaten by hellhounds. I suspect there's not much resurrection from a fate like that."

"Then whoever is raising these things obviously has enough power to raise more than one. Get over there straightaway. And tell Rhoan I need him up here to learn his undercover history."

"Will do." I hung up and glanced at my brother. "You heard?"

Rhoan grimaced. "Yeah. Look after Liander until I get back."

"Just make sure you get back, bro."

He touched a hand to my cheek lightly, then rose and left. I finished my coffee then stood, but had to grab at the back of the booth as the room swam briefly around me. Maybe I needed more coffee.

I ordered a cup to go, then climbed into the car and drove across town to the next murder scene. Whoever was behind these didn't seem to be overly choosy about their location. First Fitzroy, then Coolaroo, now the green-living, artist-friendly hub known as Eltham.

I parked the car behind the other Directorate vehicles, then walked across the grass. This kid had been murdered in the trees near the railway lines and, like before, her neck had been slashed.

I stopped several feet away from her body. The metallic tang of blood mingled with the dying warmth of raw meat, but layered in between was a scent that reminded me of solvents.

"She had a gun?" I said, my gaze on Cole rather than on the bloody, broken body he was squatting beside.

"Yes." He didn't look up as he spoke. "And it may lead to an early capture of this particular zombie. She shot off one of the creature's fingers before it got her."

"Damn shame she didn't aim for the zombie's head. That might have done her more good."

He glanced up at me. "Not everyone is as efficient at killing as you guardians."

"And some of us guardians wish we weren't as efficient, either."

He snorted softly. "Jack would have a fit if he heard you say that. You are his protégée, after all."

"It's not a job I particularly liked or wanted, Cole, but I'm stuck with the damn thing and have to make the best of it."

He raised his eyebrows. "Even guardians can quit."

"Not this guardian. It's either this or military for me."

"Why?" he asked, frowning. "It's just a job. It's not a life commitment."

"Maybe not for the rest of you." I might have accepted my guardian role, and some part of me might even enjoy the hunting aspects of it. But I didn't want to be doing this for the rest of my life, and yet I could see no way out. The drug introduced into my system so long ago was still wreaking havoc, and until we knew what the full scope of those changes were, the Directorate was the safest place to be. They could at least monitor what was going on. "Buy me a drink sometime, and you just might tempt me to tell you the whole sorry tale."

His grin crinkled the corners of his eyes, and made his whole face light up. "And I suppose you're hoping a drink would lead to sex?"

"Werewolves aren't *that* easy. I'll have you know it'd take two or three drinks, at least."

He laughed. "Good to see your standards have risen."

I grinned. "Sorry to see yours haven't. You don't know what you're missing, Cole."

"I'll survive."

I was sure he would. "Did you get enough of the finger to get a print off it?"

He nodded. "I sent an image through to headquarters. They're doing a search."

"Finding the zombie probably won't help us find the master."

"You don't know that."

Yeah, I did. The woman behind these things was not only powerful, but clever. I very much doubted she'd be keeping barely animated carcasses close at hand for someone to see and report.

"Did you find out anything about the last zombie?"

"Not much." He shrugged. "But there doesn't seem to be any connection between him and the people he killed."

"No, but remember it isn't the zombie who's going after these people. It's the person who's raising them who'd have the connection."

"Well, there's no obvious link between the first two victims, and I doubt we'll find one here."

"There *has* to be something. We just aren't seeing it yet."

"Undoubtedly." He paused a minute to pick something black off one of the woman's remains and shove it in a plastic bag. "We found some feathers at the old warehouse. They're currently at the lab undergoing DNA testing. Interestingly, there were no prints of any kind on the gantry where the crow was resting."

"If she was in crow form, there wouldn't be."

"The gantry was covered in dust and grime, so there should have at least been claw prints. All we found was feather imprints."

"Meaning she had no legs?"

"Or her legs were useless and just hung lifeless. Any scuff marks they might have left were erased by her belly feathers."

So we were looking for a paralyzed shifter? That was rare, because shape shifting actually healed most wounds. Unless her back was so shattered even shape-shifting couldn't repair it. "Maybe she's simply a lazy crow."

"Could be." He shrugged. "If the fingerprint doesn't bring anything up, you could do a search through police records and see if there's any more reports of grave vandalism. Whoever is behind this is using the freshly dead—or at least so far. They're easier to reanimate than older bodies. Their flesh still remembers life."

"Muscles don't have memories."

He gave me a wry look. "Of course they do. That's why astronauts have to spend so much time in rehabilitation after long space flights. Their muscles forget what it's like to walk under atmosphere."

"But the space stations don't have that sort of problem."

"The space stations are pressurized to earth standards. Or near enough that it doesn't matter." He paused. "Doesn't your vampire own a few of those?"

I blinked. "I don't know."

"A woman who hasn't investigated a potential partner's wealth? You're not only a rare werewolf, but a rare woman."

The words surprised me, as did the bitter edge in his voice. "Wow. Someone really *has* done you over in the past, hasn't he?"

He looked away. "Let's just say I learned some valuable lessons when I was young."

"You were young?" I said in mock surprise. "And here I was thinking you were always old and wrinkly."

"I prefer the term weather-worn," he said, the humor reappearing in his eyes. "And now, if you have no more questions, I have an investigation to get back to."

"Let me know if you find anything."

"I always do."

I headed back to the car. Once there, I rang Sal.

"Have Mel and her team come back with the reports on Garrison's murder?"

"The initial report is in. It was definitely a robbery. Garrison apparently kept a collection of precious coins and jewels in his safe, and they're gone."

And it would be easy enough to get rid of them on the black market. Which is probably why they went for the smaller items. "Have we a list of items stolen from Armel's safe?"

"It's basically the same deal. Rare coins, precious gems." Her voice broke for a moment. "He used to show them to me. He was very proud of his collection."

I frowned. "Did he make a habit of showing everyone his collection?"

"No, just his lovers."

And the man apparently had more than a few lovers. "Do you know if Garrison enjoyed showing off his collection?"

"I don't know. Why?"

"Because maybe that's the connection. Maybe they share a lover who has more than a little vampire loving on his mind."

"Armel was very eclectic in his tastes—"

"Meaning he had both male and female lovers."

She hesitated. "Yes, but I don't believe he and Garrison would have shared any lovers."

"Why not?"

"Because Garrison liked it very rough, while Armel was a gentle and considerate lover."

"That doesn't mean they couldn't have shared a lover. It is possible to enjoy both ends of the spectrum."

"Yes, but vampires do not share lightly. We tend to be very territorial."

Which was something I was *all* too aware of. "And yet you shared Armel with others."

"We're vampires. We cannot live on each other's blood, so other lovers were a necessity, not an option."

I hesitated, then asked, "Then you really did love him."

"I really did," she said simply.

"So why do you lust after Jack?" Or was it simply a matter of me misreading what she considered a bit of playful teasing? It certainly wouldn't be the first time I'd gotten the wrong end of a situation.

"There is a difference between lusting and doing, Riley. Not that a werewolf would know that."

The bitch was back, I thought with a grin. "I will get whoever did this."

"I know." She sniffed. "Cole sent me through a fingerprint and we found a match. You want the address?"

"Patch it through to my onboard."

"Sending it now."

"Thanks." I paused again. "Would you be able to get me a complete list of both Garrison's and Armel's lovers? I think it might be worth cross-checking, just to be sure there is no connection."

"I'll see what I can do," she said, and hung up.

I blew out a breath. Sal and I might never be great friends, but that didn't stop me from feeling sorry for her. I knew what it was like to lose someone—even if my someone had walked away rather than be murdered—and I wouldn't have wished that sort of pain on anyone. I wondered if she had anyone to talk to or lean on. Certainly having Rhoan and Liander there had helped me through the worst of it.

The onboard beeped as a message came through and I touched the screen, bringing it to life. It was the zombie's last listed home address and, naturally, he lived in the opposite direction from where I currently was. I transferred the North Coburg address into the nav-computer, then started the engine and drove off.

It took half an hour to get across to Coburg, and I wasted another ten minutes trying to find parking in a street already crowded with cars.

As I walked back to the house, I saw an all-too-familiar silver car cruise past, obviously looking for parking just like I'd been.

I snorted softly and shook my head.

I should have known I wasn't going to get rid of Kye that easily.

Chapter 5

So, are you going to arrest my butt, just like you said?" he said, walking toward me with a dare-you smile that played havoc with my pulse rate.

"Give me one good reason why I shouldn't." I crossed my arms and tried to ignore the fact that he looked positively edible. Faded jeans, white shirt, and a black sports jacket gave him a classy yet casual appearance, and showed off both his broad shoulders and his long, strong legs to perfection.

He stopped several feet away, but it was close enough for his scent to fog my senses.

His nostrils flared, and the spark that brightened his golden eyes suggested I wasn't the only one having trouble with my hormones. Only *he* seemed to be having a damn easier time controlling them.

He glanced up at the house. "The parents are werewolves, and they may not be too pleased with you coming to take away their son for a second time."

"I'm well aware of those facts. The Directorate doesn't send people in blind." Well, not often, anyway.

He smiled. It was a nice smile, one that crinkled the corners of his eyes and lent a warmth to his otherwise controlled expression. "And yet here you are, alone, about to face two wolf parents and God knows who else."

"I've coped with worse." And I had the missing finger to prove it. I glanced up at the house and saw the curtains twitch. I looked back at Kye. "Why are you here? The zombie isn't going to be able to tell you anything about his mistress."

Presuming he was here, of course. We wouldn't know until we got into the house, but while it seemed an illogical place for the witch to hide her creature, people in deep grief sometimes didn't question miracles—even if that miracle was a son they'd freshly buried appearing on their doorstep.

"You don't know that," Kye said.

"I do. It's *dead*. The blood of others fuels its body, and the thoughts of whoever raised it provide its direction."

"So it really *is* the walking dead?"

"I'm afraid so."

He considered me for a moment, probably judging whether I was telling the truth or not. "The parents might know something, though."

"They might not, too."

He nodded in acceptance of the point. "We can't stay

here all day. Short of cuffing me to the car—and I assure you, that will not be an easy task—you can't really stop me from following you inside."

He had a point. I didn't really want to create a scene—or expend that sort of energy—and that's exactly what would happen if I tried to force the issue.

And to be honest, what would it gain me? Even if I arrested his ass, I had nothing to hold him on. Not that it would stop Jack from detaining him if he became a real problem.

"Besides," he added, "I have a legit press pass. That means I can be here talking to the parents anytime I wish."

"With their approval."

"I'd get it, trust me."

Meaning one way or another he was going to get his information from them. Meaning it was probably better for him to come inside with me, because at least then I could have some control over what was said or done.

"I guess you'd better come in—as long as you shut your mouth and let me do the talking."

"That I can do."

"Let's see, shall we?"

He smiled and opened the small metal gate, then ushered me up the path with a hand to my back. The warmth of his fingers flushed across my skin and the need to step away from his touch warred with the desire to enjoy it.

I knocked on the red-painted door. The sound seemed to echo, as if the house was empty. There was no response for several seconds, though there were at least two wolves inside. I could smell them, as they could undoubtedly smell us.

Eventually footsteps approached and the door opened, revealing a tall, brown wolf with a pinched face and hawklike nose. "Yes?"

"Mr. Habbsheen? Riley Jenson from the Directorate." I showed him my ID then slid it back into my pocket. "I need to talk to you and your wife about your son."

"Our son is dead."

He tried to close the door on us, but I slapped a hand against it and stopped him. "Mr. Habbsheen, as a guardian I don't need a search warrant, and I *will* force my way into this house if you refuse to cooperate."

Anger flared deep in his brown eyes and for a moment the threat of it filled the air. It was a threat that drew a deep rumbling growl from behind me. Kye wasn't appreciating the response. And I know who'd I'd be putting money on in any fight that arose.

Not that it would. Habbsheen's gaze went from me to Kye and back again, then he visibly forced himself to relax.

"I guess you'd better come in, then." He opened the door wider. "First door on the left."

The house smelled musty, a scent that was both wolf and aged air. And it was cold—icy cold.

Maybe to stop the kid's flesh from rotting too quickly?

My nostrils flared as I drew in the deeper aromas of

the house. Underneath the dust and cooking scents, there was another.

Dead flesh.

He was here all right.

I glanced at Kye. *You smell him?*

Yes.

He stopped slightly behind me, the warmth of his strong body flowing across my back, heating me more than was wise given the situation. Maybe it *wasn't* such a great idea to let him accompany me.

"What is this all about, Ms. Jenson?" Habbsheen was propped in the doorway and basically blocked our exit.

"As I said, we're here about your son."

"Our son is dead. What possible interest can he have to the Directorate?"

"Your son may be dead, but we've reason to believe he has been raised from the grave."

He didn't blink, didn't react in any normal way. But then, I wasn't telling him anything he didn't already know. "No one can raise the dead, Ms. Jenson."

"Certain sorcerers can."

"Magic doesn't exist."

"As vampires and werewolves don't exist?" I gave him a polite smile. "Mr. Habbsheen, the body you harbor is not your son. It is simply reanimated flesh that remains in control of the person who raised it."

"Ms. Jenson, I told you. Our son is not here."

"Oh, I agree, your son isn't here. However, his reanimated flesh *is*. We can smell him," I added softly.

"And what if he is?" Tension rolled across his shoulders and crossed arms, and again the scent of his anger flowed around him. "He's done no harm. We've done no harm."

Kye didn't respond to the growing threat in Habbsheen's stance, and yet I felt the tension in him rise. Felt his readiness to move.

"That thing you're protecting murdered a teenager last night. It slashed her throat then sucked the blood from her body."

The blood seemed to flow from his face. "Rob wouldn't do that."

"Rob probably wouldn't have. But as I've said, that's not Rob down there. Not anymore."

His mouth tightened. "I don't believe you. Get out."

"I'm afraid we can't leave without Rob's body."

"And I can't let you leave *with* it."

I didn't have the chance to reply, because Kye was suddenly past me, launching himself bodily at the other man. The two of them crashed into the far wall of the hallway, denting the plaster and sending a white puff of debris into the air.

"Go," Kye said, as he grappled with the other man.

I jumped over them, avoiding Habbsheen's flailing arms and running down the hallway, following the aroma of decay. It led me through a kitchen and on into a laundry. The scent of female sharpened abruptly, seemingly surrounding me even though there was no one but me in the room. I reached for the back door, but at the last moment became aware of air stirring, and of something approaching the back of my head.

Fast.

I dropped hard, jarring my knees on the tiled floor. The axe aimed at my head embedded itself into the wall instead, the force behind the blow enough that the whole metal head buried itself deep into the plaster.

I swung around, sweeping out with a leg, knocking the woman off her feet. She screamed as she went down, but it was a sound filled with fury rather than pain.

I grabbed her legs, pinning them under mine, but her arms were another thing. She screamed and bit and flailed like a mad thing, her blue eyes wide and without any sense.

A wolf protecting her cub, whatever the cost.

"Damn it," I yelled, as her nails raked my arms. "It's *not* your son down there. You buried him. It's just flesh that resembles him. Nothing more, nothing less."

She didn't say anything, just kept on fighting.

I avoided another blow, then drew back my fist and hit her hard. Not enough to truly hurt her, but enough to knock her out.

When her body went limp, I blew out a breath and studied the shadows out of which she'd come. A small trapdoor led down into deeper darkness—and it was here that the aroma of decay was coming from.

Just to make sure she couldn't get up to any more mischief while I was investigating, I grabbed a shirt from the nearby washing basket and tore it into thick strips—lots and lots of strips that would be hard to tear as a whole—using those to tie both her hands and feet. Then I stepped over her trussed body and ducked through the trapdoor, walking cautiously down the short flight of stairs.

It was a small cellar area. Shelving lined one wall, stacked with dusty wine bottles, many of which looked older than me. In the middle of the room sat a small table and several chairs, and on this, wineglasses and a tub of old corks. In the far corner was a bed, and on this lay the zombie.

I walked across. He was dressed, his clothes freshly ironed and smelling a whole lot cleaner than he did. His skin had a waxy, marblelike appearance, and his veins were so close to the surface I could trace them with my fingertips. Not that I actually wanted to.

I stepped closer and studied his hands. There were more obvious signs of his death here. His fingertips were black, and the rot was spreading down his remaining fingers, threads of darkness that suggested to anyone paying attention that things were *not* what they seemed when it came to this wolf.

That and his eyes. There was no life in the filmy blue of his eyes. No understanding, no intelligence. Just a blank emptiness as he stared up at the ceiling.

I hesitated, then carefully reached out telepathically. Nothing but emptiness and the shadows of death.

I shuddered and dug my phone out of my pocket to call the Directorate. "Sal?" I said when her face came online. "I found our zombie. You want to get some of the magi out here? They might be able to trace back the magic used to raise him or something." And give him a proper ending, rather than the beheading I'd have to do if I took care of him. And I didn't think his parents would appreciate *that*. "Roughly how long will it be before someone gets here?"

"Give us half an hour."

"Thanks, Sal."

She hung up. I shoved my phone away and looked around as noise vibrated above me.

"Fucking hell," Habbsheen shouted. "What have you done to my wife?"

"Nothing, Mr. Habbsheen," I said, not bothering to raise my voice. He'd hear me no matter where he was in the house. "She's merely knocked out. Although technically, I should arrest her ass for trying to kill a guardian."

And if I wanted to get *really* technical, I could have just killed her. She was interfering in Directorate business—had actually tried to bash me over the head with an axe—and given she wasn't human, the law didn't give her the same sort of protection and rights that humans got. Sad, but true. But Jack preferred an arrest over a kill in these sorts of situations, and I sure as hell wasn't about to argue.

Although there were some in the Directorate who did.

Habbsheen's face appeared in the hatchway, and a second later he was hustled down the stairs by Kye. Who, although a bit rumpled, looked more like a man who'd gone for a quiet stroll rather than having gone several rounds with a wolf determined to protect his own at whatever cost.

"So you found him," Kye said, voice flat and show-ing no sign of the effort it must have been taking to keep Habbsheen under control. His gaze went from me to the zombie and back again, and something deep inside trembled at the intensity so obvious in those amber depths. "You can't get anything from him?"

"He has no brain, Kye. No thoughts or memories or impulses that are his own. He's just rotting flesh surviving on magic and other people's blood."

"That's not true—" Habbsheen began, then stopped as Kye shook him hard enough to rattle his teeth.

"I thought maybe the witch might have left some sort of telepathic link with which you could trace her," Kye said. "She has to have some sort of link, after all, to control his actions."

"True, but if she's not currently connected to him I can't trace her." She wasn't connected at the moment, and I had no intention of trying to delve deeper into the mush that was the remainder of this body's mind. I glanced at Habbsheen. "When did you realize your son had been pulled from the grave?"

"Only last night, when he walked in the door." He hesitated, looking at the body on the bed. "He was naked, and confused, and he didn't really say anything."

Meaning the witch had made him dump his undoubtedly blood-splattered clothes before he'd gotten here. "I would have thought a son two weeks buried would have caused a serious amount of panic."

Or did the witch know these people well enough to be sure that the mother would never turn away the son, supposedly dead or not?

He hesitated. "My wife was too happy to see him to even remember that we buried him not long ago. He's our only child you see." His gaze met mine. "She was determined that no one was going to take him away from her again."

Meaning that, deep down, she probably knew the truth. "Mr. Habbsheen, you surely must be able to smell the rot. You can certainly see it if you look at his fingertips and toes."

He didn't say anything. Ultimately, he knew the truth, too.

"Let him go, Kye."

Kye raised an eyebrow, but did as I asked. Habbsheen slumped down on a nearby chair and rubbed his hands across his eyes. "It's going to kill her to lose him again."

It was on the tip of my tongue to say there was no "again" about it, because the thing laying on the bed wasn't their son, but what was the point? "Did your son make any new contacts in the days before his death? Were there any problems or incidents that you can remember him mentioning?"

Habbsheen shook his head. "Nothing. Rob was an easygoing kid, well liked by everyone."

"And there were no strangers at his funeral? Someone who seemed out of place?"

He hesitated. "I didn't know a lot of his friends and work colleagues, and many of them were there."

"Where did he work?"

"Coles. He was a shelf stocker."

"I very much doubt our witch is working for Coles stocking shelves," Kye said, amusement lacing his tone.

I met his gaze with a smile. "Probably not. But it still makes me wonder if these are random raisings, or if she has a pattern." I hesitated, and glanced at Habbsheen. "Where was he buried?"

"Fawkner."

The other zombie had been taken from a cemetery as well, although I wasn't sure it was Fawkner. Maybe there was no pattern except that they were fresh burials. Maybe the witch was simply going to whatever cemetery gave her the best options. "And there was a notice in the paper?"

He nodded. "If what you're saying is true..." He paused, glancing at his son's remains then swallowing heavily. "Who would do this to us? Why choose our son? He didn't do anything to anyone. *We* didn't do anything to anyone."

"Whoever is raising these people doesn't seem to have any particular reason for doing so." At least, not one that he'd like to hear. It was bad enough having a son raised from the grave. Knowing that he'd been raised solely to murder other people would be an absolute kicker.

"Then Rob's not the first...zombie?...you've found?"

"No, Mr. Habbsheen, he's not. But we're hoping he'll be the last."

"Good." He looked at the body of his son. "What happens to him now, then?"

"I've called in the Directorate magi, Mr. Habbsheen.

They'll be here soon, and hopefully they'll be able to undo whatever has been done to your son's body, so he can be reburied in peace."

"And my wife?"

"If she causes no more problems, I won't press charges."

"So I can untie her? She won't cause any more problems, I assure you."

"She may not, Mr. Habbsheen, but for the moment I think we'll leave her tied. You can seat her more comfortably though, if that's any help." I glanced at Kye. "It might be a good time for you to leave."

"Are you sure you're going to be okay here with the two of them?"

I glanced at Habbsheen. The man had slumped shoulders and a defeated look about him. Of course, it could be all an act, but I doubted it. Still . . .

"As I said, the Directorate crew will be here shortly, and unless Mr. Habbsheen wants to see his wife arrested, or worse, he *will* make sure she causes no more problems."

Habbsheen's shoulders slumped a little more. Kye's gaze met mine briefly, then he nodded and turned, making his way up the stairs.

I followed him to the front door.

"You really need to keep your nose out of Directorate business." I grabbed the door as he flung it open, preventing it swinging back against the plaster.

He stopped and gave me the sort of smile that would surely melt the panties off most regular females. As it was, it damn near scorched mine.

"We both know that's not going to happen. Not until I catch my target." He raised a hand and gently cupped the left side of my face, his touch so light and yet somehow so erotic. "You'll have to arrest me to stop me, Riley."

The heat of him washed over me, caressing my skin, my senses. He hadn't even moved, yet suddenly he seemed so much closer.

I licked my lips and tried to ignore the unsteady racing of my heart. The way every breath seemed filled with the musty, all-male scent of him. "I *will* do it, Kye. Have no doubt of that."

"I have no doubt you'll try," he said softly, and then he kissed me.

Not like before. Not heatedly, not desperately, but gently, sweetly. As if we were two sweethearts kissing for the very first time, unsure of our emotions and each other.

And it was *good*.

And wrong.

And I didn't care.

I just wanted the sweetness to go on and on and on. Desire rose, but it was no instant burn despite the nearness of the full moon, rather a gentle flame as pure as the kiss.

When we finally broke apart, neither of us said anything. We simply stared into each other's eyes, looking for God knows what, our breath mingling and our lips still so tantalizingly close.

Then he smiled, and it, too, was a sweet thing. "I do

not think we should explore what lay beyond that kiss."

"No," I agreed softly. I didn't need another attraction in my life. Didn't need *him* in my life. Not in any way, shape, or form.

Damn it, I didn't even really *like* the man, so why the hell was I even kissing him in the first place?

His fingers slid down my neck, then he slowly let his hand drop. "Till next we meet," he said softly, and walked away.

"If we meet again, your ass will be history," I muttered, watching said ass walk down the path. The man moved with a fluid grace that in some ways reminded me of a vampire. A dangerous vampire.

Only he was all wolf.

And if I wasn't very careful, a *whole* lot of trouble.

Once he'd climbed into his car and driven away, I turned and moved back to the cellar to keep an eye on the zombie and his parents.

Mrs. Habbsheen was sitting up against the washing machine, her hands and feet still tied. Her husband sat beside her, talking to her softly, obviously trying to calm her. It wasn't working, if the hateful, angry look she cast my way was anything to go by.

"Keep those bindings tight," I warned, and stepped over the pair of them to grab the axe. I wasn't about to leave it embedded in the wall, just in case she got loose. I took it out to the car and dropped it in the trunk. As I walked back toward the house, a Directorate car pulled up behind mine and three women piled out. I knew two by sight and one by name, having helped all three magi restrain a vengeful spirit.

"Marg," I said, shaking the older woman's fragile-looking hand. "Sorry to drag you out like this, but I need to know if there's any way to trace the magic that raised the zombie back to its owner."

"So Sal said." She waved me forward. "We won't know until we feel the magic, but I very much doubt we'll be able to trace it. The best we can probably do is block it and let the poor boy go back to his eternal rest."

"That would be better than nothing." And certainly better than the option I would have used.

We single-filed through the house and down into the cellar. Mrs. Habbsheen hurled abuse our way as we passed, but her husband managed to restrain her more violent tendencies.

"What's wrong with her?" Marg asked, her gaze on the body laying on the bed.

"Refuses to believe that her son didn't come back to her, that it's a shell with no thought and no feelings."

Marg snorted. "She'd believe soon enough once bits of him start rotting and dropping off. Most magic can only contain the decomposition of flesh for a limited amount of time, you know."

"And how long would that be?"

She shrugged as she squatted beside the bed. "Couple of days, depending on the strength of the sorcerer."

"Is there magic that can contain them longer than that?"

"Yes, but it takes very powerful—and very dark—

blood magic to do it. More so than what you'd use raising fresh bodies."

Great. So I was dealing with not only yet another nut, but an extremely powerful one at that.

I leaned a shoulder against the wall, crossing my arms and watching as she ran a hand down the zombie's body. There was barely an inch between her hand and the zombie's cold flesh, but it was filled with a greenish glow that had a decidedly unhealthy look about it.

"Okay," she said, pushing to her feet. "I can't trace the source of the magic. Whoever is behind it knows enough to muddy the signature. The best we can do is bind the body, so that her magic will not get through a second time and reanimate the flesh."

"Do you need me here for that?"

She hesitated, then nodded. "The sorcerer will feel the threads of his or her magic pulling away, and may try to stop it."

"Then I'll stay."

"Good." She glanced at the other two women. They pulled sacks out of their backpacks and began to empty candles, little packets, and God knows what else onto the floor.

Marg knelt down beside the bed and placed her hands on the body. As she did so, it twitched.

"Shit," she said, pushing back so fast she landed on her butt. "Riley, the sorcerer is contacting it."

"Through magic?"

"I can't feel magic."

Then it had to be via its mind, or what shattered remains there were of it. I reached out with my own psi skills, making sure my shields were as tight as possible. I had no idea how strong the sorcerer was and no intention of laying myself open to a possible attack. I dove down through the darkness that had once been the zombie's mind, feeling nothing more than the chill of death and a decaying emptiness. This creature might move and kill, but the spark of humanity had well and truly left for greener pastures.

But in the deeper darkness, something whispered. Words rolled through the void, unclear at first but gradually gaining strength as I drew closer.

An ache formed behind my eyes, and a droplet of sweat rolled down my cheek. I swiped at it without thought. Closer, closer . . . I pushed myself toward the voice, until the words were clear.

And they were chilling.

Kill her, kill her, slash her throat and drain her veins. There can be no mistake. She must die. Kill, kill, kill.

The mantra was repeated over and over, and the voice—though soft—was one that I knew.

It was the woman I'd heard in the old warehouse. The woman who could take the form of a crow.

But it wasn't only words I picked up. There was an image—a young woman in her midteens.

Enough, I thought, and pushed more power into my psychic probe, letting it spread and grow until it skimmed his ruined mind, wrapping it in a field of power through which nothing—not even the thoughts of a sorcerer intent on murder—would get through. It would warn the sorcerer that something was wrong, but at least this zombie was now out of action. For as long as I could hold this net, anyway.

"Move," I said to Marg. "Do whatever you have to do to deactivate this thing."

She scrambled back to her feet and began to chant. I ignored them, concentrating on the zombie, feeding energy into the net. Something hit it hard and power flared, a dark sensation of evil that crawled across my psychic barrier, as if seeking a break in the field.

The ache behind my eyes began to feel more like a stabbing pain, but I held firm. The probing darkness faded. Soon there was nothing but the chanting of the magi filling the shadows.

"Okay," Marg said, what seemed like an eon later. "You can release it now."

I did so, and it was as if all the energy drained from my body. Not only did my head feel like it was on fire, but I felt weak and shaky, and my knees refused to support my weight. I dropped to a squatting position, one hand on the floor, closing my eyes and taking deep breaths to stop the spinning.

"You look very pale," Marg said, squatting in front of me and offering me a drink.

I took it gratefully, and felt strength flush through my body the minute the cool, tart liquid flowed down my throat. "That isn't water."

"No. But don't worry, it won't poison you." She studied me for a moment, her gaze searching mine, then cupped a hand around mine. "Your fingers are cold, and you're extremely pale. Is it possible you're iron deficient?"

"I eat plenty of meat." But I also had a vampire dining on my neck, so it was totally possible he was taking more than he should. Maybe eating red meat wasn't enough anymore.

Although given Quinn had over twelve hundred years of experience behind him, he'd surely know the limits of what he could viably take before it started affecting me. So if it wasn't an iron deficiency, what the hell was it?

I hoped it *wasn't* another indication that the drug given to me all those years ago was twisting either my DNA or my psychic talents in new and exciting ways.

"Might be worth taking iron tablets." Marg's gaze dropped down to my neck. "And talking to your vampire."

"I will." *If* it was the problem. I rubbed a hand across my eyes. The ache was still there, but not as fierce. Whatever had been in Marg's potion seemed to be helping it. "I think I need to go home to rest. Can you take care of the rest of this now?"

She nodded. "We'll be fine."

"Good." I pushed to my feet but grabbed at the wall again as the room spun around me. "I wouldn't release the mom from her bindings until the body has been removed. She's a werewolf and more than a little violent."

"She is a mother protecting her son—or what she believes is her son. It's instinct."

"Maybe, but I wouldn't be pouring too much sympathy her way, or you might just find an axe in your skull."

Marg's dark eyes gleamed. I wasn't sure whether it was amusement or determination or a combination of both. "She will see the truth by the time we leave, trust me on that."

I believed her. Marg mightn't look much of a threat, but there was an amazing amount of strength locked within her spindly body.

I got out of there. It might be the middle of the afternoon, but my bed was calling and I had no intention of keeping it waiting.

*J*ack called about eight that evening. I'd been up for all of five minutes, but I'd managed enough swallows of coffee to get the brain cells working.

"The zombie has been magically restrained and we're making arrangements with the parents to have him reburied," he said, without preamble. "And there's been another murder."

Oh, fuck. "Not another teenager." *Please, don't let it be another teenager*. I didn't need that sort of guilt right now.

"What teenager are we talking about this time?" Jack said, confusion evident in his tone. I didn't have the vid-phone activated—I figured he didn't need to know that I'd slept most of the afternoon.

"The one I saw in the zombie's mind. The one the sorcerer who raised him was planning to kill next."

"You read the zombie's mind?" Surprise ran through Jack's voice.

"Well, no, because technically the zombie is dead

and doesn't actually have a mind. I encountered the sorcerer in whatever it is that remains."

"You shouldn't have been able to do that."

I frowned. "Do what? Touch the sorcerer's thoughts and find out her intent?"

"No, delve down into the remains of a dead man's mind. Not even vampires can do that."

"Yeah, but vampires generally don't have my affinity for the dead." I paused. "Besides, it wasn't exactly easy and it left me really drained afterward."

And if I shouldn't have been able to do it, then the dizziness I'd felt afterward *wasn't* Quinn taking too much blood, it was me doing the impossible. Again.

"That's beside the point." There was worry in his voice. "We'd better schedule some more testing."

I rolled my eyes. "We're testing every couple of months as it is. Surely that's enough?"

"Not if you're now able to read the minds of dead folks."

I resisted the urge to point out once again that I hadn't actually *read* the zombie's mind, and changed the topic instead. "So who is dead this time?"

"Another vampire, although it isn't one of the older ones."

"And not someone you knew?"

"Not personally, no, though I believe the council had him marked as one to watch, as he had gained a lot of money extremely fast."

I raised my eyebrows. "Why would that make him a person of interest to your council?"

"Because he certainly didn't acquire his wealth through any known legal route."

I grinned. "From what I hear, that's not exactly unusual among the vampire ranks." Hell, even Quinn had admitted to a brief life of crime.

"These days, we prefer not to draw such attention to ourselves. It doesn't reflect well on our image."

"Boss, you're never going to change humanity's opinion of vampires. It's too ingrained. Besides, it's a good evolutionary trait not to trust things that eat your kind."

"People once thought that vampires, werewolves, and other supernaturals would never be able to come out of the closet, too."

"That's not the point." Humans may have accepted our existence, but that didn't mean they had to like it. And many of them didn't. There might be laws in place to protect both sides of the fence, but that didn't stop problems from happening. And the Directorate wasn't always able to clean up the messes.

"I'm not getting into a debate about all this now," Jack said. "I need you to get over to the latest crime scene and see if you can scent the same things."

"So who is it this time?"

"Martin Shore. A two-hundred-year-old playboy with more money than brains, apparently."

"The council wouldn't have done this, would they? To head off a potential problem, that is?"

"No. They would have informed me if they were planning anything."

I raised my eyebrows and wondered just how many

of the unsolved cases we had on our books were unsolved because they were actually looked after by the
vamp council. A council I hadn't even known actually
existed until recently, let alone knowing that Jack was
in constant contact with it.

"When was the body discovered?"

"About six. One of the women he shared the apartment with came home and found his remains. I doubt
she'll be able to give you much, but you might as well
talk to her anyway."

"I will. And I'm going to send through the description of the teenager I saw in the zombie's mind. She's
obviously next on the hit list, so we'll need to find and
protect her." She might also be able to give a clue as to
why the witch was sending the zombies after her.
"Hopefully, you'll be able to track them down through
license records or something."

"We'll give it a try. Cole and Mel's reports are
through, too, if you ever want to make a reappearance
in the office to read them."

"Boss, it's almost the full moon, and I'm afraid having me and Kade in the same small room is not a good
idea."

"You've survived it before."

"Because the moon heat isn't always as strong as it is
this time around." I probably wouldn't be kissing Kye
if it *was* just a normal moon heat.

Probably being the operative word there.

Jack grunted. "The address has been sent through to
your onboard. Get there fast."

I hung up and headed for the shower. Thirty

minutes later I was pulling into the underground parking lot beneath the Eureka Tower, which had once been the world's tallest residential building. Of course, these days, ninety-two stories wasn't much to crow about, but it had been back then. And unlike many of the older buildings that dotted the city, the slim elegance of the Eureka's design still managed to catch the eye, as did its golden top, which still shone as bright as the sun on a summer day.

Martin Shore lived on the seventy-sixth floor, in one of the larger, and more expensive, apartments. The express elevator zoomed me straight up to the floor, leaving my stomach somewhere down on the lower levels. It stopped smoothly and gently, but even so, my nerves faltered. I'd never liked being in tall buildings, and that hadn't really changed with the advent of wings.

I could smell the blood as soon as I got out of the elevator. In the pristine whiteness of the foyer, the scent seemed to hang around like some gigantic cloud of doom.

I followed my nose and discovered Cole and his team hard at work.

"Don't you guys ever sleep?" I said, stopping several feet behind a kneeling Cole.

"Not lately we don't." His voice was little more than a tired growl. "Though if you could catch at least one of the murderers we're after, our lives would be much easier."

"If it was that easy to catch these bastards, they wouldn't need us guardians. You guys could do it."

My gaze went past him to the body slumped across a

sofa. He was naked, his flesh almost as pale as the white leather couch. He was also very hairless. His chest, his arms, even the top of his head—which lay at the base of the sofa like some forgotten ball—was as smooth as alabaster. It was creepy looking in death, and I very much doubted it would have been that attractive in life. But then, the Goth look was apparently making a comeback, so what did I know?

I flared my nostrils, sucking in and sorting through the differing scents, this time finding the touch of roses winding in between the scents of blood, death, and that intensely "wrong" scent that had been present before.

"It's definitely connected to the other two vamp murders," I said.

Cole glanced at me. "You can smell the same scents?"

"Yeah." I nodded toward the piece of china he held in one hand. "You found something?"

"A thumbprint. It probably belongs to those who live here, but we might get lucky for a change."

I snorted. The chances of us getting lucky right now were about as good as the chances of me ever having kids. "Where's the girlfriend?"

"Second bedroom down the corridor," Cole said, returning his attention to the broken vase. "Her name is Anna."

"Ta." I turned and headed that way. The first bedroom was obviously Shore's. It was masculine in design—all brown leather, dark wood, and a bed that came complete with black satin sheets. Why anyone would prefer them over Egyptian cotton I'll never know. I knew from experience that everything just slid around too much on satin.

I paused to smell the room. That "wrong" scent was stronger in here, just as it had been in the bedrooms of the other victims. It had to be a clue. We just had to find the key.

I continued. The second bedroom was definitely more feminine. The walls were a very pale gray, and the furnishings a mix of white leather and linen, with hot pink accents.

A thin, pale young woman with fiery red hair and large breasts looked up as I entered, her blue eyes red rimmed and mouth trembling. "I don't know anything," she said. "I really don't."

"Anna?" When she nodded, I couldn't help adding, "How old are you?"

"Seventeen." She sniffed. "Almost eighteen."

I was betting her eighteenth was farther away than what she was admitting. Hell, I'd be surprised if she was even seventeen. She just didn't look it, despite the almost weary light in her eyes.

I sat down on the white cane chair nearest to the bed, then reached out psychically and lightly linked to her mind. Not so much to read it—not exactly, anyway—just enough to tell whether her vampire had placed her under some sort of geas. After all, she was human and young, and while the age of consent was sixteen, vampires weren't legally allowed to have a relationship with anyone under the age of eighteen.

Not that it ever stopped them.

Sifting through the layers of her mind did indeed

reveal a male imprint, so he'd definitely been messing with her thought processes. Which meant she'd have to go to the Directorate for deprogramming. I might be strong enough to do it myself, but it wasn't something I actually knew how to do. I could control or read minds right up there with the best of them, but undoing the damage others had done was work for a specialist. And that wasn't me.

But I'd been right about one thing—she wasn't seventeen. She was barely even sixteen.

"How long have you been living here?" I asked.

She sniffed and wiped a pale hand across her nose. "Nine months. He treated me very nicely."

He'd have to, given she was underage when they first became lovers. The vampire community might look the other way when it came to sex and youngsters, but only for as long as there was nothing that could draw attention to themselves or their community. A mistreated underage lover would certainly do that. "And you were lovers?"

"Of course. Me and Mandi both were."

"And is Mandi also human?"

She nodded. "Her room is the next one along."

"But she wasn't with you when you found the body?"

"No." A sob broke through. She squeezed her eyes shut, but tears leaked out regardless. "How could someone do that to him? *Why* would someone do that to him?"

"That's what we're trying to find out." I reached across and took her hand in mine. Her flesh was cool, the tips of her fingers almost blue. It made me want to ask just how often Shore had been feeding off her. "Were you and Mandi his only lovers?"

She shook her head. "We couldn't be. He had a voracious appetite."

Most vampires did, I thought with an inner smile. But some of us were more capable of handling the situation than others. "Can you remember seeing anyone new in the last few days? Anyone who you thought acted strangely?"

"No. I mean . . . He had new lovers all the time, but there was no one I'd consider strange."

"But how many of those new lovers appeared within the last week?"

She frowned. "Maybe two? There was a Rita, and I think the other one's name was Vicki. Vicki Keely, actually. Marty introduced her to us. She was young."

I frowned. "How young?"

She shrugged. "Maybe fifteen, sixteen? She looked nervous, too. Like she didn't want to be there."

Which suggested she wasn't under any sort of vampire "persuasion," because second thoughts wouldn't have shown. "If we brought in an artist, would you be able to give us an image of them both?"

She nodded. I squeezed her hand, then released it and sat back in the chair. "Do you know where he met the two women?"

She shrugged. "Probably at one of the strip clubs. He used to enjoy going to those."

Her tone suggested she didn't approve and again a smile twitched my mouth. Humans had such strange ideas when it came to sex. I mean, here she was, barely legal, knowingly sharing her vampire lover with other women, and yet she turns up her nose at him visiting strip clubs? What was with that? "Do you know which ones?"

"No. I'm not able to get into them for another couple of years."

She might be under a geas, but it wasn't as complete as her vampire had presumed, because the legal age for getting into strip clubs was eighteen.

"So he never mentioned a favorite?"

She frowned. "There was one. Man Hard, or something like that."

"Man Hard? Really?"

She shrugged. "I don't know. I told you, I never really listened when he was going on about the clubs."

"So did he ever bring home women from those clubs?"

"The strippers? Yeah, a couple of times. He seemed to like them showing us how to strip. Like we don't know how to take clothes off or something."

"Compared to a professional stripper, you probably don't."

Her blue gaze flashed up to mine. "I strip better than any of them bitches did. And I was built better."

I resisted the urge to tell her there was more to life than boobs and stripping, and said, "So, did either of the last women he brought home strip for you all?"

"No. He just shuffled them into the bedroom, like. One of them was a screamer, though."

I barely managed to contain my smile. "Which one was she?"

"Vicki. The reluctant one."

Who obviously wasn't so reluctant in the end. "And she worked at Man Hard?"

"I think that's where he met her, yes."

Then Vicki from Man Hard would need to be talked to—though whether she or the club was the connection or not was anyone's guess. "And there's nothing else you can tell me?"

"I don't think so."

I pushed to my feet. "If you do think of anything, contact the Directorate." And if she didn't, someone from the Directorate would follow up with her regardless.

She nodded and wiped a hand across her nose again. I headed out. Cole was kneeling near the victim's head. "You ever heard of a strip joint called Man Hard?"

"Now why would you think I'd be visiting strip joints?" he said without looking up.

"Uh, because you're a man?"

He snorted softly. "Being a man doesn't automatically mean I have a preference for visiting strip clubs."

"Well, being a werewolf doesn't automatically mean I'm a whore, but half the world holds that opinion of us."

"Touché." He flashed me a grin that was more than nice. "Doesn't change the fact, though. I don't visit clubs. Stripper or wolf."

"You must live a sad and lonely life, Cole Reece."

"Only in comparison to some werewolves. By wolf shifter standards, I'm very outgoing."

Then the wolf shifters had very different standards

from the rest of the supernatural community. "Found anything else of note?"

"Dust."

"Dust?"

"Yeah. Not the sort of dust that generally accumulates around houses, either. This stuff appears to be herbal."

I frowned. "There was dust at both Armel's and Bovel's, too."

Cole nodded. "It's been at all three scenes. I'd hazard a guess it's the same, but we won't know until we get the samples to the lab."

"So how is this dust important?"

"That I can't say." He paused to seal the bag. "Shore's safe has been opened, just like the rest of them, though this murder isn't as violent as the second one."

"Maybe because he has closer neighbors."

"Could be."

"You'll let me know if you find anything?"

"You know, you could read reports like a normal person."

I grinned. "But why would I do that when it's so much more enjoyable hearing your silky voice?"

"I'm not ever sleeping with you, you know that, don't you?"

"Facts have never stopped the fun of trying."

He snorted softly. "Will you just get out of here and let me work?"

I gave him a break and left. Once back in the car, I did a search on the strip club that Anna had mentioned. There was nothing on record, but that didn't mean the club didn't exist. It might simply mean that it was one of the underground ones.

And I knew exactly who would know. I pulled my cell phone from my pocket, flicked the vid-button, then rang Ben.

"Hey, how's my favorite werewolf doing?" he said, his smile like snow against the utter night of his skin.

"I thought your sister was your favorite werewolf."

"Well, she is. But I can't sleep with her. You I can."

His blue eyes shone with amusement and my stomach did flip-flops. Ben and I hadn't gotten any further than just being friends, and while the potential to become lovers was definitely there, it would never be anything more. Ben had found, and lost, his soul mate several years ago, and her death had shattered his heart. He might live, he might be marginally happy, and he might enjoy sex, but there could never be anything more for him. Could never be anything deeper.

"I don't think my vampire would be too happy about me sexing you on a regular basis."

"How about a nonregular basis?"

"Not even that, I suspect."

"You have told him I'm harmless, haven't you?"

"Yeah, but he isn't believing it."

"You really need to sit down and talk to that man. He's spoiling all my fun."

I laughed softly. "And possibly mine."

"No possibly about it, my sweet." His grin flashed again. "What can I do for you?"

"I need some information about a strip club."

"Well, the cost of supplying information is having a meal with me."

"You're just trying to get me into bed again."

"No doubt about it." The corners of his blue eyes crinkled with the force of his smile. "So, how about it?"

"Yes to a late dinner, no to sex. When are you free?"

He paused and glanced away. "I have a break in forty-five minutes. You want to meet me around at Fuzzball's?"

Fuzzball's was a little café not far away from his work. We'd met there once, for lunch, and while the food or coffee wasn't great, it certainly wasn't the worst place that I've ever eaten.

"I'll be there in forty-five."

"I'll be waiting."

I grinned and hung up. Almost immediately the phone rang again, but the number wasn't one I was familiar with. Frowning, I flicked the button and said, "Riley Jenson speaking."

"Riley, it's Mike. You said to ring if I had anything else."

It took a moment for the name to click. It was the street kid—the one with the bright blue eyes and quick mind.

"I did. What have you got?"

He didn't ask for cash, as I half expected him to. Instead, he said in a rush, "There was a woman here asking about Joe. It wasn't the same one that talked to Kaz, but I think she's going to kill him."

Chapter 6

She can't find him, right?" I said, a little alarmed by the panic in his voice. Mike was a kid who had seemed totally in control. I wouldn't have expected this sort of reaction out of him.

"But she can. She did something to me. I don't know..." He paused. "She threw this dust at me, and suddenly I couldn't stop blabbing. Anything she asked, I answered. It was unreal." He blew out a breath. "I thought she was harmless. She was in a damn wheelchair, after all."

A wheelchair. So Cole was right about the reasons the bird was resting on its belly. While shapeshifting could heal most injuries, there were a few that could never be repaired. Missing limbs didn't grow back, and broken spines were never fixed. I had no idea why, especially when most other broken bones could be repaired once set. Maybe it had something to do with nerve damage.

"Look, this woman is a sorcerer, so she's obviously used some sort of magic on you. How much head start has she got?"

"Maybe five minutes. She said she'd kill everyone if I moved or tried to warn Joe, but once I got the chance, I rang you."

"And did you ring Joe?"

"No. I mean, I can't. He doesn't have a phone with him when he's working."

"I thought you said he didn't work nights."

"Well, he doesn't normally. But he hasn't had a good run this week and needs the cash."

I bit down on the instinct to ask what he needed the cash for, simply because it was a stupid question. Even street kids needed cash for some of the necessities in life. Although in Joe's case I didn't think one of those necessities was drugs. Not yet, anyway. "Where is he?"

"He's working the hospitals. I'm not sure which one he's doing tonight, but he did the Freemasons last night, so it'll probably be the Epworth tonight."

I frowned. "What do you mean, he's working the hospitals?"

"He's a pickpocket. Hospitals are great places to work, because no one expects it."

That's because most people expected a certain level of respect in hospitals. But then, a street kid living just above the starvation line isn't exactly going to be respectful of anything but his own skin.

"I'll see what I can do, but you'll owe me one."

"Deal."

I hung up, then threw the phone down on the passenger seat and started the car. It didn't take that long to get to the hospital, but with the extended visiting hours the hospital had, parking was a bitch. I didn't even bother looking, just stopped in a no-parking zone and slapped the Directorate official vehicle sticker onto the dash. I grabbed my gun from under the seat, then climbed out.

The wind was free of any familiar scents. I jogged toward the hospital, keeping alert and using my psychic senses to feel for anything that seemed remotely out of place.

People milled around the main doors, but neither Joe nor a strange woman wearing a blonde wig were present. I hesitated, wondering if I should move up to the parking lot and investigate there, or stick to the hospital. After a moment, I moved toward the dark glass doors. If I were a thief, I'd rather go to someplace where a lone person hanging around wasn't going to be that noticeable—and that wasn't in a parking lot.

The doors swished open, and the scents of antiseptic, sickness, sorrow, and death washed over me. When combined with the overwhelming odor of humanity, the urge to gag became pressing. I hated hospitals at the best of times, and walking into one willingly had to rate right up there with walking into a cemetery. For a start, both places were filled with far too many ghosts.

I paused just to the left of the entrance, studying the foyer and wondering where the hell was the best place to find a thief.

The aroma of fried food snagged my attention, and I headed that way. Lots of people tended to get careless in cafeterias. Some flung their purses over the side of the chairs, others shoved their wallets casually in a side pocket while carrying trays of food. Either one was easy pickings for an experienced thief.

And Joe was obviously that.

Most of the tables in the cafeteria were empty, with only a few near the serving counter currently occupied. The kitchen itself seemed to be packing up, the clang of metal and rush of steam as hot trays were cleaned mingling easily with the murmur of conversation.

I walked farther into the room, just in case there was a section I wasn't seeing, and caught a trace of Joe's scent. My heart rate quickened, the wolf within eager for the chase. I followed my nose, weaving my way through the tables, moving through the cafeteria and out into a wide hall. There were more people here, but most of them were moving toward the exit. Joe's scent was fainter, getting lost in the myriad other smells.

I walked through the doors and back out onto the street. Joe's scent headed off to the left. I followed, hoping like hell he hadn't jumped onto a tram or a bus; if he had, then I'd lost him.

His scent got stronger rather than weaker, but twined within it was another. Only it wasn't a feminine scent, but rather one that was all too familiar.

Decaying flesh.

The sorcerer might have risked talking to Mike, but she was canny enough to realize she'd never keep up with a fleet-footed street kid. Not when she was in a wheelchair, anyway. And in her crow form, she'd hardly be a threat.

But why send a zombie when she had the hell-hounds at her disposal?

And what had Joe seen that warranted such an action in the first place?

The scent swung left, into a side street. I was running now, my footsteps light, mingling with the noise of the surrounding night. A mix of warehouses and housing loomed. Maybe Joe was hoping to lose his pursuer in the maze that was the Richmond landscape.

The trail swung left again, heading back up toward the hospital, then sharpened abruptly. I slowed and dug my laser out from my pocket. The building was weatherworn and rusted, its windows cracked and roofline sagging. Obviously not a warehouse currently in use—and the scents of age and mold coming from it seemed to confirm that.

I pushed the metal door open with my fingertips. Wind rushed past me, scattering the rubbish lining the floor. I stepped inside and flicked to infrared. Two blurs of heat became visible down at the far end of the factory, the brighter of the two half hidden by something large and black, the other creeping ever so slowly toward it. Joe obviously didn't realize the zombie knew exactly where he was.

I broke into a run, moving as quickly as the maze of corridors and the rubbish would allow. Ahead, the dark red blur that was the zombie had drawn closer to Joe. I was running out of time.

A door stood between me and them. I hit it shoulder

first and the thing gave way, tearing away from the hinges before clattering to the floor.

The brighter blur that was Joe jumped. The zombie didn't react. It had its orders and its prey in sight, and nothing was going to stop it from achieving its goal.

I raised the laser, the weapon humming at the pressure of my finger. At that moment, a crow squawked and the zombie instantly threw itself forward. As Joe yelped and scrambled backward, I fired the laser. The bright beam gave the darkness a red edge as it cut through the metal sides of the bin the teenager was hiding behind and sliced the zombie in half. As its body flopped to the floor in separate pieces, I raised the laser and fired a shot toward the ceiling and the shifter I couldn't see or feel.

The bright beam cut through wood and metal roofing, sending dust and rust flying. A second later, wings rustled and air stirred.

The bitch was taking off.

I shoved the laser into my back pocket and reached down inside myself for my seagull shape. "Joe," I shouted, as the magic swept through across my torso and down my limbs. "Wait here. I'll be back."

Then I was flying through the hole in the rusted roof and out into the starry sky. Luckily, a seagull's eyesight was keener than a human's, even at night, and I spotted my quarry within half a turn.

With a flick of my wings, I flew after her. The night was bright, filled with lights and bugs that teased the hungers of the gull even as the rest of me shuddered at the thought. I concentrated on the big black bird ahead, flying faster than I'd ever flown in my life and rapidly gaining ground. The flying lessons were paying off, even if I'd once despaired of ever enjoying the freedom of the skies.

I flexed my feet and wished I had something a little more deadly than webbing. Something like an eagle's talons would have been handy right now, because short of dropping down on top of her, I wasn't sure how I was going to force the sorceress to ground.

I was only several yards behind her when she suddenly looked around and spotted me. How she actually knew I was chasing her I have no idea—shifters could sense other shifters, but that shouldn't instantly tell her I was pursuing her.

With a harsh squawk, she twisted her wings and dove downward, the air almost screaming with the speed of her descent. I tipped my wings and followed, seeing sand and surf and a crowded foreshore below us. St. Kilda, I thought, and wondered if she was going to try and lose me among the myriad backstreets and trees.

She didn't sweep toward the streets as I'd half expected, but rather toward the beach. A second later I realized why. A flock of seagulls erupted from the sand, stirred to life by the swooping crow. It was all I could do to check my speed and not hit any of them, and as blinds went, it was pretty damn effective. By the time I flew free of the tangle, she was gone.

I swore under my breath, the sound coming out as little more than a harsh squawk, then headed back to the warehouse. I landed outside the main door, and adjusted my torn shirt and bra before grabbing my phone from my back pocket and heading inside.

"Sal," I said when she answered. "I need a safe house for a street kid. Nothing fancy, because he may well end up stripping the joint of anything valuable."

"Then why the hell are we bothering to protect him?"

"That's what I like about you, Sal. You're such a sweetheart." Although she probably would have been, if it had been a dog I'd been wanting to protect.

She snorted softly. "And you are a bitch. I'll send an address to your onboard. You going to be there to meet the team?"

"Ta. And no." I glanced at my watch. I was already ten minutes late for my meal with Ben and I still had to get the kid to the safe house. "And I'll need a magi team at my current location. I had to laser a zombie to stop him getting the kid, but he's still alive."

"Half a zombie isn't much threat to anyone."

"When there's magic involved, I'm not taking a chance."

She grunted. "I'll send Marg and her team."

"Thanks, Sal." I pocketed my phone and walked on through the warehouse. Joe was still hiding in the shadows of the large bin that seemed to be leaking an oily liquid everywhere. The zombie lay near his feet, lifeless but maybe not entirely dead. We wouldn't know for sure until the magi got here to take care of him.

Joe rose as I approached, and his relief was evident.

"You got her?" he asked, wiping oil-stained hands across his already grubby jeans.

"No, she escaped." I stopped and crossed my arms. "You want to tell me why she was chasing you?"

"I don't know." His gaze suddenly wouldn't meet mine as he brushed sweaty strands of hair away from his forehead.

"Fine." I turned on my heels and walked away.

"Hey," he said, voice confused. "Where you going?"

"If you can't be bothered telling me the truth, I can't be bothered helping you."

"But she'll come after me again!"

"That's your problem, not mine."

"Wait!"

I didn't. There was a pause, then footsteps as he ran after me. "Okay, okay," he said. "I think I might have called her."

I stopped and turned to look at him. Fear and defiance mingled in his eyes. "You *called* her?"

"Yeah. The first woman gave Kaz a business card, just in case something happened and she wasn't able to do the job."

"And you stole the card?"

He looked indignant, but the quick flick of guilt in his eyes suggested I wasn't far off the mark. It seemed the old adage of honor among thieves didn't always apply around street kids. "No. Or at least, only once she'd done the job. Thought it might be handy to keep if the job turned out to be real and Kaz made a lot of money."

Which she probably did, but she didn't live long

enough to spend it. "So, after our little chat, you decided to ring the woman and tell her what, exactly?"

Again defiance sparked in his eyes. "That I'd seen her, like, and I wanted money or I'd go to the cops."

"And did Mike know about this phone call?"

He snorted. "No. He would have asked for his cut, wouldn't he?"

"He saved your life by calling me, Joe. Next time, take that into consideration when you're thinking about cheating him."

"It ain't cheating—"

"It is when he's keeping you all fed and safe, isn't it?"

"I guess so," he muttered.

I smiled at his sullen expression. "So what did the woman say?"

"She agreed, like, and said she'd meet me at the cricket ground, near Vale street, at eleven. But that thing came after me before then."

And why would he not have expected that? Honestly, anyone intent on a little blackmail ought to be prepared for the fact that the recipient of said blackmail *wasn't* going to be happy about it, and just might be inclined to react. But then, I guess Joe was still a kid and somewhat green to the foibles of others, even if he had lived on the streets and learned his lessons the hard way.

"You said the first woman—does that mean the woman you talked to on the phone wasn't the same woman?"

He frowned. "I don't think it was, but that sort of thing is easy to fake, isn't it?"

It was, but I very much suspected it meant we had two different women involved in these murders. Joe obviously thought the same, given his choice of words.

"How did she find you?"

"I don't know. I was scouting possible marks and heard footsteps behind me. I look around and saw that thing coming toward me."

"How did you know it was after you?"

"Well, there was only me and the marks in the café, and when I ran, it followed. So I kept running."

So how did the zombie find him? The sorceress couldn't have gotten into the hospital in crow form, and even if she had been there somewhere in human form, how had she pinned his position so accurately? The only possible answer was magic. "Where's the card the first woman gave Kaz?"

"Here." He reached down into his pocket and withdrew a business card.

The minute my fingers touched it, I felt the magic. It wasn't strong—more a faint residue that made my fingertips tingle than anything dark and nasty. Perhaps the magic was fading.

The card itself was black, with a single staked heart sitting in the middle of it. On the back was a phone number, and a set of times. Those times suggested—to me, at least—that it wasn't even a manned phone, but one that was simply checked remotely. Whoever these women were, they were playing a cautious game.

I wondered if the other murdered teenagers had

held similar cards, although it would have been easy enough for the sorceress to direct her creature to destroy it. Maybe this one was still in one piece only because Joe had stolen it.

"She was probably using this to track you," I said, waving the card lightly. "Which means we can't take it with us. Come on."

I walked back to the zombie and dropped the card next to the top half of his body, then left the building with Joe in tow.

Once we were on the road, I started the onboard computer and got the address for the safe house.

"Why we going there?" Joe said, as I switched over to the nav-computer.

"We need to keep you safe. The sorceress will keep coming after you until she kills you."

"But she can't find me now that I no longer have the card."

"We can't know that. And she seems to have found Kaz all right without the card." I frowned at the thought. Maybe the magic on the card somehow transferred to whoever was touching it, which meant both Joe and I would have to "disinfect" ourselves from its trace.

"I guess." His face suddenly brightened. "Will this place have a TV and a fridge and a bath?"

"Yes, and we want all three to be there after we've caught this bitch and you're able to leave."

"I wouldn't steal—"

"Yeah," I said blandly. "Tell it to someone who is going to believe you."

He grinned and settled back in the seat, watching

the road and probably contemplating his next thieving exploit. I got him to the safe house, and was relieved to see that Sal had lived up to her usual efficient ways and had gotten one of the night-shift guys. I handed over my charge, rang the Directorate to tell them my suspicions about the business card, then headed off to my dinner with Ben.

Of course, I was *way* late, so I grabbed a nice bottle of wine from a nearby shop then headed up to his office.

Nonpareil—the stripper business Ben managed—was situated on the first floor of a nondescript brick building in the middle of old North Melbourne. It was surrounded by factories that looked to be carrying the dirt of centuries on their facades, and the air was thick with the scent of oil, metal, and humans.

Not the nicest of places to visit, but I knew from experience that the inside more than made up for any outside ugliness.

I pushed open the glass door and stepped through. The air was warm and rich with the scent of vanilla and wolf, the latter stronger than the former. I couldn't help a happy sigh. There was nothing nicer than the musky scent of a man—whether or not the moon was on the rise. I climbed the stairs, one hand on the shiny gold railing and my feet sinking into plush red carpets.

The lobby was all gold drapery and overstuffed, lush-looking furniture. A large mahogany desk dominated the far end of the room. Behind it was a wolf whose skin gleamed a dark amber, and who aptly went by the stage name of Goldenrod. Of course, everyone working here had stage names. Ben's was Shadow.

He leaned back in his chair, and waved a finger at the bottle I was carrying. "And you think that is going to make up for Shadow missing his dinner?"

I grinned and undid a couple of buttons on my shirt, so that the swell of my breasts and the mauve edges of my bra were visible. "How about that?"

"Much better," he said, voice low and throaty, sending a ripple of delight through me. He pressed a button on his desk, opening the door to his right. "He's in his office."

"Thanks, Golden."

"Definitely my pleasure," he said, then laughed as I worked the hips just a little bit more. "If you ever get tired of the old man, you know where to come and play next."

My grin grew, but I didn't answer as I walked through the coffee room and into the hallway beyond. Ben looked up as I entered his office, then leaned back in his chair and gave me an insolent grin. "Well, well, look what the dog dragged in."

I sat on the corner of his desk and tried to ignore all the beautiful black skin his tank top exposed. "I brought wine."

"What type?"

"Wolf Blass." It was his favorite, not mine. I was more a Brown Brothers gal.

"I guess I'd better forgive you, then." He rose, giving me a fuller view of his long, strong body. My nostrils flared as I sucked in the delicious scent of him, and my ever-dizzy hormones sizzled.

"I had to rescue a street kid from a zombie," I said,

concentrating on opening the bottle rather than on the delicious-looking man walking back from the liquor cabinet. That way lay trouble, and I had enough of that on my plate already—no matter what my hormones might think.

Ben raised a dark eyebrow as he held out the glasses. "Street kids and zombies? The Directorate has branched out."

I snorted softly. "You have no idea." I poured the wine, then put the bottle on the table and accepted one of the glasses. "Here's to a quick capture of zombie masters and vampire killers."

"Now what the hell kind of toast is that?" he said, his grin flashing brightly. "Here's to pretty redheads. May they find their way to my bed sooner rather than later."

I laughed and touched my glass to his. "Your bed is the last place I need to be right now."

"Hey, I'm versatile. I can do desks, walls, floors, whatever."

"Heard that about you." I took a sip of the tart wine, then said, "Tell me about Man Hard."

His sigh was dramatic, but the effect was spoiled by the twinkle in his bright eyes. "There's no such place as Man Hard. There is, however, a *Mein*hardt's. Different pronunciation, emphasis on the front half of the word."

"If they wanted it pronounced properly, they should have gone for an easier name."

"True." He walked around the desk and sat back down. "It's only been around for about six months, but it's doing reasonable business, from what I hear."

"So who runs it?"

"Are you sure I can't seduce you?"

"Positive. But I will treat you to a very nice dinner later in the week to make up for my no-show tonight."

"Excellent." The twinkle in his bright eyes became one of anticipation. Meaning the seduction attempts would continue full force during that dinner. And while I didn't have any immediate intention of giving in to the desire that swirled between us, part of me wondered how wise it was to keep throwing temptation in my path like this. He took a sip of wine, then added, "A guy named Brad Herrott manages the place on a day-to-day basis."

"But he's not the owner?"

"No. Two women apparently own the place, but I can't tell you a whole lot about them."

"Why not? Surely there has to be some scuttlebutt about them. Everyone gossips in the sex industry, don't they?"

He laughed. "Not as much as people think. It's an industry that does need to keep its secrets."

"So you've never seen the owners?"

"No."

"What about the club itself?"

He raised an eyebrow. "What about it?"

"Is it just a strip club, or do they also do sex?"

"They don't go as far as sex," he said, a smile twitching his lush lips. "The question is, do you?"

"I do sex. I just won't do it with you."

"Yet," he added, smile growing.

I raised my glass in acknowledgment, then said, "If

you do hear anything unusual about the club, you'll give me a call?"

"Information like that has its price, you know."

I downed the remainder of my wine, then gave him a cheeky grin. "Anything but sex."

His expression reminded me very much of a cat that had just found the cream. "Oh, there's a *whole* lot we can do that doesn't involve actual sex, you know."

"Oh, I *do* know." And part of me wanted to dive right in there and test some of those things out. I stood up instead. "But it won't make any difference to my resolve."

"We'll see about that."

We would. And right now, I wasn't placing any bets on who just might win this little battle. "I'll contact you later in the week about our dinner date."

"I'll be looking forward to it."

His expression just about smoked my insides. I turned around and got the hell out of there while I still had my pants on.

Once back in the car, I picked up the phone and rang Quinn. With the moon almost full and lust burning through my body, it wouldn't have been wise to go anywhere else but straight into the arms of my vampire. It was simply too much of a risk to attempt any further investigations tonight. I'd already experienced blood lust once in my life, and even though I couldn't entirely remember everything that had happened, the scars on Quinn's arms were reminder enough that it wasn't a place I wanted to go again.

"Hey, sexy," he said, his mellow tones sending heat

flashing through my body. "How do you feel about a midnight picnic?"

"As long as there's sex and coffee involved, you can count me in."

"Then meet me at the zoo in twenty minutes."

"The zoo is closed."

"There's no such thing as closed when you have lots of money. Oh, and be naked."

I laughed, the sound thick with anticipation. "Only if you are, vampire."

"That's hardly practical when I have to pay our entrance fee."

"So why make me be naked?"

"Because I intend to cover your nakedness with chocolate before we go in, and then I intend to lick every single inch of it off you again."

The thought had me fanning myself. "Chocolate is a food. Food and vamps don't mix."

"This is a special chocolate designed for vampires."

Meaning I probably wouldn't want to know the actual ingredients. "I'll be there in eighteen minutes."

"Don't be late."

I wasn't.

And the picnic was everything my wolf soul could have wanted, and then some.

"Well," Kade said, leaning back in his chair and giving me a knowing grin as I walked into the room the following morning. "Here's a wolf who looks very satisfied with life."

"Completely satisfied." I held up a cup and raised an eyebrow in question.

"What, we're drinking machine muck rather than the divine liquid from Beans?"

"Beans was packed to the rafters with Directorate personnel wanting the decent stuff. We'll have to time our coffee runs better." I poured two mugs then headed over to his desk.

"I won't be a happy little horse if I have to go back to drinking muck."

"There's nothing little about you, my friend. I know this for a fact."

He grinned. "So you do."

I handed him a mug. He took a sip, then grimaced. "Definitely going to have to get the timing right."

"What's been happening here?"

He snorted. "The cross-checking of the emo list continues. We can't find backgrounds on four of them."

I frowned. "What do you mean, you can't find their backgrounds?"

"Just that. No birth certificates, no death certificates, no rebirth notices. They don't exist, according to the paperwork."

"Well, paperwork has been known to be wrong." I walked over to my desk and sat down. "Where's Iktar?"

"Got the day off. Some family gathering." Kade shrugged. "How's the murder investigation going?"

"That's the question I was about to ask," Jack said as he walked into the room. He was holding one of Beans's thick-ribbed cups in one hand, and the rich scent of mocha coffee permeated the room, making my coffee smell even fouler.

I ignored his question and asked, "Have the magi handed in their report from the warehouse yet?"

He propped on the edge of Iktar's desk and crossed his legs. He looked casual—if you ignored the tension riding his shoulders or the anger lurking in his green eyes. "Not that I'm aware of. Why?"

"Because the woman behind the zombies tried to kill a friend of our second zombie victim last night—and I suspect she's been tracking them all through a magic-infused business card. I left one with the dead zombie last night for Marg to pick up."

"Did the card feel similar to the magic you sensed at the vampire murders?"

I hesitated, then shook my head. "Although it has a dark edge to it, it doesn't have the same traits as the one at the vamp scenes."

"Magic doesn't have personal traits, like scents do."

"Maybe not to someone without a keen nose, but trust me, there's differences."

"So we have two rogue practitioners on the loose." He took another sip of coffee, then added, "You don't think there's a connection?"

"Between the vamp killings and the teenage girls? Hell, I don't know." It didn't seem logical at this point, but stranger things had certainly happened. I leaned back in my chair. "But I do think there could be connections between these two women, and that would mean the cases might be, as well. What are the chances of two dark sorcerers being active at the same time in the same city?"

"It has happened, but it isn't a common event. Sorcerers, unlike witches, tend to have their territories, and they don't like rivals intruding."

"Then maybe we need to source out Melbourne's witches, and see what they know about the new dark powers on the block."

"Our magi are already onto that. So far, there's been nothing."

"There has to be *something*. I mean, aren't there ley lines crisscrossing the city, from which magi draw their strength? Surely they should feel if someone new was dabbling."

"This is more than dabbling," Jack said with a smile. "But remember, most sorcerers draw from blood or personal magic. They do not use the earth energy, as most witches do."

"Witches don't only draw from the earth, though."

"No, many use white magic, which also draws on personal strength. It depends on the strength of spell required. Earth magic is a wild thing, and not every witch has the capability to control it."

"Do any of our witches?" I asked, curious.

He took a sip of his coffee, then nodded. "I'll roust our magi for their reports and see if they confirm what you suspect about the business card. What do you plan to do next?"

"I'm going out to talk to the parents of the other victims, just to see if any of them know what sort of work their kids had been involved in before their death."

He nodded. "Did Shore's girlfriend provide any useful information?"

"She said he was a regular visitor to strip joints, and liked bringing the dancers home. The last one he took home was from Meinhardt's."

"Both Armel and Garrison were regulars there, too." He glanced across at Kade. "You feel like a little investigative trip tonight?"

Kade grinned. "Boss, anything is better than sitting behind this goddamn desk chasing names that don't exist."

"Just remember you're there to get information about our victims, not just ogle the scenery."

"I'm versatile. I can do both."

Jack harrumphed—a sound of disbelief if ever I'd heard one—then glanced at me. "Anything else?"

I shook my head. "Ben said Meinhardt's opened about six months ago, but he couldn't tell me who the owners are. I'm going to do a search through business registrations to get names, then do a background check."

"Let me know if you find anything," he said, then uncrossed his legs and walked out.

I went through the eye scan and signed into my computer, then pulled up the records for the last two zombie victims. I jotted down their addresses and the names of their parents, then I retreated to the search function and typed in Meinhardt's. As the cursor began to blink, I glanced at Kade, who was still grinning like a Cheshire cat.

"And what is Sable going to think about you going

off to some strip joint while she stays home and minds the baby?"

"It's work, so she has no say. Besides, minding babies is a woman's business."

I snorted. "I bet you don't say *that* within earshot of her."

"I enjoy sex too much to ever say that within earshot of her, trust me on that. It doesn't counter the truth, though."

"You are such a sexist at times."

"Totally. It is the way of the world."

"Maybe in the horse-shifter world, but not in the real one."

He waved a hand. "There may be a few enlightened souls in this world of ours, but trust me, deep down most men believe they are the superior sex."

"Believing and fact are two totally different things."

He grinned again. "I'm aware of that. And you will note that I've never mentioned my views to Sable."

"Wise move." Because I very much suspected Sable was one mare who packed a hell of a punch.

The results of my search flicked up on the screen. Meinhardt's was a surprisingly popular business name, with a good half dozen listings coming up. I clicked what appeared to be the latest link, and discovered the two women who ran Meinhardt's were Hanna Mein and Jessica Hardt. Two women running it, and two murderers running loose. Coincidence? It was always possible, but I just didn't think so. I clicked the next link down. The same women, same type of club, different state. As were the remainder. It seemed the two women had a habit of setting up a business and selling it nine months later.

I hunted down their license photos, sent them to the printer, and noticed with interest that one of the licenses was for a handicapped driver. Maybe it was coincidence, but those coincidences were beginning to add up. I started a search to see if either of the women had a police or Directorate record in any of the states they'd run their businesses in. I also ran a separate search for unsolved vamp murders in the time periods they'd owned their businesses. It was a long shot, but occasionally long shots did come in.

With the searches on the way, I walked over to the printer to get the pictures. Both women had dark hair, with one having green eyes and the other an odd brown that could almost be yellow. They could be described as plain looking, but given that these photos were only head shots, that didn't mean much. Hell, they could both have buxom, hourglass figures for all I knew.

What *did* strike me was the fact that one of them— Hanna Mein—bore a striking resemblance to the picture Joe had drawn of the blonde who'd recruited Kaz.

Which didn't mean she was guilty, but it was yet another pointer that the investigation was probably headed in the right direction.

I shoved the pictures into my pocket and headed out. The parents of the third murdered woman weren't home, so I went to the address of the first victim. And wondered if Kye would turn up, given these people were supposedly his friends. Or was that just another lie he'd spun?

Their home was a nondescript red-brick house that was surrounded by other nondescript red-brick houses. Fading roses littered the front garden and pencil pines lined the side boundaries, providing the illusion of privacy.

As I walked up the cracked concrete path to the front door, the blinds twitched aside and a freckled face briefly peeked out. It definitely wasn't the face of a parent—more like a younger brother.

I stopped on the porch and pressed the doorbell. The buzzer rang harshly and footsteps echoed, coming from the room where the blinds had twitched.

"What?" a surly voice said, without the door being opened.

"Riley Jenson, from the Directorate," I said. "I need to talk to your parents."

"They ain't here."

"Where are they, then?"

"Why do you want to know?"

I bit down on my impatience, trying to remember he was probably little more than thirteen or fourteen and alone in the house. Technically, he was doing the right thing—although the standard security screen door and the old wooden door behind it wouldn't have stopped many nonhumans if they really wanted to get into the house.

"I'm investigating your sister's death, and I need to ask them some questions."

"What type of questions?"

Okay, so this kid was seriously annoying, whether or

not he was doing the right thing. "I'd really prefer not to be talking to two doors. Open the wooden door."

"You going to show me your ID?"

"I will." I grabbed my ID from my pocket and slapped it against the metal mesh. "You going to tell me your name?"

There was a pause, then the main door creaked open. The kid was thin and gangly, with a thatch of carrot-red hair and blue eyes to go with the freckles I'd briefly glimpsed earlier.

"It's Josh." His eyes widened as he studied the ID. "You're a guardian? I thought only vampires were guardians."

"I'm part of a new daytime squad." I shoved the badge away. "What time will your parents be home?"

He shrugged. "Mom in an hour or so, Dad after six. They won't be able to tell you much, though."

"And why is that?"

"Because Amy and them never talked. She was supposed to be moving out next week, in fact."

"Who was she moving out with?"

"Some dumb guy she *lurved*."

I raised my eyebrows. "You don't believe in love?"

"Not when all she talked about was banging the guy."

I grinned. "Did she talk about anything else other than sex with her hot guy?"

"Not really." He shrugged as he said it, but his gaze flicked away from mine and heat crept into his cheeks.

"It's really important to tell me if you do know

anything," I said softly. "It might just be the difference between catching her killer and not."

He didn't say anything for several seconds, nor would he meet my gaze. "I promised Amy I wouldn't tell anyone."

"I think this is one promise Amy would want you to break. You don't want her killer going after someone else, do you?"

Which wasn't fair, but it had the desired effect.

"I guess not," he mumbled, then sniffed. "She was offered some big-paying job. It's how she could afford to move out of her home."

What were the odds that the job was offered by a woman wearing an ill-fitting blonde wig? "What kind of job?"

He hesitated. "She wasn't a crim or anything. She just needed the money."

"I understand that, Josh, but I need to know what she did."

"A lady paid her eight grand to bang some vampire."

I blinked. That certainly *wasn't* an answer I'd been expecting. "And did she get paid money often to bang people?"

"Hell, no. She wasn't a whore. This was a onetime job, like."

"I don't suppose you know the name of the vampire she was supposed to be with?" Maybe if we could find him, we might stand a chance of understanding what the hell was going on. And why these kids were being killed.

He shrugged. "It was strange. Arkell? Or something like that?"

Oh my God... "Armel?" I said, and almost held my breath for his answer.

"Yeah, that's it."

Armel. Who liked redheads. Fucking hell, we had a connection. But there was no way on earth any of the murdered teenagers had the magical resources needed to overpower old vampires, so why were they being paid so much money to seduce them? It had to be a part of the plot, but I wasn't yet seeing the connection. "And that's all she had to do? Sleep with him and leave?"

He nodded. "Easy money."

"Do you know how Amy was supposed to meet this vampire?"

"Some club." He shrugged.

Meinhardt's, I thought, remembering what Anna had said about Martin Shore's last conquest. Only Amy wouldn't have been old enough to get into a strip joint like that. So somewhere along the line, club security and/or its owners were involved in these cases. "And she did what she was supposed to?"

"Yeah. No problems."

Except that she never got to spend her earnings, because her life had been ripped apart by the living dead. "So where did Amy meet the woman who gave her the job?"

"At the social security office. Amy was waiting to hand in her form so she could get rent assistance, and the woman just started talking to her." He shrugged. "It went from there, I suppose."

"Did she ever mention what the woman looked like?"

"No." He hesitated. "She did get one of the woman's business cards, though. It was black, with a really cool picture of a staked heart on it."

The same card that Joe had given me. Surprise, surprise. "What happened to it?"

"Amy probably kept it in her purse. Don't know where that is."

Meaning the zombie or the sorcerer had probably removed it after the kill, because otherwise Cole would have mentioned it. "There's nothing else you can remember that might help with our investigation?"

"Don't think so." He hesitated. "Are you going to catch whoever did this?"

"We certainly plan to."

"Good." He hesitated again. "Kick him for me. The bastard deserves that. And make sure some sappy lawyer doesn't get him off easy."

"Oh, trust me, the person behind these murders won't get off easy." Mainly because he or she would be dead. I hesitated then asked, "Tell me, do you know anyone by the name of Kye Murphy?"

"Dad's friend? Sure. Why? He in trouble?"

So the bastard was telling the truth. Amazing. "No, I was just checking. Thanks for your help, Josh."

He nodded and slammed the door shut. The windows twitched as I walked away, and a freckled face watched me climb into the car.

The next stop should have been the safe house so I could show Joe the picture of the two women and check whether one was his blonde, but with the business cards all but confirmed as trackers, that wasn't the wisest move. The magic might have faded, but that didn't mean the witch couldn't still track us through it. I hoped the magi had come up with something to counter it—and had already given it to Joe.

I traveled back to the Directorate then headed for my desk and checked out the searches. Both of them were still ongoing.

I blew out a breath in frustration, then glanced up as Jack came into the room.

He didn't look happy. "You'd better get over to the safe house straight away."

Alarm ran through me and I stood up quickly. "What's happened?"

"Two more zombies have been raised, and the safe house holding your street kid has been attacked."

Chapter 7

*H*ow long ago was this?" I asked, grabbing my old leather jacket from the back of the chair. Though it was actually Rhoan's old leather jacket that I'd recently liberated.

"Five minutes, if that."

"What happened to Joe and the guardian minding him?"

"We don't know." His expression was grim. "Jacques isn't answering, nor is he picking up the phone."

"Then how do you know about the attack?" I grabbed my car keys and purse and headed for the door as I spoke.

"Because unlike some guardians, Jacques has his com-unit on during all working hours. He managed a quick report before things went silent." Jack stepped to one side to let me through the door, then fell in step beside me as I walked toward the elevators. "Two zombies apparently crashed through the front door. Jacques killed one, but then everything went silent."

I frowned as I punched the elevator call button. "But Jacques is a vamp. Surely he would have been able to cope with a couple of zombies?"

"I would have thought so. The bigger question is, though, how the fuck did these people even know where to go?"

The elevator doors opened and I stepped inside. "What about the magic on the business card?"

Jack put his hand against the door to stop it from closing. "By the time Marg got to the warehouse and the card, the magic had faded. She said that the same would probably happen with any tracking magic that had been transferred onto people."

"Obviously not, because the zombies found Joe." I hesitated. "I've touched the thing, too, so theoretically, she could track me."

"I'll get the magi working on a blocker. In the meantime, turn on your com-unit and let me know the minute you get to the safe house."

"Will do, boss."

He stepped back and let the doors close, and I flicked the little button inside my earlobe, as ordered.

I made it to the safe house in record time, thanks mainly to the fact that there was little traffic. I parked the car in the driveway of the pretty, double-story cottage, but the minute I climbed out, the scent of blood hit. It was thick and fresh, but it had the stench of evil and decaying flesh entwined within it. And it was strong enough that the wolf within wanted to bare her teeth.

Which meant that the zombie might still be here.

I reached back into the car for my laser, shoving it in my back pocket before quietly closing the door. I couldn't see any crows about, so if the zombies were in there they mightn't be anything more than lumps of unresponsive flesh. But I wasn't about to bet my life on that. Who knew what sort of orders the sorceress had given them? And given she was capable of telepathic contact with her creations, she probably didn't need to be in the vicinity for them to create havoc.

I scooted around the front of the car, ducking past the front windows then running to the door. It was smashed in, lying in splinters on the floor, a clear indicator of just how much strength these creatures had.

The air flowing out of the house was heavy with the scent of decay, blood, and evil. Bile rushed up my throat and I gagged, unable for the moment to force my feet inside. God, the stench was *vile*. And considering my wolf soul generally liked rolling around in all things rotten, that was saying something.

Once my stomach was a little more under control, I stepped cautiously inside, breathing through my mouth as I looked around. The hallway was empty of anyone living *or* dead, but awareness skittered across my skin. Magic, death, violence—it all lay waiting in the room to my left.

I heard nothing other than the gentle ticking of a clock. There was no breathing, and no sign of life, in the immediate vicinity. Only the scent of new death.

And yet...I wasn't alone in this place.

Someone was here. Someone other than the zombies.

Maybe Jacques was still alive. Maybe Joe was. A street kid would have the smarts to get the hell out of Dodge when death came calling.

Or maybe it was neither of them. Maybe it was the sorceress waiting to spring her trap.

I grabbed my laser from my back pocket and switched it on. The soft whine as it powered up filled the edgy silence, but nothing or no one moved as a result of it. If the zombie master was here, then she wasn't too worried by the weapon.

I crept forward, my footsteps soft on the dusty floorboards. At the doorway into the living room I stopped, back against the wall and nostrils flaring as I sought to capture some of the room's fainter scents. It was pretty much useless—the aroma of death and evil was just too great for my senses to handle. And it didn't do my stomach a whole lot of good, either.

I licked suddenly dry lips, then slipped low and fast into the room, laser raised as I scanned for trouble.

Only the broken remnants of life remained as a reminder of its presence.

Like our previous vamp victims, Jacques had lost his head. It had rolled to one side of the champagne-colored sofa, his blue eyes staring at what remained of his body. Unlike the others, though, his torso was intact, and his blood had created a wide dark pool around his body. There were also arterial sprays up the wall. Obviously, the sorceress had no intention—or no time—to save the blood from this kill. Meaning this was probably a straight vampire kill rather than some form of bloody retribution.

Not far from his feet lay a zombie. Its head was laying at an odd angle and all its limbs seemed to have been broken. Even so it lived, because its fingers were twitching against the carpet, as if it were trying to drag itself forward. Maybe it didn't realize its partner had already completed their mission.

That partner was close. The overriding scent of death and decay might be playing havoc with my olfactory senses, but my psychic senses were in fine working order and they were tingling with awareness. Of course, they didn't actually tell me *what* was in the house with me. That would be far too helpful.

I crept forward, carefully avoiding the blood. Jacques's dead gaze seemed to follow me and chills ran down my spine. The closer I got to the body, the stronger the scent of evil became. It seemed to be centered around Jacques himself, and yet he wasn't evil. I'd met him—talked to him—many times at the Directorate, and never once had I received this sort of feedback.

So why was I getting it now?

My gaze scanned the floor around him. Maybe it was the dust. It was on his face and sprinkled across the carpet, and given that the dust had also been present at the vamp murders, there had to be a connection. And yet here it felt slightly different. There was another scent entwined within the evil of it, and it was different from the aroma so evident at the other vamp murders.

But I didn't have the time to stand here and examine

it. I had to find Joe. Had to find out who, or what, was in this house with me.

I went through the next doorway fast and found myself in the kitchen. There were vegetables on the counter and a pot of water bubbling away on the stove.

The scent of evil and decay wasn't as strong here, suggesting the zombie and whoever was controlling him hadn't come this far. I checked the next doorway anyway—it turned out to be a small laundry area. There were clothes dumped on the top of the washer, and they smelled of Joe.

I retreated back through the kitchen and then the living room, and out into the hall. The stairs waited, leading up into the silence of the next floor. I climbed slowly, keeping my back to the wall and my laser aimed at the level above me.

Nothing jumped out at me. Nothing moved.

Yet the certainty that something or someone was up here grew, and tension twined through my muscles, making my fingers twitch against the laser's trigger. The weapon whined, the sound resting uneasily against the silence.

I reached the landing and stopped. Shadows filled the upper hallway, but nothing waited within. Four doors led off this corridor—three to the left, and one to the right, beyond the stairwell.

I went through the first doorway low, dropping to one knee, laser held at the ready as I scanned the room. It was a bedroom, and smelled more like Jacques than Joe. Not that he would have been using the bed. Vampires didn't actually need to sleep, even during the day. They just needed to keep out of direct sunlight, which is why vamps made good guards in these sorts of situations—as long as you kept them fed. Otherwise, snacking on the neck of the person they were supposed to be protecting became something of an issue.

I moved back out into the hall and into the next room. Another bedroom, and one that smelled like Joe. He wasn't here though, and neither was the source of the evil I was still sensing.

Which left two rooms.

Two rooms with their doors opposite each other.

I didn't like it, even though I couldn't sense anything living in either of those rooms. I couldn't sense anything dead, either, though I sure as hell was smelling it.

And the magic—it was *much* stronger here. It burned across my skin—a foul thing that made me want to take a shower and wash the sensation away.

Something waited in one of those two rooms. Something that had evil on its mind.

For all of two seconds I thought about firing the laser through the walls into both rooms, doing a sweep, and killing whatever waited in either of them. But I had no idea where Joe was—if he was still alive, that is—and until I *did* know, I couldn't risk anything that might kill him. And a random laser shot would certainly do that.

I flared my nostrils again and sucked in the scents surrounding me, but there was just no sorting through the sheer depths of evil and decay that filled the air. So it was a fifty-fifty proposition that I'd choose the wrong room, no matter which way I went.

I paused for a second longer, then went left, choosing what looked like the bathroom over the bedroom. I went low and fast, rolling through the doorway and coming up on one knee, the laser aimed and ready to fire. Nothing attacked me. In fact, no one was even in the room ... or was there?

Feeling something, I looked up. A hatchway sat above the basin, and there were fresh fingerprints etched into the dust. Someone had moved it recently.

A street kid desperate to escape the newly risen dead, perhaps?

I stepped toward the basin, and in that moment, as the rush of an oncoming wind stirred the hairs along the back of my neck, realized I'd picked the wrong room.

I spun, but before I could fire, the zombie threw something at me. I ducked automatically, and felt a quick flash of amusement as it turned out to be nothing more than dust.

Then the thick cloud settled around me, clogging my eyes and catching in my throat, making me cough violently, and the amusement died.

Because it smelled *foul*.

As foul as the thing before me.

As foul as the magic evident near Jacques.

The zombie lurched forward and grabbed my hand, its dead flesh surprisingly strong as it wrested the laser from fingers that were somehow half numb.

In fact, *all* of me was tingling, my muscles feeling spongy. It was the strangest sensation, like half of me wanted to sleep and the other half was fighting it.

The laser got thrown—clattering to the floor

somewhere in the hall—then there were dead fingers around my neck and fetid breath on my face. Through the tears streaming from my eyes, I could see the grin stretching his rotting flesh. Could feel the force of the woman behind it.

The bitch thought she and her creature had me.

How little she knew.

I raised my arms and knocked the zombie's hands away from my throat, then pushed him, as hard as I could, out the door. He stumbled backward, arms flailing as he tried to catch his balance, bits of flesh and God knows what else flying free as he hit the door frame and went down.

I twisted around, quickly turning on the tap and splashing water over my face. The burning eased a little, and though my eyes were still streaming, I could at least see a little better. Behind me, the zombie was scrambling to his feet. I ran at him, at the last moment launching in the air, hitting him hard in the chest, my boot heel sinking into rotting flesh, but the force of my leap enough to send him sprawling back against the wall. As I hit the floor and rolled back to my feet, there was a wet-sounding thump. I looked up to see the zombie sliding down the wall, leaving bits of hair and flesh and other things dribbling down the wall after him.

But he was still moving, still trying to attack.

Still being controlled by the sorceress.

I looked around and saw my laser in the corner. I ran for it, quickly grabbing it as the zombie's footsteps echoed behind me. I swung and fired without really looking, sweeping across the creature's legs and dropping him like a wet sponge.

It didn't stop him.

He simply crawled after me.

I raised the laser to hit him again, but didn't pull the trigger. This time I attacked psychically, diving deep down, into the darkness that had once been this thing's mind, once again feeling nothing more than the chill of death and a decaying emptiness.

But the sorceress lay in the deeper recesses, and she was whispering words of command and hate. *Kill it, kill it, it doesn't deserve to live, kill it...*

It? I obviously wasn't an "it," but I let it go as I wrapped a psychic rope around her presence and pulled it tight.

Shock rolled through the darkness, and then she was fighting, struggling, like a mad thing. A fierce ache formed behind my eyes as I fought to hold her, and the sweat already rolling down my cheeks became a river.

"Tell me who you are," I said, both out loud and within. "Tell me why you're doing this."

Even as I said it, I attacked her, trying to rip past her shields and grab the answers. But it was taking all my strength to hold her, and I just didn't have enough left to break her shields.

She didn't answer, just continued to struggle. Then something grabbed my leg and yanked me hard. I yelped as I went down, my butt hitting the floor hard and sending pain jarring up my spine. My control over the sorceress snapped, and she was gone instantly, leaving her creature to carry out her last command—attacking me.

I kicked out with a boot heel, squashing his nose back into his rotting flesh, then rolled away, climbing to one knee and firing the laser, cutting off his head with one swift slice. Without the remnants of his brain and the orders planted within it, the creature stopped moving. I don't think he was dead, as such, but I didn't think he was dangerous anymore.

I stepped over him, the tingling in my legs once again evident now that the adrenaline from the attack was fading. I had no idea what it was, though it obviously was designed to stop me somehow. And if that stuff had been used on Jacques and the other victims, then maybe that explained why they hadn't put up much of a fight before they were hacked to pieces.

Though why had it only partially affected me? What was so different about me that I'd been able to fight back and the others hadn't?

There was only one reason I could think of. I was half vampire, while the others were all full-bloods. A powder designed solely to stop them probably *wouldn't* work on me the exact same way, thanks to my werewolf heritage.

Of course, I wouldn't know for sure if I was right until I talked to the magi, but I very much suspected I was on the proper track. It was the only thing that made sense.

I walked back to the end of the hallway and checked the remaining bedroom. Nothing and no one else was there. I moved back into the bathroom and stood on the edge of the bath, shoving the hatchway cover to one side. "Joe, are you up there?"

No answer came, but that didn't surprise me. Any kid with half a brain wouldn't come out of hiding on first hearing a familiar voice. Especially after what he'd just witnessed.

"Joe, it really is me." I grabbed my badge and held it up into the hole. "Here's my ID."

There was no response for several seconds, then came a shuffle of movement, and suddenly the scent of man and fear wafted down through the hatchway. It was Joe, all right.

"Are those things dead?" he asked.

"Yes." Although technically they probably weren't. Not until the magi came in and removed whatever spell the sorceress had used to raise them.

"They killed Jacques."

"I know. You coming down?"

A pale face appeared briefly in the hatchway, and the tension lining his bright eyes eased a little when he saw that it really was me. His feet replaced his face, and he slithered through the hole and dropped to the floor.

"I couldn't help him," he said, shoving his hands in his pockets. "I just couldn't."

He wasn't meeting my eyes and his expression was a mix of defiance and guilt.

"Jacques was here to protect you, not the other way around. He died in that duty. It's not your fault or your responsibility. Besides, if you hadn't hidden, you might be dead right alongside him."

He shivered and rubbed his arms. "Are those the things that killed Kaz?"

"The same sort of creatures, yes." I touched his back and guided him out the door. He hesitated the moment he saw the zombie, then squared his shoulders and continued on, stepping over the creature like it was something he saw every day.

From downstairs came the sound of soft steps. I touched Joe on the shoulder to stop him, then slipped past him to the small landing halfway down.

I needn't have worried. It was Cole and his team.

"What have we got this time?" He'd stopped in the hallway, his gaze on the living room rather than on me.

"Jacques and one zombie are in the living room, and there's a decapitated zombie upstairs. Both creatures will probably need Marg's magic touch before they can be put back into the ground. We also have more dust—and I discovered what it does."

"Oh? Do tell."

"It freezes vampires."

"That makes events at the crime scenes more logical." He looked beyond me. "Who's that?"

"Joe, the kid we're protecting. I'm about to take him back to the Directorate."

"Really?" Joe said, his voice containing an edge of excitement as his face appeared over the railing.

"It's not that interesting," Cole said dryly.

"It is when I'm there," I said with a grin.

He snorted and glanced at his team. "We'd better get moving, boys. The bullshit meter is starting to run a little high in this hallway."

Cole and Dobbs walked into the living room. Dusty remained near the door and began setting up a crime-scene monitor. I glanced up at Joe. "Let's go."

"This is going to be cool," he said, bouncing down the stairs.

"Yeah," I said, and hoped like hell Jack thought so.

*J*ack didn't. Neither did Sal, who ended up with the task of keeping the teenager in line and safe. Although if the kid wasn't safe in a building filled with guardians, then he wasn't going to be safe anywhere.

"You know I don't like civilians down here," Jack said, tossing something my way as he walked back into the day shift's office area.

"I didn't have much other choice, boss." I caught the item with my free hand. It turned out to be a bracelet of twined rope and what looked like dried leaves of some variety. My fingers tingled at contact with it, but it was a cleaner, safer-feeling magic than whatever the sorceress was using. "This from Marg and her team?"

"Yep. The kid will be given one, too. If there's any residual tracking magic left on you, this should stop it."

I slipped it over my left wrist, then handed him the sweater I'd been wearing. "You might want to give them this. The zombie threw some sort of dust at me when he first appeared, and I suspect it was designed to immobilize vampires. I think my werewolf half saved me from the full effects of it."

He took the bundled-up sweater carefully. "If that's true, then it explains why no one has fought back."

"Certainly does." I walked across to my desk and sat down. "Did Marg say anything about how these people are getting in and out of these places?"

"She suspects the killer is using some form of transport magic to get in, but there hasn't been enough of it remaining at any of the sites for her to track down the type of spell being used."

"Bummer."

"Yeah." He glanced at his watch. "It's full moon for you tonight, isn't it?"

"Certainly is." And Rhoan, Liander, and I all planned to head up to Macedon and the strip of land Dia's clone brother, Misha, had left me when he'd died. It was huge and wild, and just about perfect for werewolves to run free without the worry of upsetting or spooking anyone.

Jack grunted. "It's useless trying to get much more out of you today, then. Finish up here, then go home." He half turned away, then stopped. "What are your dancing skills like?"

"I'm a werewolf," I said dryly. "Dancing is my life."

"Not *that* sort of dancing. Regular dancing, no sex involved."

"Where's the fun in that?" I grinned as his expression darkened. "I do the regular dancing pretty darn good, too."

"Good enough to be employed at a men's club?"

I hesitated. Having never been inside a men's club, I didn't actually know what sort of dancing went on in there. "I know someone who can give me a few pointers."

"Good. Arrange it. You might have to go undercover at the club if Kade doesn't sniff out anything tonight." He turned and left the room.

I signed into my computer and checked the results of the two searches. It turned out that neither of the women who owned Meinhardt's had either a police or a Directorate record, but interestingly enough, there were at least a dozen unsolved vampire murders in each state over the time they'd owned their business.

Another coincidence?

Given that these murders had happened in five other states already, I'd have to say coincidence was *very* unlikely. I copied the results through to Jack, then rang Ben to ask if one of his girls could give me a lesson in the finer art of strip-club dancing. I jotted down her name and address, then finished my coffee in several gulps and headed out the door.

Liander and Rhoan were both waiting for me when I got home. Rhoan's hair had been shaved for his undercover job, and his baldness was something of a shock. Oddly enough, it did actually suit him—he had a good-shaped head for being bald.

We headed up to Macedon, getting there just as the sun was setting. We stripped as the darkness swept in, bringing with it the heat of the full moon that hadn't yet risen. It tingled across my body—a power that would not be denied and would not be controlled on this one night. It swept us from human form to wolf in one surge, and with a howl in our throats and the earth between our paws, we ran. Embracing the night, embracing what we were, enjoying the freedom and the fun of running and hunting.

With dawn came exhaustion and our human forms, so we snuggled up beside each other and slept.

A ringing cell phone woke me some hours later. Liander made a groaning noise of acknowledgment but didn't seem inclined to answer it, and Rhoan was still snoring.

I rolled onto my back, shivering a little as the coldness of the morning hit newly exposed skin, then climbed to my feet and stumbled across to the pile of clothes, sorting through them until I found my jeans and the phone within them.

"Yeah?" I said, rubbing my eyes and looking up at the blue sky. The position of the sun said it had to be at least ten.

"Do you feel like breakfast after your moonlit adventures?" Quinn said, his voice so warm it sent a delicious tingle running through my body.

"Certainly do. But we're up at Macedon—"

"Which has a lovely little café that serves not only fabulous coffee, but a breakfast big enough to satisfy even the hungriest of werewolves," he said. "Get dressed. I'll be there in five."

"You know, if you were a werewolf, you could almost be the perfect man."

"There's no 'almost' about it, woman."

I grinned. "I'll be waiting near the gate."

I hung up, then hurriedly got dressed, unable to stop the silly grin that kept playing about my lips. Quinn might not be a werewolf, and therefore not a contender to be the mate my wolf soul had been longing for, but there was no denying how good he made me feel. Or how much I looked forward to being with him. And as much as I had loved Kellen, our relationship hadn't been like this. Hadn't made me feel like this. Which maybe meant that I'd been in love with the idea of him being a werewolf and therefore a real mate prospect *more* than I'd actually been in love.

He'd been right in walking away. I could see that now, even if it hurt like hell at the time.

Once dressed, I walked over to the tangled pile that was Rhoan and Liander, and gently toed Liander's side. The angry redness of his scars had long faded, but he'd always wear the puckered reminders of the day a madman decided to gut him. It still made me shiver when I remembered how close we'd come to losing him.

He didn't respond so I nudged him again. This time, he groaned softly and opened a bleary eye. "This is not what I call a decent hour to get up. Wake me in another five hours."

"Quinn's picking me up and we're going to breakfast. I've left the car keys in your coat pocket."

"Have fun," he muttered as his eyes drifted closed.

Making me wonder if he'd even remember me talking to him when he eventually woke up properly. I shook my head and made my way through the trees, sucking in the clean mountain air and the delicious scent of eucalyptus and pine. The more time I spent up here, the more I appreciated the gift Misha had given me. This place was freedom—and it would also have been the perfect place to bring up a family.

I thrust the thought—and the resulting angst the knowledge that I might never have the one thing I'd always dreamed of—away, and climbed the old metal gate, sitting on top of it as I waited for my vampire and his flashy red Ferrari.

I leaned back in my chair with a contented sigh and gave Quinn a smile. "That definitely hit the spot."

He glanced down at the three plates that I'd all but licked clean, then said, with a smile touching his luscious lips, "If there's one thing I've always admired about werewolves, it's their appetite."

A smile teased my lips. "And here I was thinking you were all darkly disapproving of a werewolf's appetite."

"Only when that appetite isn't aimed in the right direction."

I leaned forward again and crossed my arms on the table. I was wearing a low cut, V-necked T-shirt, so the action exposed not only the blue lace of my bra, but a rather large amount of breast. "The right direction being you, and only you?"

"In your case, yes." His gaze slithered downward briefly before rising, and the smile became full blown. The heat of it just about blew my socks off. "And you surely can't blame me for wanting to keep your luscious body all to myself. Any man with any sense would want to do the same."

Which left me with the perfect opening to bring up the problem of his feeding. I blew out a breath, then said, "That's something we need to talk about."

His warm smile faded as he studied me for a moment, and part of me mourned its loss.

"This sounds serious."

"It is."

"Then wait a moment while I grab a coffee to fortify myself." He signaled to the waiter, who brought over the coffee pot and filled up his mug. Quinn picked it up and took a sip, then his dark gaze met mine. "Okay, fire away."

I blew out another breath. "Several people over the last couple of days have commented on how pale I look."

He raised a dark eyebrow. "You have a vampire feeding on you nightly. It's natural that you're going to look a little paler."

"Yeah, but the problem is that it's not *just* the paleness. I've been dizzy on several occasions, and I've been lucky that it hasn't had disastrous consequences." I hesitated, then added, "Now, I'm not entirely convinced it's your feeding causing this, because my psychic talents seem to be rapidly developing new and interesting twists right now, but I still think it's something we need to discuss."

He frowned. "If it *is* the feeding, then I'm sorry. I didn't realize—"

"It's not your fault," I interrupted quickly. "Not entirely. I should have said something the minute I realized the feedings might be affecting me."

"I didn't think they would." He took another sip of coffee, his expression as neutral as I'd ever seen it, then said, "Generally, a werewolf's quick recuperation power enables them to recover more quickly than mortals."

"And it does." I gave him a lopsided smile. "I'm gathering there are not many mortals who could take a vampire feeding off them three or four times a night for several nights on end."

"No." He put down his coffee then reached forward and wrapped his hands around mine. His fingers were warm, filled with a strength that was comforting. "Trouble is, when I have sex, I feed. I can't *not* feed. It's a part of the whole equation for me."

"And you reckon we werewolves are addicted to sex."

He smiled, but the seriousness in his eyes stopped my lips from echoing his. "It's not an addiction, but a necessity. You're currently my only partner, Riley, so therefore my only source of food."

"And therein lies our problem, I think." I gave his hands a squeeze, then pulled mine away and picked up my coffee. Despite the need to talk about this, my hands were shaking. Part of me feared his reaction to what I was about to say. We'd been in this sort of situation so often before—even if the reasons had been completely different—and it had always ended with one or the other of us storming off in anger. I'd like to say we'd both grown since then, but the truth was, I doubted it. Ingrained reactions never really changed—not when there were emotions involved.

And there were definitely emotions involved here—his *and* mine.

"I don't want to take other partners, Riley." He studied me for a minute, then added, "Do you?"

I raised an eyebrow, and pretended not to understand the intent behind that question. "Do I want you to take other partners? I wouldn't be suggesting it if I thought it was a bad thing."

Something flickered in his eyes. Annoyance, and just a touch of hurt. "So there'd be no feeling of jealousy? No feeling of hurt if I was with another woman?"

I opened my mouth to say no, of course not, then actually thought about it. And the truth is, I just didn't *know*. My wolf soul might have free and easy attitudes when it came to sex, but I'd had Quinn to myself for a few weeks now, and the truth was, I liked it. More than I'd ever thought I would.

"I've never really been in that situation with you," I said. "You've been something of a steamroller in your seduction attempts, and I've always been busy turning a blind eye to what lay between us. We never had what could be termed a normal courtship, so I've never had to face the situation of seeing you with someone else. But I am a wolf, above all else, and no matter what else you might be to me, you will never be *that*."

The smile that touched his lips held a slightly bitter edge. "That's the second time today you've mentioned that."

"Because it *is* important. It's what I am." I hesitated, then added softly, "And it's what I desire, above everything else."

He leaned back in his chair. "So we're back to that old chestnut."

Annoyance surged, but I didn't say anything. I really *didn't* want to get into another argument—and I would, if I opened my mouth at that particular moment.

He stared at me for several long minutes, his face showing nothing but blankness. Yet his dark eyes fairly burned with emotion. Or maybe it just seemed that way to me because I was so in tune with the man.

"So what is it you're actually suggesting?"

"That you take other lovers when you're up in Sydney, and that you supplement your feedings with synth blood when you're here in Melbourne with me. I can't afford to get dizzy and weak in my line of work, Quinn. We both know that would be fatal."

"And you?" he said, voice tight.

"I've never promised to remain in a monogamous relationship with you, just as I've made no secret of the fact I want to find my soul mate." I held up my hand as his anger surged around me and he opened his mouth to speak. "By the same token, I don't want to fuck every wolf in sight—as you're undoubtedly about to accuse me of."

"I wasn't, actually," he said, more mildly than I'd thought possible.

"Well, it *is* your usual line of attack," I said, with a slight smile. I leaned forward and caught his hands in mine again. "Look, I love being with you. I love being in your bed. Right now, I don't *want* anyone else, physically or emotionally. But that's not saying it won't ever happen. As we both keep noting, I am a wolf, and sometimes situations happen."

"And if it does, you don't want me acting like an enraged and jealous husband."

"Well, yes."

He sighed. "I don't know, Riley—"

"You have the reputation of a playboy, so don't tell me finding other women to seduce will be a problem."

His smile sent a warm shiver across my skin. "Oh, that's never been a problem. Well, until I met you."

"What, my wild and wicked ways have turned you off women?"

"Not quite," he said, raising my hand and kissing my fingertips. "Your wild and wicked ways have made me want only you."

"Which is not saying you can't be turned on by other women."

"Indeed."

"Then there's no real problem."

"Not a physical one," he agreed.

He was still kissing my fingers, and it was making my toes curl in delight. "Then you will take other women to your bed when necessary?"

"I don't want to see you dead, Riley, nor do I want to be the possible cause of it. So if you insist on other women and the revolting synth blood—"

"And I do, because it's better for the both of us."

"*That* is yet to be determined." He gave me a wry sort of smile. "Okay, agreed. But only if you promise *not* to tell me about your own conquests. It may happen, Riley, but I don't want to know about it."

"I've never gloated about my other partners to you," I said. "And just because our situation forces us to take other partners doesn't mean we can't be the most important person in each other's life."

"Unless you find your soul mate."

I snorted softly. "You and I both know that may never happen. Hell, fate has done a pretty good job of crushing my dreams of a pack of kids. The whole soul mate thing is probably next in line."

"It's still something I worry about. As I said, I don't want to lose you."

"I'm not immortal, Quinn. You're going to lose me sooner or later anyway."

"You, my annoying beautiful redhead, are both werewolf *and* vampire. The only thing anyone can say with any sort of accuracy about your life span is that it *will* be longer than a regular werewolf's."

"Oh, God," I said, pretending horror. "Does that mean I have to listen to you nagging about my sex life for half of eternity?"

He smiled, then rose and leaned across the table, kissing me gently. "I'm afraid it does, my girl."

I smiled into his gaze. "Good. Now, I have one other vital question."

"I should have known." He sighed wearily, but the effect was spoiled by the twinkle in his eyes. "Hit me with it, then."

"Have you ever had sex in a flashy red Ferrari?"

His smile dissolved into a look that was all heat, all desire. "No, but I'm willing to give anything a go once."

"That's what I love about you." I kissed him lightly then rose. "Ready to go?"

"With you, dear werewolf, always."

I grinned, caught his hand, and led him outside.

*O*kay, so sex in a Ferrari wasn't exactly comfortable, but man, uncomfortable could still be *so* much fun if you were with the right person. I was still grinning in delight as I headed over to the house of the woman who was going to teach me some of the finer techniques of being a club dancer.

Which turned out to be a whole lot of fun, too. The woman Ben had recommended was a towering amazon with honey-colored skin and amazingly large breasts. And she sure could move her booty.

Over the next few hours she taught me that dancing naked *well* was harder than it seemed, but by the end she'd declared I'd pass general muster and get employed at any of the upmarket clubs.

Meaning, I gather, that the down-market ones employed anyone with breasts.

I thanked her and handed her a hundred for her time, after which she'd declared I was welcome back anytime for lessons.

Once back in the car, I rang Jack. "Hey boss, just had my dancing lesson, so I'm ready to go undercover if you need me to."

"We *will* need it," he said grimly. "Kade reckons there's something going on behind the scenes at the club. There's several areas that are overly protected by guards, who get rather nasty if the uninvited go near them."

"I gather he tried."

"Yeah. Got thrown out for his trouble. So you'll have to go in."

"There's one problem. If the woman who was chasing Joe either owns or works at this joint, she might well recognize me." I didn't *think* she'd gotten a good look at my human form—it had been pitch black in that warehouse, after all—but she was a sorcerer and a shapeshifter, and I had no idea how good a crow's sight was at night. We couldn't afford to take the risk.

"Which is why Liander's waiting for you at home. He's going to adjust your look."

I groaned. "Boss, I really *do* like my 'look' as it is."

"Too bad. After he's finished, get down to the club. As of yesterday, they're two strippers down. They advertised today for workers. You've got a six o'clock appointment."

I glanced at my watch. It was nearing three now, so we were cutting things close. "Isn't it a little odd to be going in for an interview? I thought you just showed up, flaunted your stuff, and you were hired." Or not.

"This place advertises themselves as a 'classy' men's club. They don't just have strippers, although that is their main business. Word is that any woman caught shooting up or prostituting herself on the premises is escorted straight to a police station."

Meaning they couldn't do it while on duty, but could go home with clients? Because it seemed likely that all our vamp victims had met lovers there. "The cops wouldn't charge them, not on secondhand evidence."

"They apparently hand over the security tapes, as well. There's been one incident there before, and the woman was fined."

"I bet the club has been clean since." Knowing the owners *would* follow through with the threat of legal action if anyone broke the rules would surely be warning enough to most. "And my profile?"

"Liander has it already. And Riley? Keep the tracker on this time."

"Will do." I hung up and headed home.

Liander was waiting for me, an array of bottles and other goodies laid out over the kitchen table. I'd barely walked in the door when he pointed an imperious finger in the direction of the bathroom. "Shower first."

I frowned and sniffed. "I don't smell that bad."

"You smell of sex, and sweat, which in itself is usually a lovely aroma, but I prefer to work with a clean subject. Besides, you need to erase your base scent, just in case anyone there is a werewolf that recognizes you. I put the soap in the shower holder."

I started stripping as I walked across the room. "Where's Rhoan?"

"Gone back undercover. I don't expect him to surface for a couple of days."

I stopped and looked at him. "So you'll be here alone?"

"I can cope with being alone," he said dryly. "I did it for many, many years before I moved in here."

"But—"

"I'm fine, Riley. *Really*."

"So no more baby-sitting?"

"No. Although you can still pamper me any old time you please."

"Ha," I said. "If you're better, you become just a regular old member of the family. No pampering, and no one running after you."

"Excellent. Now go shower."

I did, taking longer than I should thanks to the fact

that half a mountain of dirt seemed to be lodged under my toenails after last night's run.

"So, what sort of look are we going for this time?" I said when I finally sat down. One of the packets on the table was a voice modulator, and my cheek began to throb in pain at the mere thought of having it inserted.

"Brown with red and gold highlights," he said, lifting my hair and running it through his fingers. Which I knew from experience meant he was going to cut it, too. "So we'll be able to keep some of your natural color—both up top and down below."

Thank goodness for that. I mean, dyeing *that* hair was above and beyond the call of duty. "And it will wash out, won't it?"

I asked this question every single time he did this, and even though the answer was always the same, I still asked it. I liked my hair color, and I hated risking the dyes. Because one of these days, I just knew fate was going to stick me with something goddamn awful.

Liander gave a much-put-upon sort of sigh. "Of course it will, if only because you would be unbearable if it didn't, and I now have to share an apartment with you."

I grinned. "Too right, makeup man. So, are we staying with gray eyes?"

"Nope. They'll be green. And your voice will be modulated down to raspy."

"Raspy? Why that?"

"Because it sounds sexy in a semidark environment. Which the club is, apparently. Now shut up and let the master work."

I snorted softly, but let him get to it, watching him work through the mirror he'd propped in front of me.

The result was surprisingly sexy. The chocolaty brown played against my own natural color, setting it off rather than clashing, and it contrasted nicely against the warm gold of my skin. The green eyes looked startling, and although I'd feared my hair being cut, all he did was give it some shape.

It was me, and yet not.

"Okay, modulator time," he said, picking up the little plastic bag.

"Damn, I was hoping you'd forgotten about those."

"Jack would have my hide if I did. Open wide, darling."

I did, and winced as he inserted the extremely thin plastic chips in either side of my mouth. The surface of the modulators were supposedly covered with an analgesic that deadened the skin as they went in, but it always felt like he was ripping out teeth rather than shoving in plastic. Although at least once they were positioned inside my cheeks, I couldn't actually feel them. I suppose I should be thankful for small mercies.

"Why do those stupid things always hurt going in?" I asked, only to be a little startled by the sound of my new voice. It was more husky than raspy, and had a deepness that suggested it was coming from the depths of my toes. Calling it sexy was something of an understatement.

"Why do you always complain about the same damn things when you already know the answer?" He handed me a folder, and the twinkle in his silvery eyes grew. "Meet your new identity."

I opened the folder with some trepidation. The Directorate had come up with some pretty stupid cover names in the past. And, as it turned out, this was no different. "CC Buttons?" I looked up at him. "They are kidding, aren't they?"

He smiled. "CC is your stage name. Your actual cover name is Cecily Berg."

"Well, at least that's a *little* better," I grumbled, scanning my history quickly and memorizing it. Luckily, I had a pretty good recall for this sort of stuff. "These are actual clubs, I gather?"

"Yeah, but all but one have folded. And the owner of Lulu's is a good friend of Jack's, and owes him a favor. She'll rave appropriately about your performances."

"It's a wonder they let me leave," I said, reading through the more personal history. CC was an orphan and former street kid. How surprising. "You know, just once I'd love to have a nice family history for one of these jobs. I mean, it's not like there aren't strippers with happy lives and supporting families behind them."

"Yeah, but it's easier to keep the background contained with an orphan." He slapped my shoulder lightly. "Go get changed. Your interview clothes are on your bed."

I grinned as I dropped the folder onto the table. "Am I going to like them?"

"Oh, I think you're going to love them," he said, looking smug. "So scoot."

I did. My outfit turned out to be a wickedly small

black skirt, a hot red singlet top with the words "Werewolf Babe" emblazoned on the front, and matching red stilettos with a heel that reminded me of a glitter ball. There was no bra, but I guess the whole point of the outfit was to let it all hang out.

I dressed and strolled back out to the living room. "So, do you think I'll get the job?"

Liander looked me up and down, then nodded. "I think the word here is 'hot.' And I can safely say that if I were a hetero, I'd certainly want you doing a private dance for me."

"I'm sure you can convince Rhoan to give you one."

"Yeah, but his legs are too hairy to wear that skirt." He glanced at his watch. "You'd better get going. The train leaves in ten minutes."

"What, the Directorate isn't even spotting me a car?"

"Nope." He picked up a large red purse from the table and handed it to me. "I've shoved some costumes, G-strings, and toiletries in there, as you'll probably be asked to try out tonight. Now get."

I got. Catching the train again after having a Directorate car for so long really sucked. Luckily, it wasn't rush hour, but the carriages were far from empty and they reeked of humanity, perfume, and sweat. As ever, it left me wishing my olfactory senses weren't quite as keen.

I got off at the Southern Cross station and caught a tram up to the Lonsdale Street stop, then walked up toward King Street. A surprisingly discreet sign pointed me in the right direction.

The outside of the club was nondescript—just a

plain, brown brick building with demure lighting and signage. A red-and-gold-clad doorman was the only indication of the opulence that awaited inside.

The foyer was large and warm, thanks mainly to the richness of the red carpet and the dark gold walls. A redwood paneled counter dominated the far end of the foyer, and the woman standing behind it gave me a warm smile of welcome as I entered. I returned it, but continued to look around as I walked toward her. There were several couches lining the other walls, and a couple of potted plants adding greenery. The biggest indicator of what this club was about were the two nude statues dominating the far corners, and the erotic paintings hanging on the walls.

"Can I help you?" the woman at the counter said. She was tall and auburn haired, and wearing a green dress that made the most of her figure without revealing a whole lot. She also had what looked to be a nanowire around her neck.

Which was interesting. The wires were a nanotechnology development that guarded against psychic intrusion. The only things I knew about them was that they only worked when the two ends were connected, and that it was somehow powered by the heat of the body. They stopped most of the vampire population, but I knew they didn't stop Jack, and they could no longer stop me—although it took me a little more concentration and effort to get past them than it did Jack.

What was interesting about *this* woman wearing them was the fact that they weren't actually available to the general public yet, although of course—and despite the Directorate's best efforts—they were readily available on the black market. *If* you had a lot of cash behind you. If all the workers here were wearing them, then someone had a *whole* lot of money to play with.

"I have an appointment with the manager at six," I said, and glanced at my watch. It was five forty-five. "I'm a few minutes early, though."

Her expression changed from politeness to real warmth. "You here about the dancer job?"

"Yeah. I've been in Melbourne a few weeks, and money is getting short."

She pressed a button, and behind the door to my right, a buzzer sounded. "It's a nice place to work. Money's good, and the clientele are usually well behaved."

"Do you dance much yourself?"

She nodded. "Mainly just on the weekends. The clients tend to be more cashed up."

The door to my right opened before I could say anything. A short, thick-set man in a blue suit gave me a polite nod, then said, "Cecily Berg?" When I nodded, he added. "I'm Matthew. This way, please. First door on the left."

He opened the door wider, and stepped to one side. The hallway beyond was long and narrow, the plain beige carpet matching the walls, and both of them in need of a little loving care.

The first door on the right was a security room, lined with cameras and several burly guards who were keeping an eye on things. The next two doors were closed. The first door on the left led into an office area. As soon as I walked in, I felt the magic. It was only faint, little more than a pinprick of energy that swirled across my skin ever so briefly, but it was there nevertheless. And it felt *bad*. Just like the stuff in the murdered vampires' homes.

A brown-haired, green-eyed woman looked up as I entered, then gave me a polite smile and rose.

"Cecily Berg? Hanna Mein. I'm the manager here."

And one of the owners. But while the scent of roses and bad magic might cling to her like a barely there cloak, she *wasn't* the woman who'd been in the warehouse with the hellhounds or who'd sent the zombie after Joe. But her scent *was* the same as the one in the homes of all our vamp victims.

And like the woman at the front desk and the security guard who'd escorted me here, she was wearing a nanowire.

I took her outstretched hand and shook it politely. Her skin was cool, her grip neither firm nor weak, but somewhere in between. Which—according to the Directorate psychobabble they occasionally like to lob on us—meant she was a woman confident in herself, and not needing to prove anything. "Pleasure to meet you."

"Please, have a seat." She indicated the comfy-looking chair on the right, then sat down and picked up some papers. "You have excellent references."

"That's because I've worked at some excellent clubs."

"We did check your reference for..." She paused and glanced at the paperwork "...Lulu's. She said you don't do pole work."

I hesitated. "To be honest, I'm just not very good at it."

"The owner did say you were in demand for both lap and private dances."

"I'm a werewolf. It's a rarity in a strip club, and Ms. Vanderberg did play that angle up a little."

Hanna smiled, but her green eyes were neutral. I was getting absolutely nothing from this woman on either a sensory or an emotional level. Nothing except that swirly magic that itched at my skin.

"So tell me, why does a werewolf become an erotic dancer for mainly human clubs?"

I smiled. "Because I'm only half wolf, and because it's a damn good way to make money—as long as you work for the right establishment."

"And you think Meinhardt's is one such place?"

"I wouldn't be here if I didn't."

She nodded again. "We never employ people without a night's trial. Are you willing to work tonight?"

"Sure."

"Excellent. There are no house fees. We simply work on an eighty-twenty split here—in the dancer's favor—which as you'll know is rather generous. Bar receipts are not included in your take, however."

Which is probably why they could afford the generous split. From the little background included in the file Liander had handed me, the bar—or rather, the overpriced booze—was where a lot of money was made.

"We run a main bar, a showgirl's bar, a sports and billiards bar, and the fantasy rooms," she continued, "and our dancers rotate between all of them except the showgirl's room. Only our most experienced dancers entertain there. We expect two on-stage performances if you're in the main room, and lap dances outside those times."

"Do you have privacy booths or rooms?"

"Certainly. We call them the fantasy rooms. Our patrons seem to prefer the various fantasy settings."

"And security?"

"All rooms are monitored. There's a strict no-touching policy in the main room and the show room. Casual contact is allowed in the sports bar, and in the fantasy rooms the option is yours. There is, however, a strict rule about no sex and no drugs of any kind. Participate in either of those activities on these premises, and you will be marched straight down to the local police station and charged."

"Warning heeded." I hesitated. "What about the dress code?"

"Costumes on stage, G-string for room work. In the fantasy rooms, we allow full nudity if the customer is paying for it."

"Sounds good."

She rose and offered her hand. "Good luck tonight, then."

I rose and clasped her hand. The tingly magic I'd been feeling all the way through the interview rose sharply, crawling across my hand and up my arm like a thousand biting insects. As I resisted the temptation to rip my hand away, the wristband Marg had given me suddenly got hot and the biting sensation abruptly fled.

Hanna released my hand quickly, and just for a moment, surprise and curiosity flitted through her green eyes. Whether that was a good thing or bad remained to be seen. "Matthew will give you the tour and show you where to change."

"Thank you."

The blue-suited man appeared in the doorway. "This way, please, Cecily."

"Call me CC. I prefer not to use my real name at work."

He nodded and motioned me into the hallway. I walked out, oddly relieved to be out of that room and away from Hanna Mein. She wasn't a threatening or intimidating person in any realistic way, and yet there was something about her—something other than her magic—that made my skin crawl.

Maybe it was simply that blankness in her eyes.

The rest of the club turned out to be a larger echo of the hallway, at least when it came to color and feel. The main room was dominated by a large stage that reached into the center of the room, lined with several rows of chairs. Tables and chairs were scattered around the rest of the room, and a large redwood bar dominated the far end. There were a few customers scattered about, some being tended to by dancers, some watching the blonde on the stage, and others standing at the bar getting drinks or talking to the waitstaff. The sports bar had billiards tables and a huge TV that dominated one wall. There were G-string-clad ladies here, some playing pool with the customers, others simply sitting down and chatting. There was no stage here, and no lap dancing happening. Some of the women were even wearing sporting-type tops—although they were skintight, and barely covered their breasts.

The show room was smaller than the main room, and it had no tables. Just a large stage surrounded by seats, all of which were empty.

"Shows don't start until ten," Matthew said, obviously noting my surprise. "We don't start getting the main crowd in here until at least nine, so it's not worth the expense of opening this room until then."

"Do the dancers here make much money?" I didn't really care, but it seemed the sort of question someone like CC would ask.

"Plenty. A lot of men prefer the titillation factor of flesh glimpsed under clothing over full-view flesh, and they are prepared to pay big to get it."

He led me into another hallway, this one larger than the one off the foyer. Half a dozen doors led off it and each one was labeled—schoolroom, Arabian nights, boardroom, and so on.

"The fantasy rooms, obviously," Matthew said. "These are all prebooked, so if a customer wants a private dance, he has to go up to the bookings office to get the room and dancer of his choice."

"Are matching costumes expected?"

"Yeah, but you can buy them in-house if you haven't got anything appropriate with you. It's only a basic materials charge."

"Then I'll be expected to get them for tonight?"

"If you dance as well as your résumé boasts, then there's going to be a demand, so yes." He opened a door marked Staff Only, ushered me through, then began pointing to the various doors leading off the small foyer area. "Back here you have a staff lounge, locker room, and bathroom. The door to your left goes through to another office area and the costumes department. Perhaps you'd better go see them first. When you're ready, walk up to the main room and ask for Candy. She'll run through the rest of the rules for you."

"Thanks for the tour," I said.

He nodded, but before he could turn and leave, someone behind us said, "Matthew, why has the schoolroom been cleared of any bookings for tonight and tomorrow night? Is there a problem with it?"

The woman's voice was sharp, almost angry, and for a moment I froze. Not because I feared the sudden rise of tension in the room, but because the voice was all too familiar. This was the woman who'd spoken at the warehouse—the crow who controlled both the zombies and the hellhounds.

Matthew turned around and I followed suit, knowing I had little other choice. If I walked away, it might look odd. But her seeing through the disguise and recognizing me was a distinct danger. She'd have seen me in the old factory when her creature was chasing Joe, and even if crows had bad eyesight at night, Liander hadn't changed my looks *that* much.

Still, I'd trusted his work in the past and it had never led me astray, so I carefully set my features into a look of cool curiosity.

The woman who'd appeared was small, almost fragile looking, with a shock of black hair and yellow eyes that looked oddly inhuman. Her cheeks were sharp, her nose long and angular, and her mouth thin. Not a woman who smiled much, I thought.

And she was in a wheelchair. Just like the woman who'd confronted Mike.

We had yet another connection.

"There's no problem, Ms. Hardt," Matthew answered. "Hanna told me not to book the room at all. Apparently a special has been requested, but she's not entirely sure what night."

Jessica Hardt—the other owner of Meinhardt's—grunted softly, and something flashed through her eyes. Something that resembled frustration and anger combined. "She didn't mention it to me." Her gaze slipped to me, and she frowned suddenly. "Who are you?"

"CC Buttons, ma'am," I said, suddenly glad I had the modulators. She'd heard my voice in the factory and would have recognized the sound of it.

"She's on trial for tonight," Matthew explained. "Amber's called in sick, and Freddie's been given a week off work, at least."

Jessica continued to frown, her sharp gaze racking the length of me. Her fingers tapped against the arm of the chair, the movements as brusque as her voice. "Do we know each other? Because you look familiar."

"I've only just arrived down in Melbourne, but I have worked other clubs interstate. Perhaps you've seen me onstage sometime?"

"I doubt it." Her gaze went back to Matthew. "Open the schoolroom up for bookings. I'll go talk to Hanna."

And with that, she rolled away. I let go of the breath I'd been holding, and glanced at Matthew. "What's a special?"

Matthew grimaced. "Usually some dirty old vampire who likes to get his rocks off by watching younger girls simulate sex. They pay big money for the privilege, so Hanna tends to allow it. Jessica doesn't like it, though."

Which made me wonder what else Jessica didn't like. Because there was a tightness about her that suggested a woman *very* unhappy with something. "How young we talking about?"

"Eighteen. We can't legally allow anyone younger than that, but the girls who do the specials are usually our less experienced dancers."

And I was betting they weren't dancers at all, let alone eighteen. Martin Shore's girlfriend had said he'd met his last lovers here, and that one of them was nowhere near legal age.

I nodded, then asked, "While I think of it, do you have a stripper named Vicki Keely working here?"

He frowned. "I don't think so. Why?"

I shrugged. "My old boss asked me to say hi if I ever ran into her, that's all."

"Sorry, I don't think she's ever been here. Not that I can remember, anyway."

I reached out mentally, pushing past the nanowire to scan his thoughts. I could see no lie. Which didn't mean Vicki hadn't been here, just that he didn't know about it.

He walked away. I stood there for a moment, drawing in the air, sorting through the various scents for any hint of the magic that had been in the warehouse or the homes of the murdered vampires. Perfume rode the air, almost masking the heavier scent of humans. Someone was having a shower in the bathroom, and in the lounge people talked softly, though it might have been the TV given it was two male voices I could hear.

There was no familiar scent and nothing seemed out of the ordinary or suspicious. Not to my novice-stripper eyes, anyway.

I glanced around the room again, and saw the discreetly placed cameras in the corners. I was being watched, which meant standing here doing nothing wasn't such a good idea. I turned and headed for the costume department. Time to get down to work.

*D*ancing might have seemed like fun when I was practicing the art with Ben's Amazonian friend, but after eight long hours of dancing in heels and smiling so hard it felt like my face would crack, I was bone tired and ready for sleep.

I slung my bag over my shoulder and headed for the back exit. The bouncer stationed there gave me a cheery smile as he opened the door. "Will you be all right out there at this hour? Or would you like someone to walk you to your car?"

"I'll be fine, thanks."

He nodded and stepped aside as I walked through. "Be careful, then."

I smiled and walked into the night. Naturally enough, it was raining and I didn't have a coat. I did have a woolly hat, and I shoved that on, tucking my hair underneath it and pulling it down over my ears. I did likewise to the sleeves of my baggy sweatshirt, although the material was pretty flimsy with age, and not exactly warm. Shivering, I crossed my arms and headed toward King Street in the hope of finding a taxi near one of the nightclubs. If not, I could always head back down to Spenser Street and catch a bus, because the trains didn't actually run at this hour.

When I was out of earshot of the club, I pressed the button in my ear and said, "What a fucking miserable way to end a shift. Tell Jack thanks for not giving me a car on this one."

"Your character is not the type to own a car, Riley, and the Directorate cannot control the weather," Jack said dryly. "How'd things go in there?"

"Tryout went well, I earned lots of money, and they've asked me back on a permanent basis."

"Excellent. Did you learn anything?"

"We've hit the jackpot. One of the owners is the crow who's controlling the zombies, and the other smells the same as the magic I've sensed in our victims' houses."

"So we have a tag team of killers?"

"Most likely. I also found out that one of the owners runs 'specials' for certain vampire customers." I explained what apparently happened, then added, "I linked with most of the women working here tonight, and none of them have ever worked a special. To me it suggests that Hanna Mein is bringing in inexperienced teenagers to work the specials and somehow hook up with the vamps. Shore's girlfriend said he liked them young."

"Armel didn't mind it, either," Jack murmured. "Although I can't understand why they'd be killing the girls afterward. With the sort of money they apparently earned, they're not likely to say anything to anyone."

"But a dead seducer definitely tells no tales." And if Hanna and Jessica *were* behind the vamp murders, then they certainly couldn't risk even the slightest whisper getting out. It'd definitely kill the stripper business, not to mention them. The Directorate wouldn't be the only ones hunting these killers. Kye certainly was, and I suspected the vampire council would be, too.

Jack grunted. "Anything else?"

"Yeah. Most of the managerial staff is wearing nanowires, and there's psychic deadeners in every room."

"The deadeners are probably used to stop vamp customers 'leaning' on dancers or staff to get that little bit extra," Jack said, a trace of amusement in his voice. Which suggested to me he'd done more than his fair share of "leaning" over his lifetime. "The fact they've got so many wires in one place is interesting, though. We've been making sure they're in short supply on the market at the moment, and the price is sky high."

"Which only means these women are in the position to spend big."

"And yet their financial records suggest that should not be possible."

"Unless they're getting their cash flow through other means. Like raiding the safes of their victims." I rubbed my wet arms and tried to ignore the water dripping off my nose. Neither was working.

"It would explain the robberies, but not the violence. Did you get close to any of those guarded doors Kade mentioned?"

"Had no legitimate reason to, and I didn't want to do anything that would raise suspicions on my first night."

Ahead of me, a door slammed and the sharp tattoo of heels echoed across the rain-swept night. I stopped in the shadows, watching as a blonde-haired woman stepped out of the shadows and turned onto King Street. I didn't immediately recognize her, but her scent told me who it was soon enough.

Hanna Mein herself.

"Gotta go, Jack," I said softly. "I've just spotted one of our targets."

"Report back as soon as you're able."

"Will do." I clicked off the sound, then slipped off my stilettos, shoving them into my bag and padding barefoot through the cold, wet night. The woman ahead was moving quickly, her blonde hair barely visible in the thick furry collar of the coat she was wearing. The click of her heels rode across the silence—a sound that was punctuated by the occasional car roaring past on the empty street.

She turned left and marched toward Bourke Street. I dashed across the street, and followed on the opposite sidewalk. I couldn't wrap the shadows around me full time, thanks to the streetlights and the occasional car sweeping by, so there was less likelihood of her realizing she was being followed if I wasn't right behind her. Not that she was bothering to look around her anyway. She seemed more intent on simply getting to wherever she was going as quickly as possible. Not that I could blame her.

I swiped at the drips running down my cheeks and chin, but my sleeve was as wet as my face and really did little to remove the rain. My top was soaked and it clung to my skin like ... well, a second skin. It was providing so little cover that I might as well have been naked—only *that* might have drawn too much attention from the cops who were always cruising King Street at this hour. With all the nightclubs in this area, there was always some kind of trouble for the police to hose down.

So was that where Hanna was heading? She was certainly moving in the right direction for the clubs, but the rail and bus station wasn't far away—though she didn't exactly look the type to take public transport. Certainly an expensive fur coat, whether it was faux or not, wasn't what any sane person would wear if trying to avoid either trouble or getting wet. Although if she was the one hacking away at the vampires, maybe saneness wasn't in her vocabulary.

We crossed Little Bourke Street and hurried on toward Bourke. The quick-click of the blonde's heels were now mingling with the base-heavy thump of music from the clubs farther down the road. She still hadn't looked around, which was odd if she was up to no good. You'd think she'd show a little more awareness of her surroundings...

The thought faded as awareness suddenly prickled across my skin. The woman wasn't the only one being followed.

I resisted the urge to look around and flared my nostrils, drawing in the scents of the wet night and rifling through them quickly. And there it was in the undernotes—a scent I recognized. A wolf who obviously *wanted* to be found, because he knew better than to be caught upwind of another hunter.

"I know you're there, Kye," I said softly. He wasn't close, but I knew he'd hear me anyway.

There was no response, no sound of quickened footsteps, but that wash of awareness grew stronger until he fell into step beside me.

It took you long enough to realize it. His mind voice might be cooler than the night itself, but his presence was so, *so* hot.

It felt like I was walking beside a furnace, and a whole lot of me wanted to snuggle right up to it. And *not* just because I was cold.

That's because you've only just moved in direct line of scent. Which was a guess on my part. I'd like to think I'd been in this job long enough now to instinctively "feel" when I was being followed.

Which might not be the case, but hey, a girl has to dream a little.

You might never have realized I was there, otherwise. This time his mental tones were laced with amusement that sent a delicious tingle all the way down my spine.

God, what was it with this wolf? I couldn't exactly blame the moon heat anymore, because the full moon was over for the next month. So why did Kye—someone I didn't *want* to like—have my hormones dashing around so excitedly?

Maybe Liander was right. Maybe my wolf soul had had enough, and was putting her foot down to demand equal loving rights.

Maybe I was just hoping that like all bad smells, you'd eventually go away.

I don't smell bad, and you know it.

He was right, he didn't, but there was no way on this green Earth I was going to admit it.

What are you doing here, Kye?

Same thing as you. Following a target.

The woman up ahead isn't the woman who was in the warehouse with the zombie and the hellhounds, so I repeat the question—why are you here?

He glanced at me then, his amber eyes cool and judging, weighing his options, sizing up the opposition. The tension that rolled through me was part fear, part a readiness to attack.

Probably for the same reason you are. I suspect she's involved with what is going on, but have no proof.

And if he got proof, he'd kill her. I resisted the urge to rub the chill from my arms, although I was no longer sure if the cause was the cold or the man. This wolf might have me in a spin, but he repelled my saner half.

Because in him I saw a reflection of myself—a reflection of the killer Jack wanted me to be.

He was everything I was trying *not* to become.

And for that reason alone, I'd fight this damn attraction as hard as I could. I didn't need a constant reminder of the future that might be mine.

If you kill her, I replied, wondering how much he actually knew—and whether I should risk doing a full read of his thoughts. *We may never get that proof.*

Which is the reason, he said softly, *that I merely follow. So no killing tonight?*

He met my gaze again, and a slight smile teased one corner of his mouth. It didn't reach his eyes. Didn't warm the cold depths. *No killing tonight.*

Good. I paused. *Does this mean you're going home?*

I said it in a hopeful kind of way, and his smile widened. Despite the continuing chill in his gaze, the night suddenly didn't seem as cold anymore.

My wolf soul, it seemed, wasn't going to give up this attraction very easily.

No, Kye said, *it means you're stuck with me until we discover just what this woman is up to.*

Darn.

It's so nice to feel wanted.

Oh, he was wanted all right. It was just lucky the moon heat was over and I had some measure of control over myself. Not that control did much good given he could probably smell my interest. It was hard for a wolf to hide that sort of thing.

Though *he* seemed to be doing a damned good job of it.

I should be arresting your ass, I muttered. *You've been warned off this case several times already.*

You could try if you want to, but it'll cause a bit of a

ruckus, and our target just might realize she's being followed.

Which is why I'm not arresting your ass. That and the fact I was just too bone tired to muster the strength I'd probably need to haul his cute rear end in to the Directorate.

He smiled again and didn't say anything. We walked another block and crossed over Bourke Street. Laughter and voices joined the bass-heavy beat, and the scent of alcohol and humanity rode the wet night air.

"I liked your performance in the club tonight," he said after a while. I guess he figured us actually having some conversation did look a little better than utter silence should our target happen to look over her shoulder. "Even for a werewolf, you moved extraordinarily well."

I raised an eyebrow. "You were there?"

"I was."

"Disguised, obviously."

"Obviously. You didn't spot me."

"Hard to spot someone if they've erased their scent and donned a completely different look."

"True." He glanced at me. "It took me a moment to recognize you. Your look and smell was different enough that I glanced past you several times before I realized who you were. I like your regular look better, by the way."

"Then I'd better keep this one," I said dryly. "You planning to be there tomorrow night?"

"Of course." Telepathically, he added, *Now that I*

know she has an accomplice, it is my duty to track her down and kill them both.

And if he did, I *would* arrest him. No matter how horrified my crazy hormones might be. "If I spot you tomorrow night, I'll treat you to a lap dance."

"I wouldn't."

I raised an eyebrow again. "Why not? We both know you'd enjoy it."

"That is the problem." *I am not here to enjoy myself.*

Of course he wasn't. He was here to track down and kill. Just like me. A shiver rolled across my skin and I rubbed my arms. If he noted the movement, he didn't do the gentlemanly thing, like offer me his coat. Quinn would have.

As we neared Flinders Lane, Hanna suddenly swung in our direction, looking left and right before running across. She didn't even look our way as she ran past us, moving up the street with a quick glance at her watch.

"Must have an appointment," Kye murmured, his arms brushing mine as the pavement suddenly narrowed.

Up ahead, a figure waited. A slender woman who was all of sixteen or seventeen.

Fuck.

I stopped, and just as I did, Hanna looked around. Kye reacted before I could, his speed almost that of a vampire as he crushed me against the wall and began kissing me.

And oh, what a kiss.

It was urgent and hungry and filled with everything

he *hadn't* been showing, and I reacted as fiercely as I would have had the full moon been nearing completion.

For several seconds, there was nothing else in my world but this kiss and the fierce heat of his body against mine. Then sanity returned, and along with it sound, and I became aware of voices talking.

I broke away, then said, *Listen.*

I am. He kissed my neck, my ear, then wrapped his arms around my waist and drew me into a hug that was as close as two people could get without being naked.

"But what does the job entail?" the younger woman asked.

"Nothing more than sleeping with a vampire for one night." Hanna's voice sounded a lot tinnier than it had before. Maybe she was wearing some sort of cheap modulator.

I shifted my head slightly on Kye's shoulder so I could get a better look at Hanna's target. Like the other women who'd been found dead, this one was slender in build. Unlike the others, she had large breasts and a wine-colored birthmark covering part of her cheek and running down her neck.

The younger woman raised an eyebrow. "Ten grand for sleeping with one bloodsucker for one night? That seems like an awfully good deal. What's the fucking catch?"

"The catch is you have to come to Meinhardt's to meet him."

"Isn't that a strip joint?"

"A men's club is the term we prefer," Hanna said,

voice holding an edge, "and you won't be expected to strip for anyone except my client. He has a fetish for unusual body markings and I think you would be to his tastes."

"So I have to do him there?"

"No. You accept an invitation to go home with him."

"And then what?" There was still doubt evident in her tones, but even I could see the glint of anticipation in her eyes. Though not, I suspected, for the sex, but rather for the cash. "I just leave in the morning?"

"With ten grand in your hand, yes. And that's more than enough money to take that course you were talking to the employment office about."

I had no idea what course Hanna might have been talking about, but I knew for sure the young woman would never live to do it.

The slender woman made a clicking sound with her tongue, then said, "Make it twelve, and I'm yours."

"Twelve it is then." Even from where we stood, Hanna's satisfaction was evident. "Here's my business card in case you need to contact me. Be in the lane behind Meinhardt's at seven, and we'll hustle you into the club."

The woman took the card and shoved it in her pocket, then turned and walked back up Flinders Lane. Hanna watched her for a little while, then spun around and headed back in our direction.

Kye kissed me again.

It was even more electrifying than before, and it took me several seconds to register the fact that Hanna had walked past us.

"Looks like we have a tough decision," he said, his breath fast and heated on my lips. "Follow the witch, or follow her target?"

"She's a sorcerer," I corrected, and ducked under his arms, forcing some air and distance between us. "And you know as well as I do that my next quarry is her target."

He reached out and touched a finger lightly to my cheek. "I enjoyed our little encounter tonight, but it's going to make the lap dance tomorrow night all that much harder to ignore."

He wouldn't be ignoring *anything* on my shift. Which was not entirely a sane thought given my resolve to have as little as possible to do with this man. But then, maybe I wasn't entirely sane. After all, I *was* a guardian. "Don't kill the blonde."

"I gave you my word not to kill her tonight, Riley. I am a man of my word, if nothing else."

"Good. See you tomorrow night."

"If you can find me," he said, a trace of amusement in his voice again.

It was a challenge, and we both knew it. I didn't answer, simply turned and ran after the young woman before she disappeared.

Chapter 8

Fortunately for me, she didn't catch a cab, but rather the nightrider bus. I climbed on after her and made my way down to the back of the bus, my wet and clingy outfit catching several appreciative glances from the male passengers. The teenager had settled about halfway down. I sat two seats behind but across from her, and tried to ignore the reek of alcohol coming from the snoring woman in the seat behind me.

The driver had classical music playing softly and with the blue interior lighting of the bus, it was a peaceful trip. Even the drunk stopped smelling as bad—either that, or my nose had become accustomed to her.

The teenager climbed off at the Dimboola Road stop in Broadmeadows and began walking down the hill. I followed, keeping far enough back so that even if headlights tore the cover of shadows away from me, she wouldn't realize she was being tailed. Not that she appeared to be really aware of anything else but getting home. I couldn't blame her—it was a miserable night.

She turned left into a street then crossed the road and ran into a house. I waited on the corner, watching as the lights came on inside, then touched the com-link lightly. "You still there, boss?"

"I'm afraid so. What's happened?"

"Hanna Mein, the co-owner of Meinhardt's, has just made contact with another teenage girl, and has employed her to sleep with a vampire for one night. I suspect we really have found our killers."

"And it undoubtedly means she's about to do another robbery-murder. Any hints as to who?"

"Yep. A vamp with a taste for unusual body markings. This girl has a wine-colored stain on her face and neck."

"That narrows the field considerably. I'll get Sal onto it straightaway," he said. "I'm guessing you tracked the girl?"

He said that like it was a bad thing. "Any reason why I shouldn't have?"

He hesitated. "No. I just want these bitches stopped, Riley, that's all."

"And I'm working on it. In the meantime, we take away her tools, and maybe frustrate them into making a mistake."

He grunted. "Did you see the other owner at the club tonight?"

"Certainly did." I paused to swipe at the drips of rain

rolling down my cheeks. "Maybe I was reading her wrong, but she seemed awfully uptight to me, boss."

"Well, they'd have to know these murders would be attracting Directorate attention. Where does the teenager live?"

I gave him the address. "She's got one of those magic business cards, so you're going to have to make sure Marg provides her with protection before you move her."

"I do realize that, Riley. I'm not a novice at this job, you know."

I grinned at his dry tone. "Sorry, boss. It's late and I'm tired. If you don't need me for anything else, I'm off home."

"Don't be late for your new job tomorrow night."

"Like I would."

He snorted his disbelief—a sound I cut off by flicking off the com-link. I turned and headed back down Dimboola Road, wondering if I had the energy to fly home, or if I should catch a cab.

In the end, flying won, simply because there were no cabs at the rail station and I couldn't be bothered waiting for one to turn up. So I was as close to exhaustion as I'd ever been when I finally fell face-first into my bed.

When I woke many hours later, it was to the scent of roses, coffee, sandalwood, and man. One smell was definitely more alluring than the others, and I forced a bleary eye open. To discover a pale pink rose sitting on the pillow.

I reached out and carefully touched it. It was real,

not a figment of my overtired brain. "Thank you," I mumbled.

"You're welcome," said Quinn. "Now sit up so I can feed you some breakfast. Although technically it could be lunch, considering it's well after one in the afternoon."

I scooted up in the bed and gave him a grin. He looked totally divine in faded denims that emphasized the lean strength of his legs, and a white shirt that was roughly rolled up at the sleeves, showing off his arms and shoulders. His hair, usually so neat, had that mussed, just-out-of-bed look, and when combined with a sexy smile—which he did *so* well—it was just about deadly. Luckily for me, there were no other females around, because he looked so hot I'd definitely be fighting them off.

"So to what do I owe this honor?" I said, reaching for the coffee on the tray.

He pulled it out of the way. "Sorry, kisses first."

"Oh, if I must," I muttered crossly, then grinned and caught his face between my hands, kissing him gently. It might not have been as explosive as the kiss I'd shared with Kye last night, but in many ways, it was far, far better.

"Now you have earned the coffee," he said, dark eyes shining with bedevilment.

I took the cup from the tray and inhaled the scent. Hazelnut. I sighed contentedly and took a sip, then eyed the bacon and eggs still on the tray.

"And what am I going to have to do to get the food?"

"Nothing. For now, anyway." He grinned as he sat down beside me then put the tray over my lap. "So how was last night?"

"Well, if I ever gave up being a guardian, I could make a ton of money as a dancer at a men's club."

"That doesn't surprise me."

He shifted a little so that his legs were touching mine. It felt good in a way that wasn't merely sexual, but more a safe, "right" kind of sensation. Like he and I had been designed to fit together like this.

"I'm actually surprised there's not more wolves in the clubs earning money," he continued. "Wolves are innately sexy, and most have great bodies."

"But not great breasts. As a race, we tend to be slender and flat. I'm just the weird exception."

"Not weird—delicious. And not every man on this planet likes his breasts large."

"No, but the largest money earners in that club seem to be the more buxom ladies—be they natural or surgically enhanced."

"It has been my experience over recent years that most males do not care if there *has* been surgical enhancement. It's you women that often sneer."

"Given the bitching I'd overheard in the changing rooms at the club, that's certainly true." I put the coffee down and began munching on breakfast. "I found our sorcerers. They own the club."

"Are you sure both these women are involved in the murders?"

"Pretty much. One of the women is definitely hiring teenagers to sleep with vampires—and I presume, let the sorceress into the house somehow—and the other is using the zombies and hellhounds to kill the girls."

"So you're dealing with two sorcerers, hellhounds, and zombies—not a good mix if you ask me. Which is why I got the holy water you asked for."

"Excellent." I popped a quick kiss on his cheek, then grabbed some bacon.

"I also acquired a silver knife."

I raised my eyebrows. He knew silver and I weren't compatible, so it seemed an odd purchase. "Why?"

"Because a silver knife will more easily slice through the hellhound's flesh and bone, making it simpler to decapitate them. I would suggest blinding them with the holy water first, though."

Blinding any other creature might work, but hellhounds hunted as much by scent as by sight. "So they're as allergic to silver as I am?"

"Most magical creatures have problems with pure silver. It's just more commonly known when it comes to werewolves."

"So, burn their eyes out, then cut their heads off. Easy stuff," I added with a wry grin. "Of course, me even holding a silver knife could be problematic."

"It has a bone handle. You should be able to hold it long enough to use it. When it's not in use, keep it in the sheath supplied. It has a thin lead lining, so I think it should give you enough protection."

"For an old man, you think pretty well."

"I'm not too old to teach *you* a thing or two, my pretty young werewolf."

"You reckon so?" I teased, one eyebrow raised.

He picked up the tray and put it on the floor beside the bed. "Obviously, I'm going to have to prove it."

"Obviously," I agreed.

Luckily for me, he did.

*M*y shift at Meinhardt's was again uneventful, and try as I might, I couldn't spot Kye. I had no doubt he was here—every now and again awareness would wash across my skin—but I could never pinpoint the exact location. The man was a will-o'-the-wisp, and obviously had no desire to catch the promised lap dance. Which, while disappointing, actually left me quite relieved. I wasn't entirely sure either of us was strong enough to resist such a close and intimate situation, and neither of us could afford the trouble it would give us if things got out of hand.

I did see Jessica several times through the night, and again I sensed that odd air of desperation about her. It was anger and helplessness and frustration combined, and it was stronger tonight than it had been last night. And I caught her watching me several times, although she watched the other acts, too, so maybe I was just being overly nervous.

I didn't have much luck getting close to the locked and guarded doors, however, and *that* was damned frustrating. The only thing I actually learned over the course of the night was that the cameras monitoring the doors were also infrared, meaning they could pick out a vampire—or even a half vampire—wrapped in shadows. What lay beyond them had to be vitally important to those running the club.

Of course, it might be something as simple as living quarters or the money-counting and safe areas, but instinct suggested it was something a whole lot more sinister.

After all, the sorcerers had to be performing their magic somewhere, because they weren't likely to want to be setting up new pentagrams every time they had some evil deeds to perform. And I couldn't feel the caress of magic anywhere else in parts of the building I had access to—beyond what I'd felt when Hanna was interviewing me, anyway.

It was close to one by the time I showered, changed into warm clothes—I wasn't about to end up half frozen as I had last night, so this time I'd even brought a jacket with me—and headed out the back entrance. It was Saturday night—well, Sunday morning, technically—and King Street was a whole lot busier than the previous night. This time the heavy beat of music mixed with the raucous sound of men singing off-tune, and their noise overrode the roar of cars passing by this back alleyway.

I shoved my hands into my coat pockets and began to sing softly along with the drunks, my voice no less off-key than the men ahead. Only I wasn't drunk, just tone deaf.

After a few minutes, that odd sense of awareness washed over me again, and I couldn't help smiling. "I was wondering when you were going to come out of hiding, Kye."

He appeared out of the shadows to my right, and fell in step beside me.

"I thought I'd better, or you might just keep singing."

"Smart ass."

"Someone had to tell you. Even the rats were running for their lives." He glanced at me, eyes glowing like bright embers in the darkness. "So, are you going to arrest me?"

I glanced at him. "What would you do if I did?"

His gaze swept me briefly—a look that was almost impersonal. Almost. "A fight would ensue if you tried, and I'd hate to see bruises marring that luscious body."

"You're presuming you'd get the chance to land the first punch. Trust me, that won't happen."

"Maybe. Maybe not." He shrugged, like it didn't matter.

And really, it didn't, because I had no intention of arresting him or getting involved in a fight with him. Sal might not have come back yet with any deep and dark secrets about this man, but every instinct I had suggested he was dangerous in ways I couldn't even *begin* to imagine. Getting involved with him in *any* way was not on the agenda—unless it was absolutely necessary.

I just wished my wolf could get that particular message.

"You didn't find me tonight," he commented into the silence.

"I had too many men wanting a dance to spend time finding one lonely little killer."

Kye's amusement swam around me, warming me in ways I couldn't even explain—and certainly didn't *want* to examine.

"So you looked, but couldn't spot me. Excellent."

Up ahead, near King Street, something scraped softly against the concrete. It sounded like the nail of a dog or something similar, yet there were no animals of any kind haunting the shadows or scrounging around the overflowing bins. There didn't even appear to be any rats—maybe they *had* fled due to my tone-deaf singing.

"I'll find you tomorrow night," I said, concentrating more on the surrounding darkness than on what I was saying. "I'm told Sundays tend to be slower, so I'll have more time to play."

"I'll tip you a hundred if you do find me."

I glanced at him and shook my head in mock sorrow. "Overconfidence gets them every time."

"You've got to find me first."

"I will."

He smiled a disbelieving sort of smile. "Have you found out what's behind the locked doors yet?"

"Have you?" I countered, my gaze searching the night again, but still finding nothing. And yet my uneasiness was growing.

We swung onto King Street and headed down toward Flinders, as we had last night. This time I had every intention of catching a cab home—my arm muscles were still aching from last night's flight.

"Anyone who gets near those doors, even accidentally, is swiftly thrown out of the club."

He touched my arm, the contact electric as he pulled me sideways a little. I glanced down, saw the puddle of vomit, and muttered "thanks" before moving free of his grip. But the heat of it still burned my skin regardless.

"I haven't seen the blonde at the club, either," he said, "Though her scent is quite strong in various rooms."

"I've seen both of them." I didn't add where, because I didn't want him storming the offices and possibly warning her and her accomplice that we were onto their hideout.

Again that odd scratching noise whispered across the silence. I frowned and glanced over my shoulder. Nothing and no one followed us, and yet . . . the shadows didn't seem to be quite so empty anymore.

Something was there, watching us.

Kye stopped abruptly, but his gaze was on the road ahead rather than on the shadows behind us.

"What?" I said, halting beside him.

"Magic," he said softly.

"Magic?" I frowned, letting my senses roam ahead, feeling for anything out of place. There wasn't anything immediately obvious. Yet the unseen drunks didn't seem to be singing as loudly and an odd sort of tension was rolling through the darkness.

Then the meandering wind brought with it a familiar scent.

Sulfur.

"Oh, fuck."

"What?" he said, his gaze still ahead, his body alert.

"Hellhounds."

He glanced at me. "The ones that were at the warehouse with the crow and the zombie?"

"I think so. They've obviously come to finish the job." And Jessica had obviously suspected me a whole lot more than I'd figured.

I swung my bag around and began picking through the mess of clothes to find the small containers of holy water. I dragged out two and handed one to Kye.

Kye shook the container, then gave me a somewhat dubious look. "Water?"

"Holy water. It burns them like acid and will blind them if it gets in their eyes."

"You really are a most surprising woman, Riley Jenson."

His expression was an odd mix of amusement, excitement, and hunger. The hunter was ready for his kill—and I wasn't entirely sure who, exactly, was his prey. Nor was I sure whether the shiver that rolled across my skin was excitement or fear.

"So how do we kill it?" he continued.

"Them," I corrected, shoving the container into my jeans pocket, which freed up my hands but kept the water within easy grabbing range. "I think there's two—one in front, one behind. And decapitation is the only way we can get rid of them."

"Do we attack, or do we wait for them to come to us?"

He didn't seem perturbed either way, but then he hadn't fought these things before. I *had,* and I'd prefer not to relive the experience if I could avoid it.

"Let's keep moving. They may not be here for us at all."

"You don't believe that any more than I do."

Well, no. And I couldn't help wondering why they were stalking me tonight. If they'd been at the club all along—and I had no doubt their mistress would keep them close, for safety's sake if nothing else—then why hadn't they come after me last night? She'd suspected me then, too.

And the hounds couldn't have picked up my scent at the club because I'd used Liander's special soap both times . . . Then I stopped and cursed myself for being a fool. I may have used Liander's soap before my shift, but I hadn't used it when I took a shower after work. Which meant I'd washed away the neutralizer and allowed my own natural scent to come through.

That's why they'd picked it up. It was a stupid, *stupid* thing to do, and one I'd make sure never to repeat. *If* I got out of this situation okay, that is.

We walked on, our footsteps light on the concrete. Cars rushed by, their headlights tearing through the surrounding shadows and revealing nothing more ominous than discarded soda containers and old hamburger wrappings.

I flared my nostrils, trying to catch the scent of sulfur, but it seemed to have disappeared as easily as it had come. Yet they were still out there, still watching. I could feel them, like a blot of evil growing on the horizon.

Kye stopped again. "The feel of magic just got sharper."

I viewed the street ahead. I still couldn't sense anything more than I had moments ago, but that didn't mean much. "You're sensitive to magic?"

"Yeah, something like that," he said, voice clipped. "There's people walking this way, too. Unless you want to endanger them, we'd better bring this thing to a head in a more secure spot."

"And here I was thinking you didn't care about anything or anyone else but yourself," I said, then pointed up Little Bourke Street. "There's several small alleys there that aren't really used at night. It'll limit the possible damage to others."

"That'll do, then."

We headed across the street and down to the first alley. The sulfur scent drifted past again, sharper and closer than before. I still couldn't feel the hellhound in front of us, but there was definitely one behind.

The reek of rot and rubbish from the nearby bins filled the air, overriding every other smell. As I stared into the darkness, I reached into my bag for the knife, drawing it from the sheath and out into the darkness. The silver blade seemed to glow with its own blue fire, and markings I hadn't noticed before suddenly appeared along the blade's length. But its closeness burned my skin. I wouldn't be able to hold it for very long, bone handle or not.

"More magic," Kye said, voice flat and all the more dangerous for it. He was looking at me rather than at the knife. "That's an interesting looking implement you've got there."

"It's a gift from a concerned lover."

Something flared in his eyes—something dark and very, very dangerous. "I'd like to meet this lover sometime and find out where he got it."

"It's silver, Kye. Silver and werewolves are never a good mix."

"Neither are werewolves and vampires, but that doesn't seem to have stopped you."

His comment surprised me enough that all I could do for several seconds was stare at him, then anger surged and I lashed out. He caught the blow in his fist, holding it tight. "Don't ever hit me, Riley."

"Don't *ever* creep around in my head," I snapped back, pulling my fist from his. Surprise flickered briefly through his eyes before the mask returned. "Or I'll fry your fucking mind to a crisp."

"It's not like I want to," he said, voice still flat, and yet sounding oddly frustrated. "Trust me on that."

"You're a telepath. You have the *choice* to intrude or not. Trust me, the *not* is the best option here."

"I'm not a telepath, Riley. I've told you that—"

I clamped a hand over his mouth, stopping his denial. Not that I believed it, anyway. "Listen."

For several seconds there were no sounds beyond the usual for this time of night. Then it came—the soft scrape of a nail against concrete.

They were on us.

But they weren't just coming from the main street. One of them was above us, on the roof.

Kye swung around and pulled out a gun from under his coat. The burn of silver suddenly became stronger.

"You carry silver bullets?" I asked, slipping my bag

over my shoulder and tossing it into the shadows, out of the way.

"In certain situations, yes. Back to back, Riley. They're going to come at us from two angles."

"Thanks for telling me that. I would never have guessed otherwise," I said sarcastically, but he didn't answer.

I looked at the rooflines above us. A shadow moved in low and fast, and then it leapt.

"Drop," I said, doing exactly that, trying to scrunch myself into the smallest possible ball. As the hound flew over the top of us, I slashed with the knife. The blue fire on the blade seemed to blaze even brighter as it scoured the creature's stomach, burning through hair and flesh and down into gut. Blood and God knows what else gushed, thick and black and putrid, splattering across my clothes and burning like acid. I swore and tore off my coat, but by then the creature had turned and was leaping again.

Two shots ran across the night. The creature jerked and twisted away from us. For a moment I thought the shots had missed, then I saw the hole in the side of its jaw, the blood and bone splattered across the nearby wall.

It snarled, revealing wickedly sharp teeth. Kye twisted around and fired off a third shot. It took the creature in the chest, ripped through flesh and bone, then clean through its body, smashing into the wall behind it. The creature howled and leapt.

I grabbed Kye, pulling him sideways, both of us falling to the ground hard. Again the creature flew over us, but this time it lashed out. Claws raked my side, spilling warmth down my hip.

I bit back a yelp of pain and slashed with the knife, missing its belly but getting a hind leg. Toes and gleaming claws plopped down onto the pavement beside me.

"Oh, fuck, here comes the other one," Kye said, scrambling to his feet before reaching down to grab my arm and haul me upright.

"Use the holy water. We have to blind them if we're to have any hope at all."

"Whatever else these things are, they're hounds," he said grimly. "They hunt by scent."

"They can't if you destroy their sensory center as well."

He didn't look convinced that would work, and in honesty, I wasn't, either.

"You take the injured one," he said.

"Kye—" But I was already talking to the air.

Soft padding steps echoed behind me. I twisted around, the knife held in front of me like a blazing lance. I wished it *was* a lance—long and strong and wickedly sharp—because it was the only way I was going to beat this thing without getting too damn close.

The bloodied hellhound stalked toward me, its steps measured, its gaze on mine, luminous and deadly. Fear stirred in my stomach, but I pushed it away. I'd beaten these things once before. I could do it again.

It sprang. There was no warning, no bunching of muscles. One minute it was walking, the next it was in the air. I twisted out of its way, slashing at the soft flesh of its neck, hoping to at least sever something vital.

Again the blue fire erupted along the blade, but the hellhound shifted at the last moment, and the knife barely skimmed the creature's flesh.

It snarled and slashed out with its claws. I leapt backward, crashed into some bins, then spilled sideways along with the rubbish. I caught my balance and backed away, down the lane, drawing the creature away from Kye, who seemed to be having no more luck with his creature than I was with mine.

The hound shook its head, spraying droplets of blood that hit the brick walls of the buildings on either side of us and began to sizzle. These things had acid for blood. What the hell kind of hound were they? At least the other hounds I'd faced in the past hadn't possessed deadly bodily fluids.

It leapt again. As I ran backward, out of the way, I drew the small container from my pocket and popped the top. But I didn't throw it, holding steady as the creature hit the pavement and launched again. When it was near enough that I could smell its fetid breath, I threw the holy water. The liquid arced across the air like a silver ribbon, hitting the creature across the snout and splashing upward, into its eyes.

The hellhound screamed, the sound so high and piercing that I had to resist the urge to thrust my hands up to my ears to muffle the sound. I twisted out of the creature's way, but it was too close and moving too fast. It hit with incredible force, lifting me off my feet and throwing me backward.

I smashed into the wall, cracking my head against the brick and driving the breath from my lungs. Pain hit like a truck and blood spurted, the metallic taste filling my mouth. I spat it out and scrambled sideways, somehow avoiding the creature's slashing paws. A weird bubbling sound rode the air, accompanied by the scent of burning flesh. The holy water, doing its stuff, but nowhere near fast enough for my liking.

I twisted around, knife once again in front of me, and saw the mess that was the creature's face. It wasn't dead. Wasn't even stopped. Its olfactory senses might be in the process of being destroyed, but right now it could still smell me. And it attacked—hard, fast, and low. I leapt out of the way, rolled to my feet, and slashed at its neck with the knife. This time it cut deep, and black blood spurted from the creature's wound, spraying across my face and arms, stinging like acid.

I swore and scrambled away, stripping off my shirt and hastily swiping at the blood. It did little more than smear the stinking black fluid, but at least the sting lessened. The scrape of nails against concrete echoed across the night—the creature, coming after me again. I kept running, gathering speed, then leapt, as high and as hard as I could. I grabbed the gutters of the nearest building and hauled myself up onto the roof.

The creature leapt after me. I sidestepped and swept the knife down hard. The blazing blade sliced through flesh and bone with little effort, and the hellhound's head dropped at my feet. Its momentum kept the body flying past, so that it crashed back down several feet away. Blue flames spread quickly across its remains, consuming its flesh until there was nothing left but ash.

Ash the wind quickly scattered. Even the smeared blood on my arms disappeared.

One down, one to go.

I leapt over the remaining bits of soot and ran across the rooftop. Below in the alleyway, the second creature howled, and this time there was no answering shot. Kye was running backward, slashing at the creature with a short knife, chipping at the claws that threatened to rend him in two, but doing little else to stop it.

The hellhound's face was ruined, its nose rotting and ready to fall off, its eyes mere holes. It didn't matter, it was relying on sound and its ears were in perfect working order. I stopped, took a deep breath, then, as Kye passed my position, leapt.

I landed on the creature's back and wrapped my legs around its belly. It roared and began to buck, twist, and turn. I held on, raised the knife, then plunged it down as hard as I could, thrusting the blade deep into its neck before twisting it hard. As one side of the creature's neck began to split away from its body, I pulled out the knife and hacked at the remaining skin.

The creature crashed to the ground, taking me with it. Kye leapt in, grabbed my arms, and hauled me free from the creature, but already it was beginning to disintegrate, the blue flame of the knife crawling over its body, consuming it, until there was nothing left but ash blowing away on the breeze.

"I really am going to have to get one those knives," he said, lifting me upright with little effort. "They do a rather efficient job on hell's beasties."

"That they do." I stepped back then moved across to

the bins to retrieve my bag. My hip ached in protest, and blood gushed warmly down my leg. But I couldn't shapeshift when I was holding silver, and I wouldn't have done so anyway. Kye might have fought by my side, but I didn't entirely trust him.

Though I wasn't sure what he could do when I was in wolf form that he couldn't do when I was in human. I shoved the knife back into its sheath, then picked up the bag and my coat and swung around.

"Will the witch sense the death of her hounds?" he asked, his crossed arms slashed and bleeding almost as much as my leg.

Maybe *he* didn't trust *me* enough to change shape and stop the bleeding.

It was a somewhat cheery thought, if only because I didn't think there was much that made this wolf pause. Certainly the hellhounds hadn't fazed him.

"From what I understand, sorcerers use a lot of 'personal' magic as well as their own blood to raise the sort of magic required for the hellhounds. So yes, she will probably feel their deaths."

"Meaning she might come here to investigate."

"I doubt it. Whatever else these women might be, they aren't stupid. And that would be a stupid move."

"Still, it's worth staying here to check. If the bad guys never did stupid things, then we good guys would never catch them."

I snorted softly. "I hardly think you can stand in line with the good guys, Kye."

"Depends on who's paying me at the time," he said,

without the slightest trace of humor. "Right now, I'm on the side of the angels."

"I don't think the angels appreciate it." Or wanted it.

"Tough," he said, leaving me wondering if he was answering my spoken or unspoken comment. If I'd had more energy, I might have retaliated and found out, but right now, I just wanted to go home, have a shower, and grab some sleep.

"Well, you can have this watch all to yourself. Although I would appreciate being told if anything interesting happens."

"If anything interesting happens, I'll give you a call."

"You haven't got my number." And he wasn't going to get it, either.

He smiled. It was the sort of smile that suggested getting information like that wasn't a problem. And for someone like him, it probably wasn't. Hell, he'd probably already snatched it in his sneaky mind raids.

And *how* he did that, when I supposedly had shields strong enough to keep out the likes of Quinn and Jack—who were the strongest telepaths I'd ever met—is one of the many things I wanted to know. But not now, when I was so bone tired.

"Good night, Kye."

"Don't let the vampires bite."

"Why shouldn't I?" I countered sweetly, "when that only adds to the overall pleasure? And trust me, it *is* pleasurable."

He didn't say anything, but there was a fierceness in his eyes that made something deep inside tremble. I had an odd feeling I'd just flung a challenge his way, and I was going to regret it.

Or worse still, *not* regret it.

I hitched my bag up onto my shoulder and walked away before I got myself into deeper trouble.

Getting a taxi when I looked like something the dog had thrown up proved to be problematic. So was flying home clutching a bag filled with clothes, holy water, and a great big silver knife. Which meant I ended up walking—not fun, and a pretty crappy way to end the night.

I slept the sleep of the dead when I got home, and it was well after three by the time I dragged myself back to the land of the living.

The apartment was quiet, but the scent of coffee lingered in the air, tantalizing my taste buds. Hoping Liander had left the percolator on for me, I flung the blankets off and climbed out of bed. My hip twinged a reminder to be careful, and I glanced down. Three pink scars stretched from the top of my hip to my thigh—a stark reminder of just how close I'd come to death again last night. One of these days, my luck was going to change.

I shivered and thrust the thought away as I walked into the kitchen. The coffee was still warm, and I breathed deep, sucking in the delicious scent, feeling it flow down through my body, waking and revitalizing.

Coffee on call, without having to wait for the kettle to boil, had to be one of life's greatest pleasures. Of all the good things Liander had brought to our lives, the coffeemaker had to be among the best of them.

I poured myself a cup, then splashed in some milk, taking several sips before I shoved some bread in the toaster. My cell phone rang, and I knew without doubt it would be Jack. He always seemed to pick the worst possible moments to call with an update.

I walked into the living room, dug my phone out of my bag, and hit the receive button.

"I was going to call in a report right after I had a coffee, boss," I said.

"I'm not ringing for a report," he said, voice flat and annoyed.

Which couldn't mean that anything good had happened.

"Then what's the problem?"

"We've got ourselves another dead vampire, and this time it's really bad."

Chapter 9

 thought you were going to bring in the teenager with the birthmark to stop her being used," I said, voice sharp.

"We did. And we tracked down the five vamps who I know like body imperfections. This isn't one of them. I think it was a last-minute deal."

Or an outpouring of anger that the sorcerer's plans had been frustrated.

"So how much worse than decapitation and body parts being hacked away can it be?" I said, half wishing I'd stayed in bed and *not* answered the phone.

"Lots, from what Cole is saying. He's there now. I want you to head over and see if you can feel anything."

"I haven't felt any souls up to now, so why do you think I'd feel one at this murder?"

"Because this time, they killed the woman who was

with him. She was human, and *she* just might be confused enough about her death to still be there."

"We don't know that both women are involved in
the vamp killings. You'd think Cole would have found
some evidence of wheelchair use in at least one of the
murder scenes by now."

"Not if she was using her crow form."

"The worst a crow could do is peck someone to
death."

"When we're talking about sorcerers, anything is
possible."

I guess that was true. "It'll take me fifteen minutes to
get ready."

"I want you there by four," he said, and hung up.

I glanced at my watch. He'd given me a whole
twenty-five minutes. How generous of him. I downed
my coffee then headed for the bathroom.

Although I got ready in record time, it still took me
thirty-five minutes to get through the city traffic to
Brighton.

Cole glanced around as I walked into the third-floor
apartment, then made a show of looking at his watch.
"You're late."

"Bite me," I muttered, in no mood for frivolities
right now. The metallic tang of blood was thick in the
air, but it was the reek of magic that turned my stomach. It was so strong my skin crawled against the sensation. "So who did they kill this time?"

"Our vamp is one Jason Burke. He's got a reputation
as a philanderer, and has only just moved down here
from Queensland. Apparently things were getting a lit-

tle heated up there for him." Cole paused and smiled. "From what I heard, there were several husbands armed with sharpened sticks coming after him."

I didn't smile. I didn't have the energy. "Where are the victims?"

"In the bedroom."

Which was where the other victims had been caught, even if they hadn't all been killed there. At least there was one constant. "What time were they killed?"

"Approximately eleven last night."

Jessica had been in the club giving me the evil eye at that time, so she couldn't have been involved, no matter what Jack might think. "Any reason why Jack would say that these murders are worse than before?"

Cole snorted. "Because they *are*. They look as if they've been torn apart by dogs, although the tear marks don't actually match any dogs that I know of."

"Not even hellhounds?"

"Haven't had a whole lot of experience with them, but it seems to me they don't actually leave pieces. They consume it all."

"They seem to. And the woman who controls the hellhounds was at the club at the time of the murders."

"Doesn't mean she couldn't have sent her beasties here."

"Or that the other sorceress couldn't have raised her own little beasties."

"True." Cole's gaze was still on me, still intent. Although he couldn't see the injuries I'd received last night, I had an odd sense he knew about them anyway. A suspicion he confirmed by asking, "Are you okay?"

"Had a brush with said beasties last night. They're now ash blowing on the wind." I gave him a lopsided smile. "But I actually think it's the late-night working. It's done me in more than the hellhounds' efforts. I'll be glad when this job is over."

"Yeah, irregular working hours can be a bitch." He waved a hand toward the bedroom. "Dobbs and Dusty are in there at the moment. That's not going to interfere with your psychic radar, is it?"

I shook my head and grabbed a pair of plastic shoe covers from the little box on the table. I'd need them if this murder was as bad as everyone was saying. "Do we know who the other victim is yet?"

"Denita Lowe," Cole said, carefully picking up a hair and placing it into a plastic bag. "A forty-six-year-old woman with a hubby and two kids."

So Burke had continued his philandering ways despite his trouble up in Queensland. "The husband been told yet?"

Cole shook his head. "I think Jack is waiting until we find enough of her to get an official ID."

I frowned. "If you haven't got enough, how do you know who she is?"

"Purse over by the door."

"Oh." Of course. I turned and headed for the bedroom. There was no use delaying it any longer. Besides, I had to report to the club in an hour.

The intense sensation of vile magic hit the minute I walked into the room. It was stronger here than at the previous murder scenes, but maybe that was because the crime was fresher, too. But there was another scent that mingled with the feel of magic—the faint whiff of roses.

Hanna Mein's scent, not Jessica's.

The room itself was a mess. It might once have been painted a very pale blue, but you'd hardly know it. Blood had been smeared from one end of the room to the other, and larger chunks of flesh and bone dribbled off just about everything—the beds, the lamps, the ceiling lights, even the painting frames. It was in such a state that it was hard to tell which bit was male and which was female.

Bile rose and goose bumps prickled my skin. I might be a guardian, but scenes of gore and guts like this were not something I was used to yet. And I hope I never did get used to them. Hoped I would never be blasé about useless, wanton destruction of life.

I rubbed my arms, half wishing I'd grabbed my coat out of the car, then stopped as power began to caress the air and an odd tingle raced across my skin.

There was a soul here.

I looked around the room, but for several minutes saw nothing remotely "otherworldly." Yet the ever-sharpening tingle of energy told me something waited.

Then a faint wisp of white appeared in the far corner of the room. It was little more than a curl of smoke, barely visible in the sharp sunlight pouring through the window. Certainly it was nothing that could be defined as ghostlike, and could easily have been mistaken for a puff of dust from the nearby chair Dobbs was moving.

But it wasn't.

And the power that spun all around me, as well as the growing chill in the air, only confirmed it.

Tentatively, I reached out with my thoughts and asked, *What happened to you?*

Not so long ago, my ability to sense and hear souls had developed to where I could now converse with them telepathically—although not all souls seemed to have the strength to talk. Those that *did* seemed to be drawing additional strength from me, often leaving me feeling drained. Cole, who'd seen it happen a number of times now, thought it was dangerous—that the souls might just end up drawing me into the lands of death if I wasn't very careful. Jack and the magi weren't so sure that was possible.

I didn't know who was right, but I wasn't about to take any more risks than necessary. Death was one thing. Lingering on the plane of death—or wherever else it was that souls who were killed before their time went—was not on my agenda for the moment. Or any moment, actually.

The soul didn't answer, although the energy in the air was increasing. Frowning, I tried again. *What happened to you?*

Death happened, came the reply, the voice feminine but as strong and as powerful as the energy that spun around me. *What do you wish to know?*

I frowned. Unlike most of them, this soul wasn't confused by what had happened, nor did she seem particularly angry. Which was odd, given her fate. And the energy that crawled all around me seemed to be more than just the energy of the dead—though how that could be possible, I didn't know.

I need to know what you saw. I want to stop this killer before she kills someone else.

The soul didn't answer immediately. I waited, watching the wisp of smoke, wondering what went on in the mind of the newly dead. She seemed calmer, more accepting, than any of the other souls I'd come across, but I had a suspicion that appearances were deceiving.

I do not have the time to tell you all that I saw, the soul said eventually, *for even now, my final journey calls.*

Then tell me what you can.

It is easier if I show you. The wisp of smoke moved, drifting out from its corner, and the chill in the air increased until I was shivering with it.

How do you plan to show me? But even as I asked the question, I pretty much knew the answer. And I wasn't entirely sure I wanted anything to do with it—even if the cost was not getting a much-needed lead on our killers.

She wanted to merge with me.

It will not be painful, the soul said. *Just . . . different. Exhausting.*

You can't know that.

Yes, she said, her voice softer than before, suggesting her strength was fading even if the energy that pulsed all around me was still diamond bright. *I can. I did it many times when I was alive.*

She was drifting closer and closer, and I had to resist the temptation to step back.

You were a clairvoyant? I asked, surprised. *How come you didn't see this coming?*

I communed with the dead, like you, she said. *I was able to become one with them, to see and remember what they remembered. My own future was not something they—or I—could have ever predicted.*

If they had, would she have avoided the vampire? Or would she have accepted her fate because it was meant to be? I very much suspected the latter answer was the correct one.

And then she was on me, in me, filling me with the cold of the afterworld, chilling me down to the bone, to my very soul. Then there was nothing but images and sensory details—details that flashed by almost too fast. A man's face, soft in the aftermath of lovemaking. The sensation of evil rising, combined with the fleeting scent of rose. The spurt of fear as a sphere of darkness formed at the end of the bed, and the face of a woman, her body merging into the blackness. Dust, thrown by pale hands, scattering across the bed, settling in a choking cloud. The woman stepped forward, revealing dark hair and green eyes that shone bright with power. Power that flashed from her fingertips—lightning bright and razor sharp. Power that tore, without thought, without care, through flesh and bone alike. The world became one of pain, nothing but pain, until the relief of death...

That is all, the witch said, her voice broken and fading away. *Catch her. Stop her.*

I didn't answer. Couldn't answer. My energy was as drained as the soul's, and as she faded away, so did I.

When I came to, I was lying on one of the leather sofas in the living room. Cole was close to my left side, a bloodied cloth in one hand and a take-out cup of coffee in the other.

"What the hell happened?" he said the minute he saw I was awake.

"Lack of caffeine in my system," I muttered, sitting up somewhat gingerly and reaching for the coffee. I took a sip, felt strength and heat begin to flow through my body, and sighed contentedly before squinting at the cloth he was holding. "Why are you holding a wet cloth?"

"Because you collapsed into a puddle of body bits, and I didn't think you'd appreciate it being left on you."

My stomach turned at the thought, though at least it explained why my jeans were clinging to my legs. I resisted the urge to strip them off and gave Cole a wan smile. "Thanks for that."

He nodded. "So what happened?"

"The soul sort of merged with me."

"What?"

"Yeah, surprised the hell out of me, too." I grimaced. "I saw everything she saw. Felt everything she'd felt." I shuddered at the memory. "Hanna Mein did this."

"Then we can take her out," Cole said.

"Except that we have no hard evidence." I might know that Hanna had killed *this* couple—and probably the other vampires—but knowing and actually proving it enough to justify a kill was another matter entirely. Hanna Mein might be a sorceress, but she was also listed as *human*, and there was a whole different set of rules for humans. Even humans gone bad.

Now had it been Jessica who'd done this, it would have been kill first, ask questions later. She was a shifter, so all bets were off when it came to her crimes. It might not be right or fair, but it was still the humans who made the rules in this world, and there was nothing the rest of us could do about it until the status quo changed in government.

"Proving suspicions may not matter in this case. Not when one of the victims was a close friends of Jack's."

"These women have been killing vamps in other states, possibly for a very long time. I don't think either will be easy kills. They will have taken precautions of one kind or another."

He grunted then pushed to his feet. "Are you feeling better?"

"Well enough that you can stop baby-sitting and get back to your job."

"Good." But he said it with a smile in his blue eyes.

I swung my feet onto the floor and sat up. Weakness washed through me and, for a moment, the room spun. Being infused by the dead had taken more out of me than I'd thought.

"Are you sure you're okay?" Cole asked, standing back but looking ready to catch me should it be needed.

"I'm fine. Really." I glanced at my watch and saw that it was after five. "I'm going to be late for my new job if I don't get a move on."

And I couldn't *not* go there, even if Jessica now suspected me. We needed concrete evidence before we could move against the two women, and to get that, I needed to be near them. And at least if she was watching, and worrying, about me, she wasn't out there sending zombies after innocent kids. I doubted she'd try anything in the club. There were too many possible witnesses.

Cole grabbed my elbow as I rose, and thankfully held me steady as the room spun around again. "God, that's unpleasant," I muttered.

"Maybe you shouldn't drive—"

"I'll be fine," I interrupted, pulling away from him. "I just need more coffee and some food."

"Figured you might need something to eat, so I brought some hamburgers. They're over near the door."

I smiled and rose up on my toes, kissing his cheek lightly. "If you're not careful, wolf, I might begin to think you actually like me."

"Then you'd be thinking wrong," he said, blue eyes twinkling. "Get, woman, so I can go back to work."

I left, grabbing the bag of burgers on the way out. Of course, traffic was hell and it took me forever to get back home. By the time I'd showered, changed, and caught a cab to the club, I was a good hour late.

They weren't happy, but I mollified the night manager somewhat by promising to make up the time working a couple of extra hours on the following night.

I changed into my almost nonexistent dance gear and shiny stiletto heels, and headed into the main room. I checked the board to see my stage times, and saw that I'd been allocated shifts in both the main room and the sports bar. Which would enable me to have a closer look at both the locked doors while keeping an eye out for our two murderers. Who, according to the minds I'd briefly scanned, hadn't been seen at all during the day.

Fate was obviously giving me a break for a change.

The crowd in the main room was smaller tonight, but no less noisy, and the bartenders seemed to be running to keep up with the drinks orders. I couldn't immediately spot Kye, nor did I get that surge of awareness that suggested he was near—although that didn't mean he wasn't here. He could have been in one of the other rooms. I talked to various patrons as I made my way around the room, dancing for some and having drinks bought for me from others—a practice management encouraged because that's where the real money was—all the while working my way toward the locked and guarded door.

There was an old guy sitting at the table nearest the door, and for a moment I thought it might have been Kye. He was the right height and had the same broad shoulders, but this guy's hair was a matted brown, and he reeked of booze, stale sweat, and humanity. I doubted even a werewolf as stoic as Kye would stand that odor for very long. Besides, the sharp awareness that always warned of his presence, even if it didn't pinpoint a location, was absent.

At any other time, I might have avoided the old guy like a plague, but he happened to be sitting in the perfect position to study the door more closely without raising suspicions.

I walked around the table so that I was upwind of him, then pulled out a chair and sat down beside him.

"Don't want a dance," he said, voice sharp and crackly. "I ain't gonna pay you anything, girlie, so you can just be off and harass someone else."

I was about to ask the old grump what the hell he was doing here if he didn't want any personal attention, but the guard was in earshot and I doubted they'd be happy with a dancer bad-mouthing the customer. Even a grumpy, stinky, old one.

So instead I took off a shoe and rubbed the ball of my foot. "I'm actually just giving my feet a rest. But if you mind, I'll move on."

He harrumphed. "I ain't buying you a drink, either. Not at them bar prices."

I continued to rub my foot, surreptitiously studying the door lock as I did so. It wasn't only fingerprint coded, it had an iris scanner as well. Which in itself wasn't a problem, except that all the guards wore nanowires. I might be able to get past them and force him to open the door, but it would mean a concerted effort on my part, and that would certainly be dangerous considering that the cameras were constantly checking out the room. A dancer standing still apparently concentrating on nothing was sure to attract attention. Which meant I'd have to find a way to short the cameras out first—all without raising an alarm in the security room.

No easy task, whichever way I looked at it.

I sighed and glanced at the old man. His brown eyes were still regarding me suspiciously, and they had an oddly flat look about them. Contacts, I thought, for no particular reason. And wondered again if it was Kye.

After all, it'd be just like him to go for a disguise that he knew would turn me off. And he *had* told me a number of times he didn't want a lap dance.

"So, do you come here often?" I leaned back on the table to ensure his view of my breasts was unobstructed by the short, gauzy jacket I was wearing.

"First time," he said, his gaze sweeping my body then moving away swiftly. Pink tinged his cheeks.

If it was Kye, he was a damn good actor.

"Are you enjoying yourself?"

"Don't mind the stage shows." His gaze raked me again, and he licked his lips. I couldn't smell his excitement. Couldn't smell anything except that overriding, unwashed, boozy scent. "Don't like all the table attention, though."

"It's part of our job to talk to all the customers." My gaze moved past the grumpy old fart as one of the money men moved in our direction. The various club tills were regularly cleared out of big notes—a result, I'm told, of the club being hit by robbers within the first few weeks of its opening. If he was heading this way, then maybe the vaults were behind door number one rather than any sort of secret magic chambers.

"Just as it's a part of your job to wrangle money out of them," the old guy said. "But you ain't wrangling anything out of me, young lady, so you might as well not waste your time."

I shoved on my shoe and switched feet. "As soon as my feet stop aching, I'll leave you in peace."

"Well if you wore sensible shoes, sore feet wouldn't be a problem."

"Sensible shoes aren't pretty," I said, my attention more on the guard than on what the old guy was saying. The money handler had reached the door, and the camera above me whined as it began to rotate. I glanced up, watching it do a complete circuit of the club. Only when it had finished did the guard press his hand, then his eye, against the scanners.

There was a pause, then several clicks, before the door opened ponderously. I leaned sideways a little to catch a glimpse of the hallway beyond, and saw the old guy do the same.

Saw his intent expression.

And knew, without a doubt, that it was Kye.

I'd seen that intentness too often now to mistake it.

Why I wasn't getting that surge of awareness I had no idea, but right now, that wasn't important. Seeing what was beyond that door was.

I leaned further, placing a hand on his leg to support myself. Felt the muscle and the strength underneath the stained and ratty pants, as well as a surge of electricity and awareness that just about short-circuited every sense I had. I hadn't been wrong. This was definitely Kye.

"You owe me a hundred," I said softly, making it look like I was whispering sweet nothings when all the time I was eyeing the hallway.

It wasn't much. Just a short, concreted area that led to another large door, this one metal. A vault, not a sorcerer's secret place of mischief.

The guard shifted and I flicked my gaze to Kye, who was looking at me like I was nuts.

"I don't know what you're talking about," he said, still sounding like a man who drank and smoked too much. A voice modulator, obviously.

I slipped my shoe back on and rose. "Of course you do," I said, stepping past him then stopping to add softly, "and that door is not our target. Meet me in the sports bar at eleven."

He didn't check his watch. Didn't do anything but scowl at me. I smiled and headed for the stage to do my floor show.

By the time I'd finished, Kye had gone, but that didn't surprise me. With the first door out of contention, he'd probably already moved into position to check out door number two.

I could only hope he stank less when I found him again, or I wasn't going to be able to talk to him long, let alone do the promised lap dance.

Although now that he knew I was onto him, he might very well change his look. He might be on the prowl for his targets, but I didn't think he was above providing a challenge in the process.

For the next few hours, I continued my shift in the main room, chatting up customers, giving them lap dances, earning money, and fending off the occasional grab. When I'd finished my second stage show, I headed to the staff lounge for my break and to eavesdrop on the local gossip. To date, the topic of conversation had consisted mainly of bitching about the customers and very occasionally about other dancers. I was sipping my coffee and only half listening when one of the busty blondes said, "God, wasn't the boss in a bitch of a mood last night? I'm glad she hasn't turned up tonight."

The other blonde—whom I only knew by her stage name, Sammy—snorted softly. "I could hear her screaming all the way down in the dressing rooms. Do you know what happened?"

The blonde sniffed. "Rumor is that she had a special lined up and the girl didn't appear. She took her frustrations out on a customer in another room and beat him up pretty bad."

"One lawsuit coming up." Sammy shook her head, though her expression was one of amusement more than disgust. "I thought she'd given up dancing."

"Apparently she likes to keep her hand in." The blonde hesitated, then leaned forward conspiratorially and whispered, "She likes the younger ones, so she's always on hand to help out when we have some young bucks in."

"She can have the young ones. They're all hands and no damn cash. Was an ambulance called?"

"No. And the cops didn't show, either, so it couldn't have been more than a few slaps."

"So why did they shut the room down? It's been out of action all day, apparently."

I continued to look at the paper, but I wasn't really reading anything. Instead, I reached out telepathically, linking lightly with the blonde's mind. I delved stealthily but deeply into her memory centers, fishing though quickly until I caught the images she was talking about. I wrapped around them, drawing them into me, remembering them as she remembered—not only seeing and hearing, but smelling.

What I smelled was blood. Lots of blood.

Hanna Mein hadn't injured. She'd killed.

So, did that mean the couple she'd slaughtered had been nothing more than a last-minute substitution for the special that had been canceled? Or had they been just another release for the anger, as the man she'd danced for—then killed—had been?

I continued to sort through the blonde's memories, but she hadn't actually seen anything. She'd been stopped at the doorway, and had gotten the information from the guard stationed there.

I withdrew and flipped over the page as I took a sip of coffee.

The blonde shrugged. "It was due for refurbishment. Now there's a new chaise lounge and a fresh coat of paint on the walls." She glanced at her watch and rose. "I get to christen the new surrounds in five minutes."

"Give him hell and make him pay," Sammy said with a grin.

"Always do, love, always do." The blonde dropped a kiss on the other woman's cheek then walked out.

I finished my coffee, rinsing the bitter dregs in the sink before heading down to the change rooms to get into my other outfit for the evening—a soft striped silk that looked like something a jockey would wear, except that it didn't fully cover my breasts. Every time I raised my arms even slightly, out popped the girls. And even though there were plenty of women walking around without covering tops of any kind, the outfit had proven to be extremely popular with the guys despite its impracticality.

The sports bar was half full, which wasn't bad considering it was a Monday night. There were a heap of men sitting at the tables near the big screen, watching some boxing match, but there were many others playing pool or simply chatting with various dancers at the other tables. The name of the game in this room wasn't pool or chatting, but getting the customers to spend money on drinks, or interested enough to spend big in the fantasy rooms.

I scanned the room as I walked around the edge, looking for Kye in his grumpy old man outfit. Not a sign of him. Which meant either he wasn't here, or he'd changed, and I was betting on the latter.

I was three quarters of the way around the room when awareness of Kye washed over me—a short, sharp caress that was gone almost as fast as it had arrived. I turned and saw a spiky-haired blond man walk into the room and then stand, arms crossed, in the shadows near the door, his gaze on the big screen.

He looked totally different than before. Gone was the ratty coat, the slouched stance, and almost grimy appearance. In its place stood a broad-shouldered, muscular man wearing faded, hip-hugging denims and a crumpled, pale pink shirt that suited his golden skin and bleached hair. He looked more like a builder than a hit man, and even though I couldn't deny the surge of attraction, that was the one thing I couldn't ever forget—that he *was* a hit man. That he *was* extremely dangerous.

I stepped out of the shadows. The minute I did, he shot a glance my way. This time his eyes were green, and they gleamed like the brightest emeralds in the half-light of the bar.

There was nothing warm about his gaze, nothing friendly about the way it latched onto me, and yet the shiver that ran over me was all heat, all desire. Maybe it was simply the danger he represented that pulled at me so fiercely. The feeling that every minute I spent with him could be my last. That no matter how strong I was, no matter how fast, this man *could* counter it. That he *would* counter it, if I ever got in the way of his aims.

Danger was an aphrodisiac to a wolf, and *my* wolf was reacting to it as fiercely as she ever had.

"You're looking like a man who needs to play some pool," I said softly as I stopped beside Kye and touched his arm. The contact was as electric as ever, and only served to confirm his identity.

A smile flirted with his lips, then he glanced past me. "There's a table available over there." He nodded toward the locked and guarded side door. It wasn't the only spare table, of course, but it best suited our purpose. "How about we take that?"

"Perfect." I tucked my arm through his, letting my hips brush against his as we walked. Tension rose between us—all sexual—until it fairly crackled.

The guard didn't even look at us as we stopped at the table. His scent said he was human, so he wouldn't overhear any conversations as long as we kept it low.

Like all the other guards in this place, he was wearing a wire, but there was also what looked to be a small two-way radio hanging around his ear. Every now and again he'd murmur something, and the camera would react by moving.

It wouldn't have surprised me if they were monitoring conversations, so we'd have to keep an eye on the camera position to make sure it wasn't pointed our way. And while we could talk telepathically, that would look suspicious to anyone who might be watching.

"So what happened to the old man?" I asked softly as Kye racked up the balls.

"He's lying in a rubbish bin as we speak." He picked up the cues and handed me one. "You going to break?"

I glanced up at the odd emphasis he placed on "break" and saw the teasing, almost mocking, light in his green eyes. I arched an eyebrow. "I never break unless it's absolutely necessary."

"Really?" he drawled. "Maybe I should test that little statement."

I took the cue from him, then leaned a little closer and whispered, "This from the man who absolutely *didn't* want a lap dance."

"Oh, I still don't. But then, I'm not the one aching from head to foot, am I?"

"Oh, really?" I chalked the end of the cue then bent over right in front of him, so that my butt casually brushed his groin. The man was definitely understating his current state of desire.

"That sure feels like a whole lot painful to me," I murmured, drawing the cue back and sending the little white ball spinning into the others. Colored balls scattered everywhere, none of them going into the pockets. The cue ball came to rest close to where I was standing, so I remained where I was, forcing him to come closer.

"I think we need to check out one of the private rooms," I said. My breath hitched as he casually lined up the shot and his fingers brushed past my side.

"And why would we need to do that if you're in no danger of breaking?"

He eyed his chosen target rather than me, and I waited until he was about to play the shot before saying, "Because Hanna Mein killed someone in the Arabian room last night, and I think we need to check it out."

His shot didn't miss a solid ball, but it didn't send one into a pocket, either. I smiled.

He stood back and chalked his cue. "And how is what she did in the Arabian room related to what we're interested in achieving?"

I shifted slightly and lined up the ball sitting near the far corner pocket. "Because if someone *did* die, then the body is either still concealed in that room or there's another way in or out. No one saw anything resembling a body leaving the club."

I went for the shot, but a second before the cue tip hit the ball, his hand snaked down my back and butt, a caress so light and yet so heated that it practically singed.

Needless to say, I missed the ball.

He moved around to the other side of the table and

began to line up the same ball I had. "That still doesn't explain the connection to our current case."

"Don't be obtuse."

He smiled and drew back the cue. I waited until the last possible moment, then shifted my arms so that my top rode up my breasts, and leaned over the table, giving him an eyeful.

He missed the ball even worse than I did.

He swore under his breath, then said, "So you think this hidden doorway could lead to one or both of our sorceresses?"

"They haven't been seen in the club all day."

"Maybe they're simply resting at home."

"Maybe. Except that this place is listed as their residential address as well and given there's not another floor, we're left with the possibility that either they're behind the locked doors, or there's other hidden areas." I quickly lined up the ball and made the hit before he could do anything to distract me. There was a satisfying clunk as it went into the pocket.

"You play dirty," he murmured.

"No dirtier than you, wolf," I returned. "Remember that."

His gaze met mine for several seconds, and it was hard to know what he was actually thinking. And while I *could* raid his mind, that just might leave me open for a mind raid attack from him. Which *shouldn't* be possible—given my shields and his lack of telepathy skills—but this wolf kept doing things he wasn't supposed to be able to. Which was a pain in the ass. I had a *bad* feeling that I really needed to know what was on his mind right now.

When he smiled, it only increased my sudden wariness. "Then I guess I'd better go book that room, hadn't I?"

"I think that's a good idea. We can always come back here if it proves a bust."

"Oh, I'm sure something will bust if we're not very careful." His gaze skated to my breasts and his desire surged, so strong I could almost taste it. "The rooms are monitored, so there isn't going to be much of a chance to look around without raising suspicions."

"Oh, I'm sure a clever wolf such as yourself can do something about the cameras without raising too many suspicions."

I glanced at my watch. A good fifteen minutes had passed since I'd been in the staff lounge, so the blonde's appointment in the Arabian room should be finished by now. I hoped no one else had booked it in the meantime.

"I'll see what I can do," Kye murmured.

"Well, you'd better hurry," I said, putting a little tartness in my voice. "I'm a much-in-demand dancer, you know, and someone else just might grab me."

"Then I'd have to beat them up, wouldn't I?"

"That would work," I agreed sagely. "You get thrown out, I get inside the room and investigate without your interference. Clever."

His smile was cool and calculating. "You're not finishing *anything* without me, wolf."

And one look into his eyes made me realize he

wasn't just talking about the case. A shudder that was half anticipation, half fear, rolled through me.

He put down his cue. "I'll go book now, then see what I can do about the cameras."

"Sounds like a plan."

"Meet you there, then." He walked away without a backward glance.

I let out a breath, then smiled at the eager young man who rushed to pick up the abandoned cue and who couldn't have been any older than nineteen. I played out the game, giving him lots of little touches and glimpses of breasts and butt, leaving him flushed and smelling of desire. But he didn't say anything about a dance—either private or lap—so I walked over to the bar.

"Any bookings come through on my card?" I asked the heavy-set bartender.

He pressed a couple of keys on the computer, then nodded. "One for twelve in the Arabian room."

Twelve was a good hour away, so either he was taking time to cool down, or it was going to take him longer than I'd thought to take out the cameras.

"That's it?"

"Yeah, it's been a pretty slow night, although the patrons are drinking well."

Which was good for them, bad for the dancers. "Thanks."

He nodded and served another patron. I turned around, saw two guys playing at the table I'd evacuated, and headed over there to chat them up and keep an eye on the door.

The money men did go through with the hourly clearings, but I didn't get a glimpse of anything more than another corridor. I couldn't see a safe let alone private living accommodations.

But if these doors just led to vaults, then where was the sorceresses' den? It *had* to be here somewhere, if only because both women actually lived here. I couldn't imagine they'd want to be too far from their place of deep magic.

Just before midnight I headed down to change into my "Arabian" costume, which consisted of a barely there bodice with filmy sleeves, and a skirt piece that consisted of detachable scarves that were gradually stripped away to reveal a tiny jeweled G-string. Then I reached into my bag and grabbed the remaining bottles of holy water, taping them under my breasts. Big boobs, I thought with a grin, certainly had their uses, but hiding little bottles under them had to be one of the more unusual ones. I closed my locker and walked down to the hall to the private rooms.

The Arabian room was probably my favorite of all the fantasy rooms. Scrumptious golden curtains lined the four walls and framed the ceiling, so that it felt like you were standing in some sultan's luxurious tent. The furnishings enhanced this feeling, mixing rich wood tones with gold paint and deep red fabrics. The carpet was thick, lush, and patterned—just perfect to walk barefoot in—and the air had a light rose and cinnamon scent.

Kye was standing in the middle of the room when I

walked in, and said telepathically, *So what do we do now?*

Obviously, he trusted the paper-thin walls as much as I trusted him.

I closed and locked the door. *We pretend to discuss what you want while actually talking about why we're here. How long have we got before the cameras go down?*

Ten past twelve. Thought it was safer to seem "involved" when the lights go out.

I raised my eyebrows and said out loud, "How long did you take the room for?"

"A full hour." He gave me a wicked smile that would have blown my socks off had I been wearing any. "You'd better be worth it."

I smiled slowly, and flared my nostrils as his desire surged. Such a sweet, sweet scent. "Why don't you take a seat on the chaise lounge, and we'll find out."

"It looks rather skinny," he said, barely even glancing at it.

"But it's perfect for what we need." I added telepathically, *And if you don't sit soon, they may think something is wrong."*

As he sat down, I muted the lights and turned up the music. With the erotic, exotic music filling the silence, I walked over and straddled the lounge—and him.

"Now I see why it's smaller." A smile teased his luscious mouth as he lay back on the lounge and watched me with hungry eyes.

"It would be awfully hard to be sexy when a normal chaise lounge is considerably wider," I agreed, and slowly began to move in time to the music, my dance as sensual and erotic as the music.

I was only straddling his legs at the moment, allowing him plenty of time to admire my body and movement. As the tempo of the music increased, so did mine. Little by little, I edged my way up his body toward his crotch.

"Can I ask a question?" he said after a while, his voice several tones huskier than normal.

So much for being unaffected. "You can ask anything you want. Whether I answer is another matter."

What are those strange bulges under your bodice, or is that a trade secret?

I smiled. *A woman has to keep her holy water somewhere close and safe, because you just never know when another hellhound is going to pop out at her.*

He snorted softly. *You really are a most intriguing woman, Riley Jenson. It's a shame you work for whom you do.*

And why is that? I shook loose one of the scarves and tossed it lightly at his face.

He caught it with a smile, his nostrils flaring as he drew in the scents on it. *Because you and I would make a rather good team.*

No, we wouldn't. We're totally different.

We're both killers, Riley, whether you like to admit it or not.

That may be true, but I kill to save others. You kill for profit.

You kill because you like the kill. Admit it.

I kill because I've learned the hard way that others suffer

DEADLY DESIRE   285

or die if I don't. I don't deny I enjoy the chase, but the kill?
Never.

I don't believe you. You're too good at what you do for it not to be enjoyable.

I opened my mouth to refute his statement, but the words never came out because the room suddenly got colder.

Colder in an all too familiar way.

Goose bumps raced up my arms and I looked away from Kye, my gaze doing a sweep of the room. There was no smoke, no insubstantial wisps, hiding in any of the corners, and yet there was no mistaking the fierce chill that suddenly rode the air.

There was a soul here somewhere, and it wanted to speak.

"What the fuck?" Kye said, his head suddenly whipping toward the right corner.

There was no soul to be seen there, yet it *did* seem to be the main source of the chill.

But how the fuck was *he* sensing it?

I glanced at him sharply, briefly stopping the dance then forcing myself to keep going as I remembered the watching cameras. *What do you feel?*

I don't know. He frowned. *It feels like death. Cold, cold death.*

And *he* should know, having dished it out often enough.

How the fuck are you feeling that? I wanted to grab him and shake him—hard—and finally get some answers out of the damn man. He *wasn't* clairvoyant—hell, he even admitted to not being telepathic—and yet here he was, telepathic one day and clairvoyant the next. He might be listed as having no psychic talent, but something sure as hell was going on. And maybe, just maybe, I knew what it was. *Have you got some weird ability to siphon the talents of others?*

He glanced at me, and though his expression had suddenly gone blank, he gave a short, sharp nod. *Tell me what I'm—we're—sensing.*

Tell me the fuck about your talent, I snapped back. *Just how far does it extend?*

He didn't answer. I clenched, then unclenched my fist. *Tell me, Kye, or I will call in the Directorate and get your ass thrown in jail. And trust me, it wouldn't even blow this operation wide open, because the Directorate has guardians who can seize control of every man and woman in this place, regardless of whether they were wearing wires or not.* And they wouldn't even remember it.

Hell, *I* could probably do it if I put my mind to it— Jack kept insisting I'd be one of the strongest telepaths he had if only I'd apply myself a little more.

Which is precisely why I *didn't*. I didn't *want* that sort of power. What I had was scary enough.

For the longest of moments, Kye didn't answer. When he finally did, it was flatly, grudgingly, done. *I'm what you call a sipher. If I'm in the presence of another person with a psychic talent, that talent becomes mine for as long as I am with them.*

So when you're with me, you're telepathic.

And I can shadow, because that is also a psychic talent— one that is very handy when stalking vampires.

Which is why he was such a skilled hunter of vampires. Most vampires wouldn't expect a werewolf to be able to shadow, and by the time they heard the rush of life and realized Kye was near, it was already too late.

And now you're sensing the soul?

Is that what it is?

Yes, I snapped, stripping off several scarves and tossing them across his face. *And hang onto your hat, because it's about to get a whole lot worse.*

And with that, I reached out to the soul and said, *Who are you?*

The chill got fiercer, until it felt like fingers of ice were creeping into my soul. I didn't know why it always felt like these souls brought the chill of the underworld with them. Maybe it was because they were trapped between two worlds, neither here nor in heaven or hell—or wherever else souls went to.

Something stirred against the soft, golden light infusing the corner—a wisp of thicker air that held no shape and couldn't even be defined as smoke.

Billy. Billy Cardwell, it said, the insubstantial voice young and confused.

I continued dancing, only half concentrating on the music. Another scarf went. Kye caught it and tossed it to one side, his gaze heated and expression intent. He looked for the world like a man who was enjoying his dance, but I knew the only thing he was intent on was listening in on my conversation with the soul.

Do you know what happened, Billy?

The soul stirred softly, a wisp with no features and no body that gently rotated.

She went ballistic, he answered. *She attacked me.*

Do you know why?

For a moment there was no answer, but the energy continued to build in the air, giving the soul the strength to speak.

She kept screaming "the bitch. I'll get the bitch for this."

Had she meant the teenager who hadn't shown up? Or me? *What time was this?*

He didn't answer for several seconds, then said, *I had the room booked for seven-thirty, so it was just after that.*

So the rage—and Billy's subsequent murder—had definitely happened before she'd gone on to slaughter Jason Burke and his lover. Meaning her rage, or her need to tear, had not been assuaged with Billy's death. Or maybe we were simply dealing with a mind that wasn't exactly chummy with sanity. *Is that all?*

The energy in the air was still building, until the small hairs along the nape of my neck were standing on end. Only then did the words come again.

She said something about no one stopping her from making them all pay.

Thank you, Billy. I hesitated, then added, *It's safe to move on now. We'll take care of her for you.*

Maybe that was what he was waiting to hear, because the energy abruptly fell away, and the soul disintegrated, fleeing to whatever region of afterlife it was bound for.

I took a deep, shuddering breath that did little to clear the sudden wash of weakness from my limbs. Maybe Cole was right. Maybe the energy these souls were using to talk wasn't coming from the air around us, but from *me*.

Fuck, that was unreal, Kye muttered, suddenly looking as washed out as I felt. *And I hope I'm never with you when another one of those pops up.*

Oh, I don't think that's going to be a problem, I snapped back, although I wasn't entirely sure whether I was annoyed more with him, or with myself for not having the gumption to call in the Directorate and get this man locked up. It was too late now, despite my earlier threat. We were in the end game and simply couldn't afford to stop right now.

I just had to hope that my reluctance to do something about the man didn't end up being the biggest mistake I'd ever made in my life.

Chapter 10

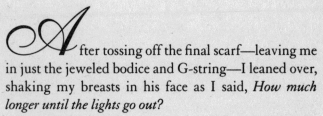fter tossing off the final scarf—leaving me in just the jeweled bodice and G-string—I leaned over, shaking my breasts in his face as I said, *How much longer until the lights go out?*

Even as I asked the question, the lights went out. As they did, Kye wrapped a hand around the back of my neck, dragging me close, and kissed me. This was no gentle kiss—it was fierce, hungry, and very erotic. A promise of what was to come, of what he wanted.

He let me go with the same sort of suddenness, and I staggered back a little before catching my balance. My lips felt puffy with the force of his kiss, and my body was in turmoil, desire fighting with common sense, one part of my soul fighting against the other.

Let's find this door, if there is one, he said, mind voice flat and controlled.

But *he* wasn't. I could feel the turmoil and desire raging through his body, and it was every bit as strong as mine. This wolf might want me, but he didn't *want* to want me.

We were fighting the same fight, and we were both losing.

I didn't answer, just walked across to the door and unlocked it. With the lights and security out, they'd probably evacuate the building, so maybe they'd think we'd already left the room.

I turned around and blinked to switch on the infrared of my vamp vision. The outline of the door was instantly obvious, tucked away in the far left corner.

Over here. I walked across and pulled the curtain back. The door was handprint and iris coded. *Well, fuck.*

The emergency lighting flickered then came on. The generators had obviously kicked in. *Will these doors still be functional?*

Probably.

What about the cameras?

Footsteps sounded in the hall outside, followed by gruff voices. They were still several rooms away from ours, but we were running out of time fast.

The cameras probably wouldn't be considered a priority, so I'd say no. Which is probably why they're evacuating. He bent to look at the lock. *There's no getting around it. We need a guard to open it.*

Then let's get one.

I reached out telepathically for the guards in the hallway. With the nanowires they were all wearing, it felt like I was hitting a brick wall. I continued to push telepathically, hitting the nanowire with everything I had. As sweat beaded across my forehead, my consciousness began to seep through the wire's wall, until suddenly I was through. I grabbed the guard's mind, wrapping around it completely, letting him finish evacuating the schoolroom before walking him down toward us.

He opened the door and walked into the room, and even had the cameras been active, they wouldn't have picked up anything out of place. My touch these days was so light that I could control a mind and still have that person look and act completely natural.

"I'm afraid we've lost power and have to evacuate the building," he said, gaze sweeping the room but not actually seeing anything important. He wasn't even seeing us standing at the other door—I was making sure of that.

I nudged Kye, and nodded toward the guard. He seemed to get what I wanted, because he said, "My time isn't up yet."

"All monies will be refunded, sir." He walked over to the door and pressed his hand against the scanner. After a beep, he leaned forward, letting his eye be scanned. There was a soft click, and the door opened.

I turned him around and walked him back out the door. As I retreated from his mind, I left the image of us walking away from the room.

As the hall door clicked shut, I blew out a breath and lifted a sweaty strand of hair from my forehead.

So you're one of the guardians who could walk into this

club and freeze the mind of every man and woman in this club, Kye said, eyeing me with an odd expression.

As if he was suddenly reassessing me. I wasn't sure whether that was a good thing or a bad one.

There are vamps more powerful than me at the Directorate. My reply was absentminded, my gaze on the hall beyond. It was small, pitch-black, and smelled of dust, damp, and magic. Dark, distasteful magic.

Which is warning enough that even one such as me should never get on the wrong side of the Directorate. Or her hunters.

If you want to continue living the free and easy life of a killer for hire, then that's a mighty good idea.

I don't always kill, he said mildly. *Sometimes I guard.*

Guarding killers isn't that much of a step up the ladder. I slipped off my stilettos, then blinked on my infrared vision and stepped into the hall. The faint, metallic scent of blood flavored the air, and with it the stench of flesh beginning to rot. Maybe they hadn't had time to get rid of Billy's body after all.

Well, when it comes to Blake, your pack alpha, I'd have to agree. He let the door close and darkness swamped us. Not that it mattered to me.

Then why did you take the job? I moved forward cautiously. I might be able to see in this inky blackness, but magic was crawling across my skin, pinpricks of fire that sent a continuous shudder of revulsion through the rest of me.

Because he paid more than the usual rate, and because I was intrigued to meet the woman who had him so scared.

I snorted softly. *Blake was never scared of me.*

Then why did he hire me?

You know why—to protect his precious son, Patrin, from the death threats he was receiving.

Kye smiled. It swirled across my senses.

There were never any death threats. It was you and Rhoan he feared.

I snorted softly. *Blake and his precious sons spent most of their lives using the two of us as their expendable punching bags. Why the hell would he be scared of us before we beat the crap out of him?*

Because he feared what you could become—what you did *become.* He hesitated. *There is magic up ahead. And Blake will seek his revenge for what you and Rhoan did to him.*

We'd guessed that. Blake wasn't the type to forgive people—especially when they'd embarrassed the hell out of him. *So is this ability to sense magic another skill you're siphoning from someone?*

I felt Kye smile again. *No, this time it's a talent that's inherited from the pack.*

This would be the pack that supposedly has no psychic skills whatsoever?

That's the one. I'm sensitive to the presence of magic, but I cannot use it like I can psychic talents.

But that's how you tracked that sorcerer to the warehouse?

That and the smell of death.

I nodded. At least it explained how he'd come to be watching the sorcerer from within the shadows of her black wall rather than walking straight through it and getting sprung as I had.

But then, I hadn't expected to find hellhounds or a sorcerer—just a dead man walking. Kye obviously had a better idea of what was going on than I did when he'd walked into that place.

The farther we moved down the hallway, the staler the air felt, and I had the odd sensation that we were moving down into the earth itself. There was little noise in this place, and the silence felt heavy, as if it were carrying a weight that it didn't want and we couldn't see.

The floorboards beneath my feet gave way to colder concrete, then to a mix of dirt and stone. Grit wedged in between my toes, forcing me to pause every now and again to shake it loose. Despite the earth flooring, the walls and ceiling were still concrete—although it was rough looking, as if it had been slapped on in a hurry, and without care.

The crawl of magic began to get stronger, its touch stinging like angry gnats. Something stark and white appeared in my infrared. I switched to normal vision, saw a flickering golden glow begin to seep through the darkness ahead. It framed a rough-hewn archway that had only been half concreted.

I couldn't sense anyone or anything waiting, but my uneasiness grew.

Looks like the sort of light you get from a torch, Kye commented. Though his mind voice was flat and without emotion, his tension rolled over me, increasing my own. *It's an odd choice when we're under the earth and there seems to be little ventilation.*

I can't smell any smoke, though. And I don't think our sorcerers would be too worried about air quality.

Or life, for that matter.

Because the magic wasn't the only thing that was getting stronger. The stink of blood and death rode the air, so powerful that even my wolf soul was turning her nose.

We approached the arch cautiously. Dust stirred the air with each step, but little else seemed to be moving.

I can't feel or smell anyone, Kye said.

No, but they may have laid traps of the magical kind. We need to be careful.

Then you go low, and I'll go high.

There was a whisper of movement, and suddenly I felt the burn of silver across my skin. *How the hell did you get a weapon into the club undetected? And how come I didn't sense it before this?*

He raised an eyebrow. *You have a psychic sense about guns?*

No, I'm allergic to silver.

We all are. We're werewolves. Amusement laced his mental tone.

Well, yeah, but I've been hit too often by it and I'm now extrasensitive to its presence. So how did you conceal that weapon?

The weapon is in a lead-lined holster, and if you know whom to pay, you can get anything you like into this club.

So whom did you bribe?

His smile flashed. *There's no need to bribe when the manager is fucking a stripper, and the wife knows nothing about it.*

And how do you happen to know that?

Because I bugged him. Made for interesting listening, I have to say.

Perv.

And as a telepath, you've never listened in to other people's thoughts or conversations, he said dryly. *It's all the same, Riley.*

We'd neared the archway, so I didn't answer, just wrapped the shadows around me and moved with vamp speed to the far side of it. Then I shook off the shadows, glanced at him, and nodded.

Go, he said, and we moved as one into the next room.

Which was actually a cavern. It was small, dank, and the air was putrid with the aroma of blood, death, and rotting flesh. The torches that lined the walls and provided the flickering light had to be battery powered, because they certainly weren't real. Nor could I see any power outlets or electrical cords. But at least they provided enough light to see by, although deeper darkness still haunted the more distant corners. Without them, and with no natural light, even my infrared would have been useless.

A stone table sat in the middle of the cavern, its top stained a dark reddish-black and its sides streaked with the same heavy color. I had no doubt that its source was blood—blood that must have been spilled over years and years rather than merely the few months they'd been here in Melbourne.

Black candles sat around the base of the table, each one marking the point of a pentagram that had been etched into the stone flooring.

Which meant this wasn't the hideaway of the sorcerers.

It was their place of deep magic.

Nice setup, Kye said. His gaze paused on the bloody table, then he looked at me. *This where they raise the zombies?*

It feels like the same sort of magic. I stopped at the end of the wide ramp, right on one of the pentagram points. There didn't seem to be any magic coming off it, so maybe it wasn't active, but the room itself still burned with energy. With death.

My gaze moved across the stone table to the rough-hewn wall on the far side. Hollows had been carved into the stone, and in each one sat several items. A little pile of hair and a football in one. A brush and a football sweater in another. A pair of Nikes and a hubcap in yet another. All things men would generally have owned, not women.

Had these things belonged to the men raised from the dead? Did part of the ritual require something that was precious to them?

My gaze went back to the table. All I knew about zombies came from fiction and Hollywood, and I had firsthand experience at just how wrong they could get it. But there was *one* thing that remained absolute, regardless of the truths and half-truths that might abound—and that was the fact that life required blood. Hell, even *un*life required blood.

The question here was, whose blood was she using to reanimate her dead?

Kye walked past me, his clean musky scent like

heaven against the foul stench of the room. Though he was careful to avoid the pentagram and candles, his attention seemed to be on the ground itself.

Which piqued my interest. *What's wrong?*

These. He squatted and pointed a finger toward the dust-covered stone.

I walked over and stopped beside him. What he was actually pointing at looked like two wheel marks.

It's probably tracks from Jessica's wheelchair, I said, dismissing it.

He glanced up at me. *One of our sorcerers is paralyzed?*

The zombie raiser is. That's why she was resting on her belly when she was in crow form at the warehouse.

At least it explains the ramp getting into this place. He rose and followed the tracks around the room. *There's a lot of tracks going from the pentagram to these hollows in the wall.*

Meaning this is her workplace, not Hanna's. I walked around the opposite way.

Maybe. His voice held an edge of doubt. *Trouble is, the pentagram doesn't feel active.*

And maybe we should be grateful for that. The stink of rotting flesh got stronger once I'd passed the ramp again, and I studied the shadows intently. I couldn't see anything resembling a body but, given the smell, it had to be here somewhere. Besides, given how careful these women tended to be, it wouldn't surprise me if they hid their victims in walled-up hollows *and* with magic.

I stepped closer to the cavern's wall, and felt the firefly press of magic against my skin. It was a magic that was slightly different from the other magic fouling the room, yet it was one I'd felt before.

I raised a hand and watched my fingers disappear into blackness. It was another wall like the one I'd encountered in that first warehouse—the one where Kye had rescued me from the hellhounds.

I followed my hand into that blackness, and once again the air had the consistency of glue. The blackness pulled at me, resisted me, making every step difficult and progress minuscule. As before, I pushed forward as hard as I could. This time it didn't take as long to get free of it. Maybe it simply wasn't as deep.

Beyond it were the bodies. Not just one, but several, all in various states of decay. Like the trophy items, most of these bodies each had their own little hollow, but none of them were stretched out comfortably. Some lay curled into a fetal position, while others simply looked as if they'd been stuffed into their holes any old way, leaving bones jutting out and body fluids staining the stone. And unlike the trophy holes, some of these spaces remained empty. Although nine cavities had been carved into the stone, only six had occupants. And there was one body still sprawled out on the floor.

I squatted down beside him and tried not to gag at the wretched smell of decay that, for some odd reason, seemed stronger near the floor line.

This body was young—maybe no more than eighteen or nineteen—and I swear there was a look of terror frozen onto his slack features and wide-open eyes. Blood had matted his dark brown hair and splattered down his white shirt. His dark blue pants were similarly stained, but smelled slightly of urine. It had to be Billy. From the look of it, the poor kid had taken quite a beating before he'd died.

But why was he here, on the floor, rather than in one of the holes like the others? Was it simply a matter of not having the time to stuff him in, or did they have something else planned for him?

Given it was a question I was never likely to get an answer to, I searched through his pockets, finding his wallet and car keys. Neither looked to have been touched in any way, though I guess I wouldn't know for sure until we got them to the lab for fingerprinting.

I reached forward and gently closed his eyelids. As I touched his skin, magic caressed my fingertips. It was the magic of the room, magic that burned my skin and made it crawl in revulsion.

Maybe Billy wasn't quite dead, after all.

Maybe none of them were. Maybe this was Jessica's emergency supply of bodies should resources start drying up elsewhere. Hell, for all I knew, these bodies could be the remnants of interstate kills and graveyard robbings. Some of them certainly looked as if they'd been kept in this half-animated state for a while.

I glanced back down at Billy. There wasn't a whole lot I could do to prevent the reactivation of his flesh, if indeed that was what that magic was about. That was a job for the Directorate magi.

What I *could* do was stop him from becoming a problem if he did rise while we were still here. It wasn't something I really wanted to do, but at least the kid was dead and his spirit had moved on. He'd never know—

and probably wouldn't care—about what I was about
to do to his cold, unresponsive flesh.

I blew out a breath, then grabbed Billy's right leg,
one hand on the ankle, one hand just above his knee.
Then, as sharply as I could, I pushed—one hand down,
one hand up. The knee cap shattered, the sound making me wince. I did the same to the left leg, then
grabbed his wallet and keys and retreated back
through the black wall.

Kye was standing within the pentagram, examining
the bloody table.

Find anything? he said without looking up.

The source of the decaying flesh scent. I put Billy's
items down beside the ramp, then dug the bottles of
holy water out from underneath my bodice. *I don't
think you should have done that.*

Done what?

Step into that pentagram. I uncorked one of the bottles and began sprinkling the water onto the pentagram
etched into the floor. Steam began to rise and the stone
itself began to bubble.

The magic wasn't active.

*But there is magic here, and we have no idea how any of
it might be activated.* I emptied one bottle over three
quarters of the pentagram, then stepped into the ruined
circle and uncorked the second bottle. I raised it above
the stone tabletop, then let the water pour down along
its entire length.

As the stone began to bubble and steam, something
shrieked. A high, inhuman noise grated at my nerves
and made me want to cover my ears. I spun around,

looking for the source of the ungodly sound. Nothing appeared to have changed. We were alone in the room, and the shadows remained empty of life or movement.

And yet...something *had* changed, but I couldn't define what. Maybe it was just the air. It felt heavier. Angrier, if that made any sense.

The uneasiness that had been riding my insides since we'd stepped into this room suddenly increased, and I had a bad feeling we'd just overstayed our welcome.

I think we need to get out of here. I tossed the bottles under the table, then stepped away from it.

In that moment, the magic spiked and the walls exploded, sending a rain of deadly rock shards ricocheting through the room.

I yelped and ducked under the table, using it as a shield against some of the stones as I covered my head with my hands and curled up as small as I could to present less of a target. The sharp little—and not so little—missiles hit me regardless, pounding my arms and body, drawing blood wherever they hit.

It was over within minutes, leaving a silence that made my skin crawl. Because there was something within that silence, something that felt old and filled with magic. The same magic that had infused the room before the explosion.

I think the shit just hit the fan, Kye said.

I had an odd feeling that he wasn't talking about the explosion. I moved my arms and opened my eyes.

We were no longer alone in the room. At least a dozen bodies had stepped free from the shattered remains of the walls and were moving toward us, their movements reminding me of sleepwalkers.

Only I suspected *these* walkers were a whole lot more dangerous to us than to each other.

I guess our sorceress wasn't too impressed with me destroying her pentagram and table.

I guess not, Kye said, mind voice calm. A shiver went through me. I had a feeling the switch had been pulled, and he'd just become the perfect killer. *I only have six bullets.*

Then don't waste them. Bullets won't stop zombies—you can only do that by deprogramming them from the magic.

Then what are our options?

We stop them, which means breaking their limbs. All their limbs. If Kye had been a real telepath rather than just a siphon, it might have been worthwhile trying to break the connection Jessica had with them. Granted, such an attempt would have been *hard,* considering how many of them there were, but it just might have been possible. But with Kye having no real expertise with telepathy, it wasn't worth the effort.

He didn't reply, simply launched himself at the nearest pack of walking dead men, hitting them feet first and scattered them like so much rotting meat.

Fingers grabbed at my bodice and I spun, grabbing the hand and shoving the zombie back as hard as I could. Then I ran and jumped, kicking one zombie in the head before dropping to the ground and, sweeping with a leg, knocking a second off his feet.

More of them came at me. I broke the fingers off

one, then jumped back, pulling him with me and throwing him sideways, into others.

An arm wrapped itself around my neck and the fetid breath of flesh long dead washed over me, making me gag. I tried to pry his fingers away, but his entire hand seemed to be covered with something that was thick and slimy, and it was impossible to get a grip. So I dropped to my knees and tried to flip him over my head. The body went over but the arm remained, and it was still squeezing, still making it harder and harder to breathe. I reached back, grabbed the limb, and forced it away from my neck. His flesh was rotting, covered with a putrid mix of goo that was flesh and body fluids and God knows what else.

I flung it away with a shiver, and wished I had something to wipe my neck with. I could still feel him, still feel his slime on my skin, and it was *horrible*.

Two more grabbed at me. I punched one, smashing in the side of his face and sending him flying away from me. Then I pushed backward, as hard as I could, crushing the second zombie against the wall. There was a sharp crack of bone, but I didn't bother turning around to see what had broken. I simply finished the job, breaking his arms, then his legs. He dropped to the ground, but still tried to get to me, flopping around like a fish out of water.

Revulsion rolled through me, but I swiftly pushed it to one side as more of the stinkers came at me. I kicked and punched for all I was worth, breaking the limbs of some and shattering the backs of others. Bits of flesh and bone flew, covering me and the floor in their stinky goo, until the stench made me want to throw up.

And the worst part was, all my fighting didn't seem to make a goddamn bit of difference. The bastards just kept coming at me.

I blew the sweaty strands of hair away from my fore-head and cast a brief glance Kye's way. He didn't seem to be doing any better. There were three zombies flopping at his feet, but that still left another three, and those creatures seemed just as fast and just as strong as he was. Maybe they were simply fresher.

I jumped over the leap of a creature, then hit the ground and spun, knocking another on his rotten ass. I jumped on his leg, smashing his kneecap, then spun as another lashed out. Despite the speed with which I could move, I simply wasn't fast enough. The blow landed on the side of my head and sent me flying toward the wall.

Several of them hit me in the chest and drove me back against the wall. Fingers grabbed at my body, my throat, my hair, until all I could smell and all I could feel was the dead. A scream rolled up my throat but I clamped down on it, hard. The last thing I needed to do was alert anyone still inside the club that someone had gotten into one of their protected passages.

Although I'd probably done that the moment I'd destroyed the pentagram and table.

I raised my arms and smashed theirs away, then dropped to the ground and crawled, as fast as I could, between their legs and away.

Kye, I think we need to get the hell away from this cavern and regroup.

He didn't answer immediately, punching several zombies away from him before saying, *I'm thinking that's a fucking good idea.*

I flipped upright and spun, lashing out with a leg and knocking one charging zombie into another. *At least in the hallway they can't come at us from all angles.*

And that would give *us* an advantage. Right now, there were just too many avenues for the things to keep jumping us. And though we'd reduced their numbers, the ones that remained were the least rotten, and the strongest. And they just wouldn't *stop*.

I grabbed another arm and twisted it backward, hearing bone crack as I kicked out at the creature's kneecap. These things might be dead, but somewhere deep in their brainless skulls, a sense of self-preservation still survived, because it jumped backward, out of the way.

Make the charge, Kye said, *I'm right with you.*

Then I'm going. I put my head down and ran. Right into a zombie, knocking him down hard, then leaping over him as I raced for the door. Kye appeared beside me, as covered in slime as I was, and reeking to high heaven. We neared the ramp, our steps lost in the pounding of the zombies coming after us.

At the top of the ramp, the shadows moved, and the scent of humanity—of a woman—washed over me. Jessica, not Hanna. Then I felt the burn of silver and heard the soft click of a safety being disengaged.

I slid to a stop. Kye did the same, barely missing running into my back. The zombies behind us crowded close, providing a wall of flesh through which there'd be no easy escape. Not that there was anywhere to go behind them. Our only way out was the tunnel. *If* we could get past Jessica and whatever form of backup she'd brought with her.

She rolled out of the shadows, the gun held unwaveringly in her hands. There was a zombie at her back holding a second weapon.

"I underestimated you," she said softly, her voice cool but still holding that edge I'd noticed earlier.

"I get that a lot," I said, even as I added telepathically to Kye, *the weapons are loaded with silver.* "Tell me, Jessica, why are you killing the teenagers? It makes no sense, given Hanna has already paid them handsomely for their silence."

"No monetary payment ever guarantees silence one hundred percent. If any of them had opened their damn mouths about how they got the money, Hanna's game was up."

"But why would you even care? Why would you go to such lengths to protect a woman who's not exactly chummy with sanity?"

"Sane or not, she cared for me when no one else would, and for that I owe her loyalty." She gave me a twisted half-smile that was part sadness, part acceptance. "Which means I get to clean up her mistakes and keep her safe."

Then she pulled the trigger. I threw myself sideways, even as Kye hit me, making me lose my balance. He stumbled then went down, hard. There was blood on his face, blood in his hair, blood on the ramp, and something inside me went numb.

For too many seconds, I couldn't react, couldn't think. I just stared at his unmoving form and thought *no, no, no.*

Then movement caught my eye. The gun, aimed my way.

I twisted around and lunged for the weapon that had fallen from Kye's hand. I grabbed it and fired, all in one swift motion. Saw the woman jerk, then go limp, as the wound in her forehead began to leak blood and brain matter. I fired a second shot, shattering the wrist of the zombie holding the gun, tearing it clean from his arm.

I closed my eyes for a moment, releasing a deep, shaking breath. But the danger wasn't over yet, I realized as fingers began to dig into my flesh. I twisted around, wrenching myself free, then jumped upright and lunged forward at the rest, hitting them front on and sending them flying.

Then I turned and ran back to Kye, dropping to my knees beside him and feeling for his pulse. It was there, fast but strong, and some of the tension that had been twisting my insides relaxed a little. But only a little. The bullet had hit at an angle, smashing through his right shoulder before making a trench across the side of his head, and both wounds were bleeding profusely. If he didn't wake up, didn't change shape and stop the bleeding soon, he would die.

I pinched his earlobe as hard as I could, then said, "Kye, get up."

A zombie lunged at me, I twisted around, sweeping

with my leg, knocking him off his, then pinched Kye's ear harder. "Damn it, wolf, wake up. You have to shift shape."

He didn't respond, and the fear that had been partially mollified when I realized he was still alive began to rise again. I didn't care for this man, didn't want to get involved with him, but something deep within simply didn't want to see him die, either. But then, my wolf had a bad habit of latching onto—or rather, lusting after—totally unsuitable men.

I kicked away more attacking zombies, then jumped to my feet and grabbed Kye's armpits. Jessica had obviously given her creatures final orders before I'd killed her, and I couldn't concentrate on waking Kye with the zombies continuing to attack from all angles. I needed to at least restrict their options. So I hauled him upright and began to walk backward up the ramp.

And suddenly I realized that there was someone else in the room. Someone who was alive and who breathed, and whose scent was all too familiar.

Hanna.

I shifted my grip on Kye and twisted around, the gun in one hand and my finger on the trigger. But for the second time that night, I simply wasn't fast enough.

The bullet hit with the force of a hammer, tearing into my shoulder and smashing me sideways, away from Kye and into a wall.

Pain flared, red hot and burning, and I knew then that the bullet was silver.

Then that thought died and there was nothing.

Absolutely nothing.

Chapter 11

aking was a slow and painful process. My head throbbed so badly it made me want to throw up, but it was almost matched by the burning ache in my right shoulder. An ache that pulsed down my arm as it went numb.

Fear hit me—a fear so deep that for several seconds I struggled to breathe.

I knew that burning. Knew it all too well.

I'd been shot with silver and the bullet was still lodged in my flesh.

I forced reluctant eyelids open, needing to know where I was and what had happened while I was out of it. A white ceiling loomed high above me, meaning they'd moved me from the cavern. But that ceiling didn't actually look like one of the club ceilings, either. The cornices were too ornate, the ceiling itself too high.

Plus, the air here smelled different. It was fresher, with undertones of baking and roses rather than the club's seedier aroma of alcohol and lust.

Which didn't mean there wasn't magic here. There was, but it wasn't as strong. It was more a wisp of darkness that occasionally stained the fresher scents rather than something that overwhelmed and completely fouled.

I shifted slightly, trying to ease the ache in my hip, and realized I was lying on something cold and hard. I shifted my left fingers and touched the surface.

Metal. And unlike the table in the cavern, this one didn't smell like blood—although that aroma was in the air, if only faintly. I drew in a deeper breath, sifting through the smells in the air, finding strong hints of antiseptic swirling around the tang of old blood. This table and this room had been washed down many, many times.

As full awareness began to return, I also realized that the burning numbness in my right arm was matched—to a lesser degree—by similar sensations at both ankles and my left wrist.

I turned my head, saw the silver shackles and chains attached to my arm, and swore softly.

Behind me, someone chuckled.

"I'm glad you're awake, little werewolf," Hanna said, her voice friendly, almost conspiratorial. "I did so want you to see your death coming."

"That's another mistake in a long line of them, Hanna. Always kill a guardian when you get the chance, because we don't give you a second go."

"Well, this time the bad guy wins, not the guardian. And your blood will provide excellent fuel for my magic and potions."

Like hell it would. I twisted around, trying to see her. The movement not only caused chains to pull at my wrist and dig further into my skin, but sent a stab of agony through the rest of my body as my shot shoulder protested the action. Sweat broke out across my forehead, and my breath hissed out through clenched teeth. It took several seconds for the tears to clear enough to see her.

Hanna was standing behind me, a tall, willowy woman who looked far older than she had in the office. Maybe it was the lack of makeup, or maybe it was the fact that her only items of clothing were a pale green ribbon tying her dark hair away from her face and the thin strand of wire around her neck. Her green eyes had a wild sort of look to them, and her skin was unnaturally shiny, as if she'd covered herself in oil of some kind.

"What have you done with Kye?"

She raised an eyebrow, green eyes cool and amused. "I'm guessing you mean the man who was with you?"

"Yes."

"Oh, he's probably bled to death by now."

Something within me wanted to curl up and die at the thought. It was weird—I might have lusted after the man, but I didn't actually like him, and yet here I was, wanting to weep for his loss. The wolf sure was strange at times.

"It's a shame, really," Hanna continued, "to waste

all that good blood, but shifting three bodies would have placed too much strain on both my magic and me."

"You'll regret letting him die, Hanna."

"Oh, I'd be a little more worried about your health, if I were you."

I was worried all right, but I'd been in worse situations than this and had survived. And I had no intention of dying today, either.

Whether fate agreed with my decision was another matter entirely, but I wasn't worrying about that right now.

"Tell me, how did you and Jessica meet?"

It obviously wasn't a question she was expecting, because she looked up in surprise. "Why do you want to know?"

"Just curious." I shrugged, the action sending pain rolling across my skin.

"We grew up together," she said after a moment. "Like me, she had a gift for darker powers and was ostracized by her family because of them."

I could understand the two odd peas clinging together for safety and companionship, because in very many ways, that's what Rhoan and I had done. But why go on to become such violent murderers?

"And you looked after her when she had her accident and became paraplegic?"

"It was no accident," she said, voice a little tighter.

"What do you mean?"

"I mean," she said tightly, "that the rich young bastard who paralyzed her first seduced her mother before he beat them both up and drained her mother to death."

I guess that explained why she seemed to be going after the more affluent vamps rather than any old vamp. "Why didn't he kill Jessica?"

"Her back was broken—shattered—so badly that shifting couldn't heal it. She started screaming for help, and their neighbors heard and called the cops. That's the only thing that saved her."

"So you started killing vampires as revenge for what happened to her?" I shifted my head a little more, until my ear pressed against the hard stone. I didn't know if that would actually turn on the com-link's sound, but I had to at least try it. I'd left tracking on as ordered, but the Directorate wouldn't actually come running unless they realized I was in trouble. Sal might be good at guessing when that might be, but with the way fate liked playing games with me, I could place money on the fact that the one time I needed Sal to act would be the one time she didn't.

"It wasn't the only reason," Hanna said, her concentration on whatever she was crushing in a small earthen bowl rather than on me.

As concoctions went, it smelled rather nice, reminding me of forest and herbs. And *that* set all sorts of alarm bells ringing.

A dark sorcerer mixing up something that smelled good, when every other ounce of her magic smelled so foul? It had to be an illusion of some kind. And if *that* was, maybe everything else was, too.

I squinted up at the ornate ceiling, trying to see a

shimmer or a wobble, or anything else that would suggest it was little more than a fancy trick rather than a reality. But it stubbornly remained looking like plain old plaster. In fact, if not for the fact that this was the domain of a dark sorcerer, I'd swear we were just in a windowless room of an ordinary house. An almost empty one, granted, because the only bits of furniture were the table on which I lay, the large metal cart she was using, and a cluttered metal shelving unit that lined the wall opposite the door.

Would a sorcerer intent on blood sacrifices do so in the middle of suburbia?

But then, why wouldn't she? An ordinary, unassuming house would be as good a hiding place for evil deeds as any dark cavern.

I looked back at Hanna, the movement rattling the chains tying me to the table and sending yet more arrows of pain rolling through me. I tried to ignore it, but that was almost as impossible as ignoring the ache in my shoulder. Or the numbness in my arm that would soon slip insidiously through the rest of my body.

I *had* to get out of these chains, *had* to rip the bullet from my flesh, before either began doing permanent damage. And as sensitive as I was to silver, it wouldn't be all that long.

Trouble was, with the silver on and in my body, I couldn't shift shape, so my only real weapons were my strength and my telepathy. Given that the chains felt strong, it was doubtful that strength would get me free. Which left telepathy. And while she had a nanowire on, those *could* be beaten. So I gathered my strength and hit her mentally.

This time it didn't just feel like I hit a brick wall.

This time, I hit it and bounced *off* it.

It left me reeling mentally and for several seconds I felt like my head was going to explode.

"Oh," said the witch, her voice somewhat smug. "I should perhaps warn you that this room has been proofed against telepathy, both via magic and electronically."

"How can you proof a room against telepathy via magic?"

Speaking hurt. In fact, the words seemed to bounce around my brain like sharp little knives. But I *had* to get her talking. The more I delayed her plans, the more time it gave the Directorate to find me. And I had to hope they *were* on the way, because it was looking less and less likely that I was going to get out of this by myself.

"Dark magic can achieve anything if you're willing to pay the price for it."

"And what have you been willing to pay, Hanna?" The pain in my head had receded a little, meaning it hurt less to speak. Which might have been a good thing if it hadn't meant the burning ache from the silver in my shoulder intensified again.

"Oh, I began paying my price long before I came into the dark magic."

She was still mixing the herbs, and the aroma seemed to be getting stronger. My nose twitched, and despite the pleasing scent, I wasn't entirely sure my

reaction was due to pleasure. That scent was still setting alarm bells off, and while I wasn't sure why, I'd
learned long ago to listen to such warnings.

I tried twisting my wrist in the cuff, and discovered
there was plenty of room to move around in them—
but a quick snap back had my fist jamming fast. Still,
maybe if I made it slick enough—wet enough—my
wrist might just slip through. It was worth trying, and
it wasn't as if I had any other option right now anyway.

Of course, the only way I was going to make my skin
slippery was to draw blood, and that wasn't going to be
pleasant. But it would surely be better than whatever
Hanna was planning.

"Is that the other reason why you're killing the vampires? Because of the price you paid personally?"

"They *are* the killers, every one of them. Rich, dead,
and killers reborn. It is an instinct with them, and they
deserve nothing more than real death." Her voice had
taken on a slightly shrill edge, and she was pounding
the mix so hard the bowl was in danger of breaking.

Obviously, vampires had done a whole lot more to
her than just paralyze Jessica. And I was curious enough
to want to know what.

"Not all vampires are bad," I said, still pulling at my
wrist. The chains rattled every time I did it, but Hanna
didn't seem to notice. I could only hope it remained
that way. My skin had grown slippery rather quickly—
thanks to the rough edges on the silver cuffs—and the
scent of fresh blood filled the air. Thankfully, I was the
only nonhuman in the room, so with any sort of luck,

she wouldn't realize what I was attempting until it was too late. "Not all vampires deserve to die."

She thumped the pestle down on the table so suddenly I actually jumped. "*You* kill vampires for a living. You've seen the very worst they can do. Why the hell would you even think any of them deserve to live?"

"Because *every* race has its good and its bad. You can't judge the entire lot by a few bad examples."

She snorted and walked over to the shelving unit. "They all drink blood. They all have the capacity to go too far."

So did humans, but I didn't think she was going to be receptive to *that* sort of logic. I gave my wrist another experimental tug and it slipped, ever so slightly, through the cuffs. Not enough to escape, but enough to give me hope that it *would* work, if I kept persisting.

If she gave me time.

"Killing isn't just the province of vampires."

She swung around to face me, her expression one of pure fury. "It wasn't a human who attacked Jessica and put her in a wheelchair or who sliced my husband's head off in a fit of anger. It wasn't a human who stole and changed my daughter."

Something in the way she said that made my insides go cold. "What do you mean, changed?"

"What do you think I mean?" She slapped a knife and another larger bowl onto the table. "He made her one of them."

Vampires *couldn't* make humans change with just a bite. That was little more than a Hollywood myth. It took a blood ceremony *and* consent for a human to cross over, so if Hanna's daughter had become a vampire, she'd done so of her own free will.

The question was, just how badly had Mommy reacted to her daughter's decision?

If the wildness in her eyes was anything to go by, the answer could only be very badly indeed.

"What does your daughter think of you slaughtering her people?"

"*Her* people?"

Hanna's voice had become so shrill it made my ears ache. She picked up an empty bowl and threw it at me. I had nowhere to go and no way to avoid it, so it hit the top of my head—hard. The blow left me bleeding and stunned, and more determined than ever to get away from this crazy bitch. I yanked at my wrist harder, felt it slip through a little further. A few more tugs, and I just might be free enough to defend myself.

"My daughter was *human*," she spat. "And she *died* human."

Even though I'd suspected that outcome, her words still made me sick. How could any mother, no matter how desperate, ever kill her own child? There were always other options. *Always*. You just had to reach out and talk to someone.

Though I guess that someone whose grip on sanity had to be fractional at best, having her daughter turn into one of the "monsters" must have seemed the ultimate betrayal.

"So you killed your own flesh and blood?" I continued to yank at my wrist, the rough metal edges digging deeper and deeper into my flesh. It hurt like hell but I didn't care, because whatever this madwoman was planning to do with the goop in the bowl and that fucking long knife would surely hurt me more.

"I didn't kill her," she refuted, stalking back over to the shelving unit. "I saved her. Or rather, I saved her soul."

"How did you stop her from rising?" I gave a final pull on my wrist and it finally slipped free. The chains rattled like an alarm, and I grabbed wildly at the cuff to stop it from slipping to the floor.

With one wrist free, I could at least defend myself. But actually getting off this table and away from Hanna remained a problem. The numbness from the silver bullet still lodged in my shoulder prevented me from moving my other arm, and tugging on my ankle chains would not only create a whole lot more noise, it would be more visible.

"I bound her to the grave," Hanna said. "It cost me a lot, that binding, but at least I can sleep knowing my daughter is safe."

She selected a canister from the shelving unit and walked back over to the table. She raised the knife, sliced her scarred palm, and let the wound bleed into the smaller bowl. The sweet forest scent changed, suddenly becoming something deeper and darker, and yet still not totally unpleasant.

"Did you stake her?" I asked. "Chop off her head?"

She gave me a shocked sort of look. "Of course not! What do you think I am? A monster, like them?"

"Oh, I think you're something far, far worse, lady." The words were out before I could stop them, but she merely laughed. It wasn't a sane sound, but that was no surprise.

"Because of the way I kill them? Believe me, I'm only doing to them what they did to my husband, to Jessica, and to my daughter."

"I don't care how you kill the vampires." Which was a lie, because no person, whether human or nonhuman, deserved to die the way those vampires had died—even if they *had* been the most brutal vampires ever to walk this earth. Which none of these had been.

Of course, I don't deny sometimes wishing a more brutal death on some of the bastards we hunted, but wishing and doing were two extremes that were never going to meet. And the guardian who *did* sink to the "eye for an eye" mode of thinking soon found himself out the door and on the most-wanted list.

"Then why do you think me a monster?" She picked up the canister and added several pinches of white powder to her mix. There was a flash, like a small explosion, and suddenly the dark, foresty scent was gone. In its place was a fouler, stronger scent that reminded me of the muck the zombie had thrown at me.

But why would she try and freeze me again if she already knew it didn't work? Or was this stuff stronger than the last mix?

God, I hoped not. I might only be half free, but at least I could defend myself if worse came to worst. If that stuff actually worked, I'd be in real trouble.

Like I wasn't already.

"You're a monster because of what you did to your

daughter. Because you *didn't* kill her but instead *bound* her."

She frowned at me. "She was dead already. I bound her before the change, so what is the problem?"

She didn't get it. She really didn't. What a stupid, *stupid* bitch. "Binding a body doesn't stop said body from taking the change and rising as one of the undead. It just stops them moving out of the grave or communicating with their maker for help. What you've done is ensure your daughter a living hell of *un-*life in a coffin, with no hope of escape." I shook my head in contempt. "How could you not know that?"

And I guess it was yet another mess the Directorate would have to clean up. Although whether the daughter would actually be sane enough to rescue after years of being locked underground was another matter entirely—and not one that I'd have to decide. Thankfully.

There was a shocked silence, followed by a vehement, "No!"

"Yes," I spat back. "You would have been better off to stake her from the start."

She stared at me for several long minutes, then shook her head. "I don't believe you."

"Then go to her grave, Hanna. See for yourself."

"I have no need to, wolf." Her voice was flat. She refused to believe she could be wrong, that she could have doomed her daughter to a fate far worse than vampirism. "I know you're only lying to try and save yourself."

I didn't know how lying about her daughter's fate

would actually do anything to save myself, but she obviously wasn't thinking clearly, so there was no point in saying anything else.

She walked over to the shelving and picked up a more ornate knife and another larger container, then walked back to the table. She exchanged the knife for the smaller bowl then walked across to where I lay. Luckily for me, she chose the right side rather than the left, and didn't notice I had one hand free.

Not that it would do me any good at the moment, because she simply wasn't close enough.

She placed the larger bowl on the floor, shifting it several times until she was satisfied, then rose and looked at me. "Don't you wonder how I'm about to kill you?"

I snorted softly. "Lady, dead is dead, no matter which way it comes at you."

Besides, she'd already told me she was going to bleed me. It said a lot about her state of mind that she couldn't actually remember that.

"That, I'm sorry to say, is very true."

She didn't look sorry. She looked positively ecstatic. She raised the smaller bowl and scooped her fingers inside, gathering a handful of the powder before throwing it down the length of my body. It took every ounce of control I had not to react, not to show my hand just yet. Truth was, she still wasn't close enough. I just had to hope the dust didn't do its stuff as well as it was supposed to.

The thick cloud settled around me, clogging my eyes and making my nose twitch. And it smelled even fouler than before. My body began tingling even as my muscles seemed to relax and feel oddly weak. Like before, only worse. I twitched my fingers, wriggled my toes. Response was slow, but it was there, at least for the moment. I had to hope it remained that way.

She grabbed another handful and threw it over me again. The tingling increased, and deep down, the wolf bared her teeth and roared to life. Her strength infused me, battling the sleepiness creeping over my body, keeping it at bay if not away altogether.

"If you have any questions, you'd better ask them quickly. It's a much stronger formula this time." Her voice was conversational—like we were best friends rather than mad sorceress and intended victim. "You taught me that this powder doesn't work as well on humans and other nonhumans as it does on vampires, so I guess it's better to be safe than sorry."

I could only hope she was wrong about the strength of the formula. But I asked my questions quickly, just in case she wasn't. "Did Jessica tell you she sent one of her creatures after the street kid?"

"She was in the room when that blackmailing little bastard rang. Personally, I would rather have taken care of him myself."

I bet. "Then the business cards you gave the teenagers *were* infused with some form of tracking magic?"

"Of course. How else would I have known exactly where to transport myself?"

She gave me a serene sort of smile, then turned away and walked back to the table. I twitched my extremities again, and was relieved to discover that everything that should wriggle did. The mix might be stronger, it might make the tingling fiercer, but it still wasn't completely freezing me. Which made me wonder if the mix was wrong, or whether the fact that I was a half-breed was fouling the reaction.

She returned carrying the knife. I didn't move, just watched her. To have any sort of chance against the woman, I needed her to get closer. Needed to grab that knife and use it against *her* flesh rather than mine.

She grabbed my right arm and pulled it away from my body. The arm was numb, so it flopped around like so much dead flesh, and she made a satisfied sound in the back of her throat. I held my tongue and didn't say anything, hopefully giving her the impression the powder had done its work and stolen the power of speech.

With my arm positioned on its side and presumably over the bowl, she clasped the ornate silver knife with both hands and raised it above her head.

Fear slithered through me. The mad bitch was going to cut off my arm. Why else would she need that much leverage to cut flesh? A quick slice along the forearm from the wrist was all it took to get a decent bleed—and yeah, werewolves were tough, but we still had skin like a regular human, not a rhinoceros.

She began to murmur, the words incomprehensible. Maybe it was sorcerer talk, maybe it was a prayer in some old language. I didn't really care, because my attention was on the gleaming knife being held above my body. I'd get only one chance at stopping that knife. Once she realized I was partially free, she'd no doubt either knock me out or kill me, and I wasn't overly thrilled with either option.

She continued to murmur and tension wound through me, tightening my muscles and making my stomach ache. The pain in my shoulder seemed to have retreated, but not the numbness. It was now creeping outward, reaching toward my neck. If I didn't remove the bullet soon, I'd be in real trouble.

The words stopped. For a moment that knife didn't move, just stayed high above me, glittering brightly in the semilight of the room.

Then it came down.

Fast.

I barely caught it. Whether it was the dust she'd sprinkled over me or the weakness washing through my body thanks to the silver, the fact was, the blade was inches from my flesh when I stopped it.

And I didn't stop it by the hilt, but by the blade itself, and the metal sliced into my flesh as easily as butter. Blood seeped past my clenched fingers and began to run into the bowl under my right hand. I didn't care. I ripped the weapon from her fingers, flipped the blade, and stabbed her.

But again I was too slow. She moved at the last moment, and the blow meant to pierce her heart got her in the side instead. A nasty wound, but not a deadly one.

She grunted and staggered backward, once again out of my reach. She slapped one hand against the wound, but it didn't stop the bleeding

"For that," she hissed, "you will die horribly."

She raised her free hand and blue sparks began to

dance across her fingertips. I drew back the knife, taking aim, knowing it was a risk to lose my one weapon but having little choice.

But before I could release the blade, something hit the door—hard—and the whole frame shuddered. Hanna spun as the door took another blow, and this time the wood splintered. She lunged for the table, her fingers grasping for the second knife as another blow hit the door, and this time it gave way.

Revealing the man I'd thought dead.

Kye.

He didn't even come into the room, just raised his gun and fired in one smooth motion. The bullet hit Hanna in the forehead and went straight through, splattering the back of her head against the wall behind her.

As her body slumped to the floor, I closed my eyes and sighed in relief. I'd been saved. Maybe not in the manner I'd expected—or by whom I'd expected—but life was life and I wasn't about to grumble.

"Any other problems I should know about?" he said, still standing, gun at the ready, in the doorway.

"Not that I know of. But you're the one sensitive to magic. For all I know, this room could have zombies hidden in the walls as well."

"I can't feel *that* sort of dark magic, and there's no pentagram on the floor." He lowered the weapon and his gaze met mine. "You look like shit."

I laughed softly and dropped the knife onto the metal tabletop. The clang rang out like a bell as I squeezed my hand shut, trying to stop the bleeding.

"Says the man who's covered in blood and missing a chunk of hair and flesh from the side of his head."

He holstered the weapon and walked toward me. Despite the scent of blood and sweat that lingered on him—or maybe even because of them—he smelled good.

"Silver cuffs?" he said, eyeing the chains intently.

"And a silver bullet in my shoulder. You need to get that out first."

He looked at me, his expression all cool efficiency. "There's only one easy way to do that, I'm afraid."

"There's no easy way to do it, and we both know it."

He gave me a cold smile. "And once again, you're wrong."

"Oh, will you just cut the crap and get on with it?"

"As you wish," he said, as he raised a fist and hit me hard. I was out before I could even swear at the bastard.

When I finally came to, I was in wolf form, which meant the bullet and the cuffs were both gone. The hard metal surface of the tabletop had been replaced by an even harder, colder tiled floor. My fur might have protected me from the chill of it a little better than my human skin, but the ache in my bones suggested I had been lying there for a while.

The air itself was also cold, and ripe with the scent of blood, death, and man—one man, no more. Kye hadn't called in help and I wasn't sure why I thought he might. He was a contract killer. Helping the Directorate and its people in any way, shape, or form would be a consideration only if it suited his own aims. I had no doubt he'd helped me because it was the only way he could get his kill and claim his payment.

And removing the bullet? Well, if he hadn't it might have killed me, and that wouldn't have been good for his health. He had no idea just how much I'd told the Directorate about his involvement in this case, and he was canny enough to suspect they'd come after him if I died.

I opened my eyes. Hanna's body still lay on the floor near the table, looking more fragile in death than she ever had in life.

Kye squatted against the wall opposite, watching me, his expression that of a predator sizing up an adversary. His dark red hair was still matted with blood, as were his clothes, and his face was battered and bruised.

I wanted him. And hated myself for it.

I closed my eyes and reached for my other form. Once the change had swept over my body, I sat upright and hugged my knees close to my chest. His very nearness had awareness tingling across my skin, and I could only thank God the moon heat had passed. Otherwise my crazy hormones might not have been so easy to control.

"I need to call the Directorate in," I said, my voice clipped. "If you don't want to be involved, you'd better leave."

"We need to talk first."

"Kye, there's nothing you and I need to talk about. *Nothing.*"

Especially not the heat that simmered between us, nor the fact that he'd saved my life and I now owed him.

I dropped my gaze from his and concentrated instead on rotating my shoulder, trying to ease the stiffness out of it. At least I could move my arm and fingers again, even if the tips still felt a little numb. Given my sensitivity to silver, it was surprising the aftereffects hadn't lasted a whole lot longer. In fact, I felt amazingly strong, and given the blood I'd lost through the wound, that shouldn't have been the case.

"There's something very vital we need to discuss, and *you* know it."

His voice was flat, yet there was an edge in it that made me glance up at him again. His golden eyes burned with heat and passion, and something else, something else I really couldn't put a finger on. In any other man I would have called it fear, but this man *didn't* fear. Not anyone or anything.

"I really don't know what you're talking about, Kye."

And yet I did. He was talking about the heat and the lust that still burned. It was a flame that only seemed to be getting stronger the longer we were together. It was as if our bodies were calling to each other, something that neither of us really wanted and yet couldn't fight.

"And you really do need to go," I added. Almost desperately.

"I can't go before I know for sure."

He rose as he said it, and part of me wanted to scoot backward and keep the distance between us.

"There's nothing to know, Kye. Just leave it and go."

"I *can't*." The words were as desperate as mine. He didn't want this any more than I did, and yet this man—this wolf, who was as cold and as unemotional as any good killer could be—was as helpless against it as I was.

He stopped in front of me and offered me a hand. I ignored it, looking up at him instead. What I saw there—not just heat, not just desire, not even fear, but something stronger, deeper, and far scarier—made my heart stutter and my blood surge.

Because it was nothing less than fate looking out at me from those golden depths.

And suddenly, just like him, I had to *know*.

I placed my hand in his. He hauled me upright, into his arms. I barely had time to draw a breath against the fire of contact when his lips were on mine, the kiss harsh, fierce, and oh so passionate. The force of it drove me backward, until my back hit the wall. My barely healed shoulder took the brunt of the blow and pain slithered through me. But I didn't care, because it was nothing compared to the ache beginning to assault my body.

His hands were on me, caressing me, nipping me, teasing me. It was all passion, all heat and intensity, and I was drowning in it. Willingly, wantonly, until every bit of me was screaming for the ultimate release, and every muscle, every fiber, was so tightly strung it felt like I would shatter.

He ripped off my bodice, then the G-string. I unbuttoned his pants and shoved them down, every move as urgent as his. His strong hands cupped my butt and hauled me upward. I'd barely wrapped my legs around his waist when he was in me, and God, it was *good*. More than good.

Because it wasn't just our flesh that became joined.

This was a dance of body *and* soul, and it went far beyond mere intimacy, far beyond mere pleasure.

This was the moment I'd been waiting most of my life for, yet all I wanted to do was weep.

I didn't want it to be *this* man. I really didn't.

Then he began to move, and the pain of discovery was ripped away, lost in the glory of the moment. The rich ache grew, becoming a kaleidoscope of sensations that washed through every corner of my mind. Then the shuddering took hold and I gasped, grabbing his shoulders, pulling him toward me, pushing him deeper still. Then everything shattered and it was such a sweet, glorious relief that I wept.

Although most of the tears weren't tears of pleasure or joy.

For several seconds, neither of us moved, our breathing ragged echoes as we stood wrapped around each other. Then I released my grip on his waist and he lowered me to the floor. His expression was as neutral as my mind was chaotic, his golden eyes giving little away. He raised a hand to my face, reaching for but not quite touching my cheek, then dropped it and stepped back.

"So now we know."

"Yes." My voice was clipped. I wanted to stamp my feet and rant and rage—at him, and at fate—but there was absolutely no point. It was no more his fault than it was mine, and there was absolutely nothing either of us could do about it.

"I don't want this."

My laugh was harsh. "And you think I do? For fuck's sake, Kye, you're the last man on this earth that I would ever want to make a life with."

The smile that twisted one side of his lips was bitter. "Ironic, isn't it, that we find the one thing that most wolves spend their lives searching for, and neither of us actually wants it?"

"Oh, I want it all right. Just not with you." I rubbed a hand across my eyes. They were stinging, but no tears were falling. Perhaps I was simply beyond them. "So what do we do?"

"Do?" He reached for his pants and pulled them up. "I suggest nothing. Let's walk away and continue living our lives as we otherwise would."

It wouldn't be that simple, I was sure. There was a connection between us now, a link that went soul deep. But I guess we had to try. I didn't want this man in my life, soul mate or not.

"Then get out and don't come back."

He smiled then, but it was a cold smile, a harsh smile. "Good-bye Riley. It was a pleasure, however brief."

He gave me a slight bow then turned and walked out. I released a breath, then slid down the wall and hugged my knees close to my chest.

What a goddamn, fucking mess.

But I guess I should have known fate wouldn't give me a soul mate without adding her own nasty twist.

I should have arrested the bastard when I first had the chance, then maybe none of this would ever have happened. But I couldn't undo the past, no matter how much I might have wished to. I needed to move forward.

And that meant confronting an even bigger problem.

What the hell did I say to Quinn?

Chapter 12

Two hours later I was still at Hanna's, but I'd moved from the inside of the house to the outside, and had parked my butt on the curb. That's where Rhoan found me.

"So," he said, plopping down beside me and handing me a cup of coffee. "I heard it all went down as expected, and you caught your bad guys. Or gals, as the case may be."

I took a whiff of the coffee and smiled. Hazelnut. Rhoan obviously knew I needed a pick-me-up, even if he didn't know why.

"Well, it didn't exactly go the way I planned—" which had to be the understatement of the year—"but we stopped them, and that's what counts."

He sipped his coffee and didn't answer immediately, staring instead at the house across the road. There were three kids standing at one of the windows, and their little faces had been practically glued to the glass for the last couple of hours. Nothing like a half-naked woman and a host of Directorate vehicles and people to make an everyday suburb more interesting, I guess.

"That older kid over there is getting such a boner watching you."

"You can tell that from here?"

"His heart rate is way up, and there's a whole lot of blood heat concentrated around one certain area." He flicked me a grin. "Although it could be me he fancies."

"Either way, he's a boy with excellent taste." I took the lid off my coffee and took a sip, but the steaming liquid did little to warm the ice that had formed deep inside.

"Undoubtedly." He paused to take another drink. "Jack has sent a team to go dig up the daughter, but he doesn't think there's going to be much chance of her being sane."

"How long has she been in the ground?"

"She was declared dead eight years ago."

I grimaced. One year would have been insanity-inducing. Eight was the stuff of nightmares. "What is he going to do with her?"

"Probably send her to the vampire council. It's up to them to decide from there."

"You think they can save a mind destroyed by being locked underground for so long?"

"Maybe." He shrugged. "The magic must have kept her alive, because even the strongest vamp can't survive that long without blood. So maybe it preserved some sanity, as well."

Anything was possible, I guess. I sipped my coffee and waited for the question that was undoubtedly coming next. I didn't have to wait that long.

"So, who was with you today?"

"Kye. He saved my ass."

"And then you had sex." It wasn't a question. He could no doubt smell him all over me.

"Yes."

"Do you think that was wise?"

I snorted softly. "Brother, you have no idea just *how* unwise that little event was."

My voice broke in the middle of it, and Rhoan wrapped an arm around my shoulder, hugging me close. It felt so safe and warm—like everything would be okay, no matter how bad things got. Which is everything I should have felt with my soul mate, and everything I didn't.

"Tell me," he said softly.

I took a deep, shuddering breath, then said, "Kye is my soul mate."

For several seconds, he didn't react, but I felt his surprise as sharply as if it was my own. Then it burst out of him. "*What?* Are you *sure?*"

I laughed, but it was a harsh, almost crazy sound. I gulped back the anguish and rubbed my free hand over my eyes. They still ached, though the tears had yet to come. "As sure as you are that Liander is yours."

"Fuck."

"To put it mildly."

"But..." He paused, as if to gather scattered thoughts. "How can your soul mate be someone you don't actually like?" He glanced at me. "Or do you? Like him, that is?"

"He's the last man on this earth I would ever want to be linked with." Although I guess he was better than someone like Gautier, the rogue guardian who'd hated me as much as I'd hated him. At least he was dead and out of the picture. Hell, the way fate loved playing with my life, I'm surprised she didn't pick *him* as the one.

"Then how the hell can he be your soul mate?"

"It's not like anyone has ever tried to sit down and examine the rule of soul mates. It just *is*."

"But I've never heard of anyone actively *disliking* her soul mate. Surely there has to be some sort of connection between you both that attracts?"

Another bitter, edgy laugh escaped. "Oh, there's plenty of attraction."

So much so that I very much doubted that Kye would actually stay away for long. He couldn't, not if he was feeling what I was feeling—a cold emptiness that seemed to clutch at the heart and make it ache. Make *me* ache.

"I didn't mean physical attraction—that's obvious. I meant you've got to have a lot more in common than just physical attraction."

I took a drink of coffee and looked up at him. "And where in the rule book does it say that?"

He frowned. "Well, it only makes sense, doesn't it? Why else would the bond be a lifetime one? There *has* to be at least some common ground between the two parties involved."

"There's lots of cultures around the world that still believe in arranged marriages, Rhoan. In such situations, the families pick the mates, and often it's without input from either person." I paused for more coffee. "And a lot of the time, it's done purely for social or economic gains for the family."

"That's different."

"No, it's not, because either way the participants have no choice, whether the decision is being made by the parents, or by the moon and fate."

"Damn it, it's *wrong*. He's a killer—a cold-blooded killer. He can't be your soul mate!"

I smiled, and again it was bitter. "We're both killers, Rhoan."

"But we kill for the *right* reasons. We don't hire ourselves out to the highest bidder."

No, but we still killed, and innocent people sometimes did get hurt because of our actions, and maybe that was our meeting place. The one thing Kye and I had in common.

I rubbed my eyes again. "None of this really matters, Rhoan. It is what it is, and now we have to deal with it."

"How did Kye deal with it?"

"About as well as me. He doesn't want it any more than I do."

"So where is he?"

"I have no idea." And despite the coldness deep within, I didn't really care. I didn't *want* to care. Not about him, not ever. "He's probably off somewhere shooting someone in frustration, for all I know."

"If he did, we could hunt him down and—"

"And what?" I interrupted. "Kill him? You know the lore, Rhoan. Kill him, and you kill me."

He gave me a glance. "Ben didn't die when his soul mate died."

"But he *wanted* to. It was only his sister who kept him alive."

"And you think I wouldn't do the same for you?"

I placed a hand on his knee and squeezed lightly. "I know you would. But I don't ever want to face that decision or that situation. It's better if he's alive and out there somewhere."

Just not in my face. Or in my life.

But would fate let things go on like that? I had a bad feeling the answer would be no.

He blew out a breath and took another sip of his coffee. "So what do we do?"

"Right now?"

"Right now, and later on."

"Well, the first thing I need to do is go talk to Quinn."

"Oh, *fuck*."

"Yeah," I said, keeping my voice even though everything inside seemed to hurt. Or everything that wasn't half frozen, at least.

"What the hell are you going to say to him?"

I snorted softly. "Why do you think I've been sitting out here for the last two hours?"

"You've got to tell him. You owe him that."

"But he doesn't deserve this." *Neither* of us deserved it. Not when everything was finally starting to fall into place between us.

He hugged me harder and for several minutes, we didn't say anything. Just sat there contemplating the evilness of the universe. Or at least, that's what I was contemplating.

I drained the remainder of my coffee, then said, "There is one tiny spark of hope."

"Of what?"

"Of me and Quinn not being totally over."

Rhoan snorted. "You may not want Kye as a soul mate, and he may not want you, but trust me, he's not going to be interested in sharing, either."

"Quinn's old enough and powerful enough to take care of himself, even against the likes of Kye." Hell, Quinn had once been a professional killer himself, and for far longer than Kye had been. "Besides, Liander shares you."

"Liander is an amazingly patient and loving person. I get the feeling Kye will be neither of those." Rhoan drained his own cup, then plucked mine from my fingers and tossed both into the nearby trash can. "Besides, what makes you think that Quinn will want to share you with your soul mate, knowing that at any moment he could lose you? You ask a lot of him."

"But what if he's my soul mate, too?"

Rhoan looked at me like I was crazy. "What are you talking about?"

I took a deep breath and blew it out slowly. "Dia once asked me if a wolf with two souls can have just the one soul mate. What if she's right? What if both men are meant to be in my life?"

"I think you're asking for a whole lot of trouble even contemplating that."

"It's not like I actually want both men."

"No, but you're a wolf in all but blood. That means one soul mate, not two."

"So, I can't have two soul mates," I retorted, pulling away from his arm, "but it's okay for you to have a soul mate and play around?"

"It's different, sis."

"No, it's *not*."

"Liander won't be driven to kill because he knows, without a doubt, that he is the only one that means something to me. There's no shared emotion with anyone else. No danger that I will ever want to stay with anyone else." He touched my chin gently and made me look at him. "How can you possibly promise that to Quinn when your wolf soul mate is out there? When we all know just how desperate you are to have children, and that's the one thing that Kye can give you and Quinn can't?"

"I'm never going to have kids, Rhoan—"

"Maybe you can't carry them, but you have viable eggs frozen and there are always surrogates. Kye gives you an option. Quinn doesn't."

"I know, but—"

"No. You have to consider these things now, before you make any decisions you'll regret."

I stared at him for a moment. "You want Kye in the family?"

He snorted. "God no. I just want *you* to be fully aware of all the implications before you make any lifetime decisions."

"Kye *isn't* a lifetime decision." He was a problem I might never get around.

"Realistically, he's more lifetime than Quinn right now. He's your *soul* mate. How can you promise anything to Quinn when Kye is out there?"

"I can't, but—"

"You *can't*," he cut in. "So you're left with the possibility of two men who won't share, one of whom has already proven he will go to great lengths to make you his."

I jerked away from his touch again and thrust to my feet, taking several steps away from him before I stopped. I breathed deep, but it still didn't do anything to ease the turmoil within me.

"This might be all a moot point anyway," I said eventually, "because I might not be like you. I might not even *want* anyone else now that my wolf has found her soul mate."

Hell, Ben had been like that. He might take other lovers now, but certainly not when his soul mate was alive. And with the games fate was playing, it'd be my luck to be more like Ben than my brother—and the result would be the loss of a man I really wanted over one I didn't.

"Then this arguing is pointless. You need to uncover all the facts before you worry about the consequences."

I closed my eyes. It was a moment, a discovery, I

really didn't want to make. Because once I knew, I would face the hardest decision of all.

"It's only going to get harder the longer you leave it, sis," Rhoan said softly. "Just do it. Now. Then you'll know, one way or the other."

"Okay, okay." There really was no point in putting it off any longer, and sitting here stewing over it certainly hadn't gotten me any closer to a solution. He was right. It was better to know than to worry over what might or might not be. I turned around and held out my hand. "I need your keys."

He reached into his pocket, then tossed the keys to me. "You don't want company?"

I smiled, though it was a pale shadow of its usual self. "I think this is something I'd better do alone."

"Be careful then, won't you?"

"Quinn's not going to hurt me."

"I meant, be careful driving. I don't think you're in the best frame of mind for concentrating on the roads."

This time, my smile was warmer. "I won't dent your car, bro. I promise."

He snorted. "I'm more worried about you denting yourself."

"I won't do that, either."

"Good. Then get."

I got, but with a whole lot of reluctance.

I went home to shower and change first. Luckily for me, Liander wasn't there, because the last thing I needed was to go through the whole explaining thing again. I just wanted to get over to Quinn's, discover what I had to discover, and then make any decisions I had to make.

It was still very early in the morning, so the traffic hadn't yet reached its peak. I parked in the Langham hotel's underground lot, then made my way up to Quinn's suite.

Once there, I dug the key card out of my wallet and swiped it through the slot. The lock clicked and I pushed the door open. The suite was dark, but I could hear the soft timbre of breathing coming from the bedroom. I doubted he'd be asleep. Not now that I was in the room. The beat of my heart was a cadence that would have woken him immediately.

I took a deep breath, trying to ease the tension that was rolling through my body. It didn't help—nothing would. Not until I had my answers. I forced my feet forward, stripping down as I went, scattering shoes and clothes haphazardly across the lush carpet.

He reached for me the minute I slipped in beside him. Every muscle was so tightly wound that his caress felt like a blow. I shuddered a little and tried to relax. But how could I do that when what happened in the next few minutes might be the end of a relationship that had barely begun to blossom?

"You're later than I thought you might be," he said, kissing my cheek, my neck, my shoulder. "Were there problems with the job?"

"Let's just say there were some discoveries made that have caused monumental problems."

I ran my fingers down his cheek and lightly across

his lips. He kissed each fingertip gently. And again, it felt like a blow.

"You're very tense," he commented, his dark eyes on mine. "Would you like me to draw you a scented bath?"

"No." Because how on earth could I relax until I knew? "I'd much rather be kissed senseless until everything else just slips away."

Please let it all slip away.

Please let it be like it's always been.

"That I can also do." A smile curved his lips as he gathered me in his arms.

For the briefest of moments, something within me fought his touch. Fought *him*. And the fear surged.

No, I thought. *No.*

Then his lips were on mine, and I forced myself to relax. Thrust away the fear, and concentrated instead on the kiss, on his scent, on the heat of his body pressing so close to mine.

The tension within seemed to ease a little, and while the ice didn't melt, I didn't have any immediate urge to reject him, either.

But was I supposed to have such an urge?

Ben had never really explained the finer points of sex once he'd met his soul mate. All he'd said was that he simply didn't want another partner when she was alive.

Concentrate, I thought. *Don't think. Don't worry. Just do.*

But it was easier thought than done.

The tension continued to roll through me in waves, but as his kisses and caresses moved down my body, a dreamy sense of enjoyment soon joined it. It wasn't the heat and the fire that marked many of our encounters, but then, it didn't need to be.

Slow was good, too.

He continued to tease me, touch me, tasting and exploring every part of my body with his hands and his tongue, making every inch of me tingle. Every inch of me ache with wanting him.

Wanting not just *him,* but the truth.

I needed the answer, more than I'd needed anything in my entire life.

"Please," I whispered, with an urgency he couldn't yet understand.

He chuckled softly, then wrapped his free hand around my neck and kissed me hard. As his mouth claimed mine, he slid into me. It felt good, and it felt right, as if in that one moment of unity, our souls had merged and danced as one—and all I wanted to do was cry in relief.

It might not be as strong as what I'd felt with Kye, but it was there, and it was real, and it meant that I had the choice. That I didn't have to destroy what had only just begun.

Then Quinn began to move, and everything else slipped away, lost to the glory of the moment. All I could do was move with him, savoring and enjoying every tiny sensation flowing through me. I shuddered, writhed, as the sweet pressure built, until it felt as if I was going to tear apart from the sheer force of it. Then it all *did* tear apart, and his body was slamming into mine so hard the whole bed shook. When his teeth entered my neck, it heightened everything all over again, and I came a second time.

When I finally caught my breath again, I took his face between my palms and kissed him long and slow. "You have no idea just how much of a relief that was."

He rolled to one side and gathered me close. It felt so right in his arms that I just wanted to cry. At least I was still free to enjoy all this. Fate had left me that, if nothing else.

"There's nothing like a good dose of lovemaking to ease a body's tension," he said, a smile in his voice.

"Yes." I hesitated. The cowardly part of me just didn't want to fess up about what had happened and why I'd been so tense, but that wouldn't be fair. Besides, he *had* to know, because we'd no doubt be dealing with the consequences soon enough. "You know those discoveries I mentioned earlier?"

"Yes."

"Well, they weren't exactly work related."

He frowned lightly—something I felt rather than saw. "Then what were they?"

"Personal." I hesitated again. "And huge in so many different ways."

Tension rolled through his limbs, there one moment and gone the next. Quinn was nothing if not controlled. "Whatever it is, just come out with it, Riley."

But I couldn't. I just couldn't force the damn words past my tongue. Not when I knew they were going to hurt him so much. So instead I said, "You remember how Dia once asked me if a person with two souls can have just one soul mate?"

"Yes." His voice was cool, as controlled as the rest of him. But I still felt his trepidation. It felt like a storm cloud gathering power in the distance.

"Well, it appears she was right."

The air suddenly seemed alive with energy and emotion. For one sharp moment, it rolled over me, grabbing at my breath, my body, pummeling it, making it ache as fiercely as if he *were* hitting me.

Then it was gone, snapped behind his icy control again.

"So you've found your wolf soul mate."

A statement, not a question.

"Yes."

He pulled his arm out from underneath me and rolled off the bed, stalking naked to the window. For several moments he did nothing more than breathe deeply. There was no anger, no emotion, nothing that even hinted at turmoil. Nothing more than that controlled breathing.

Eventually, he asked, voice still as even as his breathing, "Where does that leave us?"

"You haven't even asked who it is, Quinn."

"I don't *want* to know," he snapped, and just for a moment, the calm broke and his voice became fury. Became death itself. "I told you long ago my being had claimed you, Riley. That being is willing to kill to keep you."

"You kill him, you risk killing me."

He didn't say anything. Maybe he couldn't.

"Quinn, I don't *want* my soul mate. I don't like him, and I don't want to spend my life with him."

"He's your soul mate. Whether you like him or not is really irrelevant."

"That might be the case normally, but I am not normal. This whole *situation* is not normal."

Again he didn't answer.

"Damn it," I exploded. "Whatever my wolf feels, she is *not* the whole of me. And the part of me that is vampire wants *you,* not him."

He finally turned around to face me. There were tears in his eyes. Goddamn tears. For me. For us.

I scrambled off the bed and ran to him. He wrapped his arms around me and held me so tight I could barely breathe, but I didn't care.

I wanted this. Wanted him.

Wanted us.

"We have to face this together, Quinn. I don't want to go forward without you. I really don't."

"He's your soul mate—"

"But so are you! Damn it, the connection is there, and it's real, and I don't care if it isn't as deep or as strong as what I feel with my wolf. It's *there,* and I'm going to do everything I can to hold on to it."

He laughed softly. "What you or I want may not matter in the end."

"Maybe it won't, but we can still try." I shifted my head from his shoulder, looked into the gloriously emotional depths of his dark eyes, and whispered, "Please tell me you'll try."

He took a deep breath and released it slowly. "I've fought for a very long time to make you mine, Riley.

It's not within me to give up now, no matter how impossible the odds."

The relief that rushed through me was so great that my knees felt like they were going to buckle.

He wasn't going to walk away.

He was going to remain in my life.

All I had to do now was hope fate let it stay that way.

About the Author

KERI ARTHUR received a "Perfect 10" from *Romance Reviews Today* and was nominated for Best Shape-shifter in *PNR*'s PEARL Awards and in the Best Contemporary Paranormal category of the *Romantic Times* Reviewers' Choice Awards. She lives with her daughter in Melbourne, Australia.

A murderer on the loose,
beheading his victims . . .

A vampire sex club,
whose owner excels at seduction . . .

Torn between her heart and her soul,
Riley Jenson is

Bound to Shadows

The eighth dark and sexy book
in the Riley Jenson Guardian series
from *New York Times* bestselling author

Keri Arthur

Coming in September 2009
from Dell Spectra